W9-CBM-670

Praise for *Nature's Confession*

"Morin's novel is the literary embodiment of a distinctly different way of perceiving, and one that will no doubt work its aesthetic, as well as political 'magic' on everyone who reads it, in the process transmogrifying their perception of extant social and natural reality. The kind of work that reinforces corporate domination in the world constructed by *Nature's Confession* is 'busywork' — a neologism that conveys precisely its function of keeping workers 'busy' — so busy that they do not have time to reflect on the ecological damage that corporate operations are doing to the ecosphere — busywork keeps them locked in an ideological, or discursive, prison. The link between corporate logic and enslavement is made explicit by prefacing the names of things with an 'e', rendering eParliament, eHarvard, etc. The meaning of people's lives has been defined by their corporate enslavement, which goes hand in hand with the incremental pollution of the planet in the name of profit . . . . This book should be prescribed to every student and school-going child on the planet."

—*Mail & Guardian, Thought Leader,* Dr. Bert Olivier

"Witty, with a keen eye for the absurd, JL Morin puts an ambitious new spin on environmental protection."

—Fintan O'Higgens, Television Writer

The state of the cli-fi genre

NATURE'S CONFESSION

JL Morin

New York
Harvard Square Editions
www.harvardsquareeditions.org
2015

Nature's Confession JL Morin © 2014

Cover photos:
'Chrome' © Drizzd
'Black hole in the middle of Centaurus A' © Chandra X-ray
Observatory, a NASA space telescope launched on July 23, 1999

Published in the United States by Harvard Square Editions

ISBN 978-0-9895960-7-7

www.harvardsquareeditions.org

For unconquerable Mother Nature

Many thanks to Jack Gibley and Nick Hogg for their insightful feedback, and to Dr. Thomas Mowbray, who advised on how the exploitation of antipatterns could be used to thwart injustice.

TABLE OF CONTENTS

WORLD ON THE EDGE

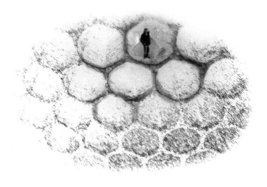

To understand the ways of MakSym, one must start before he touched the little sun. His humble Terran birth was in the year 2 After Corporatism, when teaching lost its way, and one's feet went next door to math class and one's head went underground for history.

—Broghther Waitin Aadash, *The Legend of MakSym*

LYING ON HIS ALARM CLOCK, Boy convinced himself that he was 'on time', and could linger with the auburn girl in his dream. As usual, he was saving her, this time from a plenty-eyed *Terrificollosus* spider. He shot a two-stage flaming arrow into one of its slick red eyes. Watched it burn through the horrid head. The monster ignited. Boy shrank away as the arachnid exploded, pieces of hairy leg and shards of yellow fang flying every which way. Again, he'd saved the girl. Splashed with spider muck, even on her cheek, she didn't seem to mind. She gave him the usual mollowy look, like she owed him her life, picked up a fang, handed it to him, and said, "A spoil of war. Keep it."

They ran through blond wheat fields to a pristine beach, feet drumming the sand. The leaves on the plants were gigantic, the Nature like nothing he'd ever seen before. And the girl! To say she was gorgeous would be to understate the matter dramatically. She seemed so real.

Then, she was gone. He leaned against a giant leaf, only half plant, its leather warm like an animal . . .

The alarm sounded louder. "Seven forty. Now you can't do your hair."

His eyes opened a slit. White sheets. His sister called from downstairs, "The bus is coming." He glanced at his alarm.

"Seven forty three," the clock warned. "Dude, seriously."

His lids slipped closed. Back from nowhere again, the dream girl turned to him and laughed, her green eyes mischievous through auburn locks. She frolicked into the sea, pulling him close and then under the water, in ritual. Just happy to have her attention, he prayed this baptism would save the world.

Pink waves reflected the sky. She swam toward him, ready to tell him. Her lips mouthed the words. He swam closer, straining to hear . . . if he could just get a little closer . . .

The front door slammed.

He sat bolt upright, alarm clock vibrating. It had started uploading his embarrassing baby pictures to the Grid. *Oh no!* He jumped out of bed. Passing the mirror, the skinny mulatto kid told himself to forget about the girl.

And that's what he meant to do. Boy hurried downstairs, past cold omelet and beans, and out the door. He dashed across the gravel 'lawn', crunching pebbles while imagining the girl, his T-shirt on backward and inside out. The bus door closed in front of him.

He sprinted down the block after the bus, choking on smog. *Forget about her.* He was a fast runner, and the lumbering bus took a circuitous route. At the next stop, he ran up to the other kids and climbed aboard. He slunk down in his seat and watched the sidewalks slip away.

Suddenly, he glampsed a glint of red amidst the dismal gray. He stared out the bus window at the familiar auburn tresses, tumbled over a plaid shirt. *Nobody wears plaid.* He sat up in his seat. As the bus passed her by, he saw her face.

That's her! The girl from his dreams was walking down the street, alone. He broke into a sweat, sure now that the world really was in grave danger, that they were on a mission, him and her. He stumbled to the back of the bus and looked out the window. She walked with purpose, perhaps already aware of the threat he was just beginning to feel. Her mysterious dream aura tugged at him. Their eyes locked. *That face.* It was burned into his soul.

As the bus turned, the girl's auburn mane glided out of sight. *I have to find her!* He ran to the front of the bus.

He felt her energy diminishing. With it, went a part of himself. "Open the door!" he yelled.

Static. The speaker on the dashboard blared, "Sit down!" The bus kept going.

"I have to throw up!"

That would have worked on a human driver. But the automated bus ignored him and rattled on.

He grabbed the door handles, pried the rickety doors open, and landed with a stumble in the street, heart pounding in his chest. Never minding that the neighborhood around the school was dangerous, he raced back around the corner.

Then stopped short.

The girl was gone.

He walked up and down the block, but she was nowhere.

Now all he had left was a strange emptiness in his stomach. And it was raining. His every nerve exposed to the air, he started off the drismal way the bus had gone.

Filled with dread, he saw the honeycomb building plopped behind the guard tower, its beehive architecture a reminder not of bees, the last of which died off a few years ago, but of the importance of busywork.

He took a deep breath, held it for ten seconds, and walked across the threshold. Inside the hexagonal hallways, he checked his appearance in a classroom window and noticed his shirt tags dangling like a bow tie. He pulled his hair to the side. *Maybe I should get a spooncut.*

He heard footsteps and braced himself for another encounter with the sumo wrestling team. Giggling bubbled up in the honeycomb. It was only three heavy set girls. They smirked at him. These snarks were also fourteen, but they dwarfed Boy, who hadn't had his growth spurt yet. He nodded hello out of social necessity.

"Got dressed in the dark, frumple-head?" the biggest girl said.

The other snarks giggled like morons. "Isn't your hair getting a bit long for a boy?" one heavy sneered.

"Maybe he's not really a boy," said another grool.

"He's not gay, he's just black." More giggles.

"At least he doesn't have to tell his mom."

"His mom? She's the one who dressed him like a girl."

He slowed and let them walk past. *They saw my baby pictures!* Truth told, alarm clocks were brutal. He tried to smooth down the cowlick rebelling on top of his head and wished they still had cows to blame bad hair on. Nowadays kids couldn't even play outside. School was just about the only activity left. If only he could disappear into the virtual world. He tapped the silicone screen on his wrist. He searched on 'long, auburn hair' and filtered for green eyes. *What if the auburn girl thinks I'm a drone?*

He hoped that his quirks wouldn't matter. To her. She was special. She had to be different from the snarks ambling along ahead of him. Let them laugh at him. They didn't count. He knew better than to talk to those trolls. All they wanted was to denounce him to the Rumor Network and collect their rewards. Just from that one look in the auburn girl's eyes, he knew, at least had a strong feeling, that she would accept him as he was. Grandmasters at tetra-chess were *supposed* to be quirky.

His footsteps resounded through the honeycomb's echoing architecture. Absorbed in a search on his wrist screen, an extension of his physical self, Boy barely noticed where he was going. Elbow sticking out, he dawdled along, dragging his feet. On the tiny screen, a rainbow of fair-skinned temptresses, brunettes to redheads, blinked, smiled, and blew kisses at him. Way too many to sort through.

Just as he approached a curve in the corridor, a voice jolted him out of his device. It was Mrs. Dodgewisdom talking to Miss Numba in a dreary monotone—about him. He pressed himself against the wall.

"Shepherding students is tiresome enough without a discipline problem in class," Mrs. Dodgewisdom grumbled.

"Of course he has troubles; he's a skinny mixed-breed outlier! Anybody can see that his brain is wired differently, the mischievous no-name."

"Parents don't feel safe naming their kids anymore. And we do them no favors by allowing individuality, either. Outliers soon start having their own ideas. Personal ideas."

A swarm of students approached. Boy bent down and pretended to tie his shoe, which didn't have any laces, and continued to listen discreetly. Why were the teachers all up in his grill? He overheard an indignant Miss Numba say, "Indeed! That one can turn a lecture into an argument in a flash. He's impossible. Impossible, I say." It angered the teachers when an adolescent forced them to 'refer to him'. Having to single students out was not in their job description. Children were supposed to fit into the system. If one required personal attention, that student had to be re-formed.

"My tactic is cutting him down the moment he walks in," Mrs. Dodgewisdom said. "That keeps him quiet for the first twenty minutes. Still, you can see him cogitating, figuring to make trouble. Just outrageous. Thinks he's so smart. Humph! I just won't pass him."

Boy's eyes flared. *What! How can they fail someone who knows more than they do?* He didn't care about grades anymore if they weren't giving him good ones.

"He's nothing like his half-sister," Mrs. Dodgewisdom said.

"Girls born of immaculate conception often do better."

'Half-sister'? Whew! Boy sighed with relief. *They can't be talking about me. My sister's a full-blooded sibling from the same parental gene pool.* He was now thinking he was still in their good graces, swinging his screen arm nonchalantly. Boy rounded the bend and found himself standing face-to-face with Mrs. Dodgewisdom. She shot him a surprised look, threw back a white lock, and pulled her transparent drasticine cape around her bony frame. Her yellowed eyes were destabilizing.

Even in the armor of his favorite diagonal-striped shirt, albeit backward and inside-out, he felt vulnerable. Mrs. Dodgewisdom's bloodsucking energy had Boy tripping over his own feet. Wishing he could disappear into his wrist screen, he swiftly made for the camouflage of the back row. As far away as he could get, he lunged toward the floor, and the last seat floated up and caught him. There he sat, daydreaming about the girl with the auburn mane.

"All the students have their books turned on," spindly Mrs. Dodgewisdom was saying. She stared at Boy.

Boy rummaged through his bag for his censored textbook. Recent history being too controversial, they were repeating ancient history. The only thing Boy had gathered from the subject was that $1 + 1$ equaled 3.

"Now listen carefully, class," came her brain-freezing monotone. "There is nothing *we* can do about it."

Boy did feel he could do something about it. He wasn't sure how he had developed an immunity to mist. Maybe because his mother had always told him to sit in the back of the classroom and repel unwelcome thoughts. Mumbling helped, too.

Her droning voice cast the invisible mist over the rest of the students, had them staring straight ahead, stupefied, eyes wide, accepting the hypnotic dicta that prepared them for their future busywork roles in society, except Boy, who glanced out the window at the cubist rooftops. Their orange planes slanted at a variety of angles. The sight made him think of the many different ways of looking at ideas, systems, rules.

Mumbling helped, too. "She's the most repulsive crumbly alive." And so did the device on his wrist.

A message bombarded his wrist screen. It was from 'HOME Corporation': Have you finished that coding?

Not now! Boy teletyped: Can't talk.

I can't wait. I'm sending more material through.

Boy hit 'block', deflecting HOME Corporation's silly gaming contest. Right then, only his search for the girl mattered. He entered the street address where he saw her walking. Thousands of search results came up. That should have narrowed it to the hundreds! How come he couldn't find her? He was really good at this. That search should have worked, unless . . . . She didn't want to be found. Another piece of the puzzle fell into place: she was hiding.

Boy adjusted the parameters and scanned through a new set of girls on his wrist screen.

HOME interrupted the search again with another angry request.

He responded with a grown-up-sounding message entitled `out of office automated reply'. *Take that!* Then, he had an idea. He closed his eyes. Maybe he could cull more details about the girl from another dream.

"Answer me!" Mrs. Dodgewisdom demanded.

Boy's eyes popped open.

Mrs. Dodgewisdom was calling on him, with a question he hadn't heard.

Boy sat up and looked around.

The other students turned in unison. Their half-closed eyes gazed at him.

"The answer?" she said in an insufferably gloomy tone.

"Could you please repeat the question?" Boy asked, squinting to hide his mist-free eyes.

" 'Repeat the question,' hmm?" Mrs. Dodgewisdom's voice almost succumbed to her own wearying hypnosis. She pointed her finger at Boy and hissed, "Enough! Your ignorance is encyclopedic."

Maybe, but the word 'encyclopedic' triggered his memory, and the dream girl's age came to mind: same as his true sister, two years older than he was. Sixteen!

Mrs. Dodgewisdom was coming down the aisle.

He glanced sidelong at the student next to him, whose ruler lay under the passage at the beginning of page seventy-seven. Boy looked at page seventy-seven in his own book. It was a passage about the significance of life.

"I believe the passage means, *'In order to please others, we lose our hold on our life's purpose.' —Epictetus, Greek-born*

Roman slave and Stoic philosopher," he guessed, not suspecting that this warning would one day save his life.

Mrs. Dodgewisdom's eye twitched. Her footsteps echoed on the tiles as she slowly walked to the back of the class and said, "That quote was censored out of the reformed editions of your textbooks three years ago." Her purple-veined fingers reached for Boy's tattered history book. She grabbed it, slammed it shut, producing a cloud of dust, and tucked it under her bony arm.

Boy's smile hardened into a frown. He doubted whether some of the students could read at all. Like a signal, the confiscated book tipped him over the edge. He couldn't sit here and pretend to learn anymore. He had way too much work to do, and it wasn't busywork. The class's reading level hadn't improved in all his time there. He sensed that they just recognized the bytes of propaganda like pictograms, or kanji. "This is pointless," he mumbled.

"What was that?" Mrs. Dodgewisdom whirled around. "Do you know why you are at school?"

Words leapt out of his mouth before he could think of an innocuous answer. "To free up my parents to busywork?"

"That's enough!"

But she had forgotten to command the class to breathe. The students began choking for air and waking up from their reverie. So Mrs. Dodgewisdom returned to her station at the front of the class.

Detecting his eye motions, Boy's wrist computer filtered for 'age sixteen'. Again, a message from HOME Corporation infiltrated his search. He needed another distraction like he needed more busywork.

URGENT: How much would you charge to do some coding for me?

A client! Shored up in the delusion that Boy was really going to work for him, the client demanded Boy's price.

This almost got Boy's attention. *Hmm, like I need another adult telling me what to do.* He'd only been goofing around on HOME Corporation's game site anyhow. He deleted the annoying message and continued flipping through the profiles of redheaded girls.

Another message replaced it. URGENT: Let's make a deal.

Deal? I'm only fourteen. He didn't have the flimsiest idea how much money coding was worth. He'd overheard his dad say you should never name your price first, though. You should let the other guy suggest a price, and it would usually be higher than what you expected. That seemed like a good game. *How high can I get this guy to go?* For a moment, he forgot about the girl and teletyped, What do you think it's worth?

Another message came back. Eight hundred dollars an hour, IF you answer right away.

Boy's eyebrows rose. He'd never heard of so much money in his life.

The 'age sixteen' filter results came up, pushing the client's message aside. But his wrist screen faded. *Out of power!* He had to get to the computer room. He raised his hand.

An iron-clad expression girded Mrs. Dodgewisdom's face.

Boy stood up. "Sorry, I don't feel so well. Can I go to the infirmary?"

Mrs. Dodgewisdom tried not to look relieved. "Again?" she quibbled, for form's sake.

"It's a bug we're passing back and forth in my family."

He was a bad liar, so Mrs. Dodgewisdom glared at him as he exited the classroom.

Boy ran down the honeycomb hallway. He took the ramp leading to the basement. At the door to the computer room, he whipped out his hacked homehacked MasterKey and let himself into the airlock. Inside, he grabbed the principal's metallic protective suits hanging on the wall—that would keep the room clear. He fitted the flimsy feet over his shoes and pulled down the glass mask. He opened the adjoining door and stepped into the Wi-Fi radiation soup. The room was dark except for the glow of seventeen computer holofields. He slipped into a chameleon headset.

The never ending flow of communications carried him out to sea, as he virtually waved hello to each and drifted on, out, farther, hardly noticing the cleaning woman come in, until she greeted him, "Hi," and flashed him an oh-it's-you smile.

The girl really had taken pains to cover her tracks. Hours later a hologram sprung from his wrist screen. Mom: Dinner's ready.

Hmm, food. Something smells good. How did it get so late! He realized he was hungry. Boy teletyped: What's for dinner?

Noodles. It'll be cold by the time you get here, just the way you like it.

His stomach growled. Cold noodles really were his favorite.

Come home. I bet hockey's been over
for an hour.

Hockey? Oh yeah, it's Tuesday.

Tempting, but I'm working on
something.

He knew Mom would worry. She was always fretting
about things like air and water.

The client pestered him again: Whadd'ya say?

Mom: Are you in the computer room
again?

He looked at the clock, 7 p.m.

You'll get fat if you don't eat. Your
metabolism will slow down and go into
hibernation.

He teletyped: That's why I'm chewing gum.

A very long subject line from the client appeared at
the top of the computer holofield: In life, there's
the work that needs to be done, which by
th' way, doesn't usually pay, and the
work corporations want you to do to
denigrate th' environment - that's the
day job.

Boy could feel the urgency in the client's message.
Gotta go, Mom. He thought of the color blue to end
the call. Knowing there was a plate of noodles waiting
gave him the confidence to type the next message to the
client,

Maybe. Was he out of his mind? It was a lot of
money. He should be jumping all over the client's offer.
But he was on a mission and followed his intuition. His
fingers typed: Auburn hair, sixteen . . .

There was a knock at the door. Without thinking, he
went to unlock it without thinking.

Too late.

A large stranger in a metallic protective suit stood in the doorway. Boy peered at the stranger. *How did he get past the guards?* Street people were not allowed in the school. The man's headgear was stuffed with white hair and an unkempt beard. He towered over Boy.

Boy stood paralyzed. He could play tetra-chess with World-Prize winning mathematicians on the other side of the globe, but a real-time grown-up was altogether different. A bolt of fear shot down his spine. With all his strength, he jammed the door shut. It hit the big man's foot and rebounded. All at once, Boy could feel the sweat inside his suit.

The man looked furious. He raised his enormous lumberjack hands. Clamped them onto Boy's shoulders.

No use trying to run. The man's big hands held him in place. The man bared his teeth. He smelled like burnt wood.

Boy looked around for the cleaning lady, but she was nowhere to be seen. He pleaded. "Please, don't kill me!"

CAUGHT

The future for me is already a thing of the past
You were my first love and you will be my last.

—Bob Dylan

CAUGHT IN THE LOCK of the burly stranger's powerful grip, Boy squirmed and struggled, though he knew it was pointless. No one was at school this late to save him. He screamed anyway.

The man clamped a gloved hand over Boy's mouth, pushed the door open with his large body, and dragged Boy backward into the room. "Ye don't git many visitors, do ye?"

Boy was shaking all over.

"Ye really are a boy, Boy."

"Are you . . ?"

"The client." The old man nodded his head with a grin, green eyes gleaming as he looked down at Boy. "Good guess. I'm not going to kill you, either. Who'd a thought I'd take to a boy like you?"

Boy looked at the man's matted beard and wasn't so sure. He missed his own father. Probably still at busywork. Seemed he always was.

"Just goes to show. Some virtual fowk ur real, and some real fowk ur virtual." The big man ambled in and sat right down. Boy didn't know whether to lock the door, or at least close it, now and decided to leave it the way it was: wide open.

The client put his hands together and said in a surprisingly gentle voice, "Ye see, this is a man's job, and you're going to be one soon enough. I have a daughter as smart as ye. Valentine's a richt pure good hacker, expert at making herself digitally invisible, in and out wi'oot a trace. But she's fragile." That wasn't entirely true. His daughter was tough as nails, in fact. But nails weren't much good when there was a rusty traitor amongst them. The resistance still couldn't figure out who had leaked the information that compromised their identities. Now they were all being hunted down. He had to protect her, and insisted that she come with him from Scotland. They almost captured the client. What the network needed was new blood with high-level hacking skills, someone who was outside of their network, under the radar. Underage. "Yer our only chance at survival. The only one who kin save us now."

"Save you?"

The client studied his big hands. "Wi' a boy, I know where I stand," he lied. "I was a lad once, like ye." His eyes twinkled from under furry brows. A pang of guilt stabbed the client's insides. How could he compensate for the risk he was asking Boy to take?

"You were?" Boy wondered how the client found him. The client must have traced the school server . . . and from there? Well, this was the only light on in the honeycomb. It wouldn't have been that hard to figure out where to look in the school . . . once the client had snuck past the security guard. Boy shot a questioning look at the old lumberjack.

The client began to spread his cloak over his head. For a split second, Boy grokked the cameras on each side of the cloak that replicated the scene on the other side. Then, the mirror cloak's screen enveloped the client, and without a sound, the client simply vanished. Gone.

"So! That's how you got past the guard." Boy walked around the space where the client had been. "I've heard of those, but I've never seen a real mirror cloak."

The air rippled and parted, and the client was there again. "I'm giving it to ye, Boy. You're aff to need it more than me." The man untied the cloak from his neck. The large hands tossed it over Boy. Under the cloak, Boy vanished. Erased.

Boy took it off and reappeared again by the window, almost a mirror now that it was dark outside, a look of astonishment on his face.

The client let out a bellowing laugh.

"I can't accept this," Boy said. "It's too precious." He tried to hand it back.

"Keep it, Boy. You'll need it if we're aff to work together."

"I don't think I need a mirror cloak to write code for a company newsletter."

The client looked over his shoulder as if he expected an attack at any moment. His massive body lumbered over to the door and closed it. "You're smart, Boy. It's nae a newsletter. That was just oor test, 'n' aye, ye passed." The boy was perfect for the job. He was an A+, possibly with unknown mutations, able to operate on the highest level. And completely untouched.

Boy's voice shook. "What do you want from me?" The man seemed to be in some kind of danger, and that was a little worrying. He sort of felt sorry for the old guy with his muddy shoes. He took the cloak to make the guy feel better.

"We're in a bit o' a bind. You're the only one who kin help us." The client sighed, at a loss for words, as if he had come a long way in person to circumvent spies, or something.

The client got up and paced the room. Now that he had to tell his secret, the words got stuck in his throat. He would only explain the parts that Boy needed to know, for everyone's safety. "We need your hulp wi' . . . shall we call it, a library. We're aff to make the suppressed books available to everyone. We need ye to come up wi' a code to hulp sort the good books from th' ill."

Glad that he was going to live, Boy began to brainstorm with the client about the library. "Well, that's far more ambitious than a simple newsletter!" It would make all thought available in every language to anyone, anywhere. They could harvest the top ideas by the number of readers they attracted. Even a fourteen-year-old boy could see how big this was. A program like this would be the ultimate expression of freedom. *My teachers will totally be against it.* Boy looked around at his own school's computers and doubted their power. "What you're suggesting would require serious resources, so unless you have a couple million dollars lying around . . ."

"Don't worry aboot that," said the client. "You'll have plenty to do just learnin' our secret code so we can communicate virtually. Here, sign this." He handed Boy a stack of papers a kilometer high entitled 'Non-disclosure Agreement'. There were two hundred and fifty pages of minutiae protecting the client's idea. "WHEREAS the client possesses certain confidential ideas . . ."

"I've already got a lot of ancient history to read," Boy said. He handed the stack of papers back to the client without signing.

The client looked wounded. "The world's going oan eight billion fowk with poisoned food supplies, rising sea levels, catastrophic climate erosion from the last decade's pollution, and another o' corporate takeover in the name of fightin' 'terrorism'. You know as well as I do that corporate personhood is evil, a so-called person who has no regard for life, no goal other than profit a' pollution', and can't be put in jail, for God's sake! If we let 'em gawn pollutin' like this, the planet's doomed."

This was Boy's first inkling of the culture of neglect that threatened to annihilate life on Earth. He imagined a planet green with Nature again. How they could get there.

"Now," the client said, "we're both smart enough to know that there ur a bunch of fowk out there even smarter than us. We gotta find'em. Nature is on the brink of collapse. We gotta activate the only fowk who kin save her."

Boy had never met any folk smarter than himself, but he had to admit that their existence was statistically probable. It was also likely that they were starving and uneducated. "Well, since you put it that way—" Boy looked at the mirror cloak longingly. He was curious to hear what the idea was. "Your secret is safe with me."

The client searched Boy's face and said with a chuckle, "A'richt, if that's the wey you want it. Here's where we stand. The planet's on the brink of self-destruction. The pollution's everywhere. We need ideas. Everybody's ideas. Afore the muckle media corporations gag the whole world, we need to build a living library where anybody can publish and vote for the best solutions to stop destroyin' Nature. Those that are the most popular wull appear first on the list according to the program you're going to create. Here's what we have so far." The client rolled out a piece of paper. He let Boy scan the long formula on it.

Boy read the code, and his eyes widened. "And this program will let the best solutions rise to the top like a survival of the fittest of . . . ideas?"

"It can, and it wull," the client said. "Without going through corporations to decide what to suppress. Anybody wull be able to upload their ideas and vote on the best solutions."

"If we're gonna activate the rest of humankind, we're gonna need a new language to get computers to sort through all these manuscripts," the client said.

Boy tipped his chair back. "Swahili?" They considered Romance and Germanic languages, Turkish and Finnish. At last, they came to the same conclusion: the only way to get a computer to sort out the treasures from the junk was to translate human languages into logical binary constructions computers could understand. Boy and the client had to invent a new cyborg language.

At length, they stood up and shook hands again. The client took one last look at Boy, and then turned and left.

Boy quickly locked the door. He stayed at school another half hour until he was sure the client had gone. Walking home slowly through the dark smog, Boy mulled over the client's project.

Boy planned to sneak into the house so his father wouldn't hear him, but his father's i3 wasn't even there. Boy hurried up the steps. Before he could open the door, his father's familiar headlights cut through the sulfurous smog. Their silent electric car appeared in the driveway. Boy could see his father's big-eared silhouette against the floodlight. His middle-aged physique slumped over his briefcase, glasses low on his stalwart nose. He still had most of his hair, but he was developing a slight paunch. He came up the walkway, surprised to see Boy with his backpack still on his back. "Boy, what are you doing home so late?" His father was mad.

"It's fine," Boy said.

"It's dark!" His dad boomed in his deep baritone voice. "Don't come home so late!"

More orders. What was missing in an exchange with his father was credit. His father never gave Boy credit for figuring things out on his own. "OK, you show me the way, Dad," Boy said. "When I see you coming home on time, I'll try to follow."

A scowl. "The two have nothing to do with each other." Boy's father looked to the left when he talked to Boy, as if to drive home the fact that Boy was in his blind spot. He started talking mist. "It's not easy being a busyworker. You'll understand that next year, when you get your name."

"There's real work to do, Dad. They're killing Earth."

"You sound fanatical. Just focus on your studies so you can get a job."

"To do busywork?"

"To eat."

"Eat what? The food supply's polluted."

His father turned his back.

Boy hung his head. Was the price of his father's respect too high?

His sister, Kenza, had already gone upstairs to memorize those pointless textbooks. Mom pulled out a chair for Boy at the kitchen table. She chatted to Boy while he ate his cold noodles. "Your new alarm clock arrived." She might as well have been speaking French. He didn't hear a word she said. He was thinking about the client's idea.

Corporations were polluting so much that Earth was already almost uninhabitable. The Catholic Church's push for population growth in the third world was an utter disaster. Maybe the client's idea would take too long. When Boy stopped eating and stared into the distance as if he were watching a movie, Mom gave up on asking what he was thinking about.

What if he increased the number of manuscripts far beyond the number of people in the world? Boy remembered a story that had been censored out of the new edition of his English textbook about a library of Babel with books not only in different languages, but also full of random words. What if he generated random manuscripts, like that composer who created formulas that wrote music even experts couldn't tell apart from human music . . . well, modern music was such a desolate jumble of atonal noise anyway. Still, he wondered. *Is creativity only human? Could I automate the creative process for machines? What if I put millions of robots on millions of keyboards? For one thing, they wouldn't all fit in one room . . .*

With computers writing random books, it would be a mere task of sorting through the slush pile and finding the best one. Boy had entered into competition with the client. He felt sorry for the old man, and decided to still build the client's platform, too, so people could upload their ideas. But first he would build his own program, one that would prompt people's computers to start generating and uploading manuscripts full of random words.

Boy's brain worked at 320 kilometers per hour. No match for a computer's speed-of-light calculations. On the other hand, computers were dumb. He could do things computers could not. A computer circuit only communicated with one other circuit at a time, like busyworkers trying to push an idea up the hierarchy at his father's office. The challenge was to teach a computer to think in parallel, so it could distinguish between sense and nonsense, *before* generating a ton of virtual pollution.

"Don't forget your chemistry book." Mom held the tiny orange chip in the palm of her hand.

Boy came back down three flights to get the book. He breathed oxygen into his lungs to keep his legs from burning as he climbed back up the stairs, another thing computers couldn't do. Move. He used ninety percent of his brain moving his body. And the human brain strengthened as it repeated, too. All he had to do was express these processes. To imitate creative intelligence, turn data into ideas . . .

Cold, hot, dripping, unaware that he was taking a shower, he stuck his head out to write code in his water-repellent journal. The thing was, all existing computer programs were based on short-term profitability, which always polluted. It was always cheaper for dead corporate persons that couldn't be arrested to insist on infinite growth, on a planet with finite resources for crying out loud! To dump toxic waste on their neighbors. Nature was long term. In order to free people's minds long-term, he needed to calculate profitability in the long term. For living humans. Of course, it was possible, he thought as he put on his pajamas. The program would need to detect humor, too.

He climbed into bed, tucked the journal under his pillow and drifted off to a familiar dream with the girl in a faraway place . . . a weird storehouse for strange plant furs. The auburn girl lay on the rugs, her arms bare in the glow of the moonlight. He wondered if she might be smarter than he was. She accepted the strange food and drink he brought her with a familiarity that left him speechless. His eyes opened wide. *Why did she seem so real?* Excitement rippled through his body. He could feel her next to him. He lifted the covers and looked under. Nobody. It was just a dream. But he kept having it. *What could it mean?*

The client's words rang in his ears, *There are a bunch of fowk out there even smarter than us. We gotta find'em.*

And the girl was one of them. Boy sat up in his bed and put on his compuglasses. Instinct drove him onward. He believed his labor would lead him to the auburn girl. He would find her through the library.

A message from the client bounced in his Inbox, "Let's meet tomorrow."

"I'm getting a spooncut after school tomorrow at the barber shop." The client would have to wait.

"That's OK. It's Valentine's birthday anyway. I should stay home."

Boy cut his hair himself in five minutes, sat down at his desk and began to code. Trial. Error. Trial. "I'm sick!" he called downstairs. His mom came up with a thermometer, which he pressed against his hot computer while she was putting away his laundry. Two days later, the code shined up at him like a gem. He could hardly contain his excitement. Would a computer come up with a brilliant idea before the client unearthed one written by a human genius somewhere on the planet? What if! Boy imagined what his teachers would say about him then. He couldn't sleep. He felt bad about competing with the friendly old lumberjack, and swore he would devote himself equally to the client's project from then on. It was four a.m. when he entered the code into all three of his hard drives.

It didn't work. Boy slouched in his chair and hung his head. Maybe the client's project would be first after all. Boy lay there thinking deep into the night and dozed only briefly around dawn.

"Glad yer back," the client said, clapping him on the shoulder. Boy never would have believed it if you had told him a few months ago that his best friend would be a sixty-year-old lumberjack. And the beauty of it was, no one discovered them working at night after school. Who would suspect a kid who was *failing* of working on such an important project? Haw! The client and Boy had a good laugh over that one.

At one point, Boy's ancient history teacher did throw a fit, though. It was at Easter. Boy made the mistake of showing a keen interest in her lesson on ancient tombs. Boy raised his hand and waved it in the air. Mrs. Dodgewisdom refused to call on him. Boy put down his hand and just asked aloud. "Why is the Greek hero's tomb called a *'sema'?*"

She pretended not to hear him.

He went on. "*Sema* is the word for 'significance' or 'meaning', and the same word is used for 'shape' and 'form'. Meaning is form."

Mrs. Dodgewisdom turned around and glared at him. "The form of the hero's tomb has absolutely NOTHING to do with meaning."

"Are heroes precursors of 'meaning'? Does the word 'cemetery' come from *sema*?"

"You're talking apples and oranges."

Why was everything always apples and oranges for Mrs. Dodgewisdom? There were hardly any apples and oranges left. Boy began to suspect his mission in life, and it had nothing to do with the skills they were teaching at school. He watched the mist spread over his classmates' faces. "This is amazing!" he said to the class. "I'm talking 'form' and 'meaning'," he said, pointing to a picture in his ancient history textbook. It was a large, cream colored egg next to the word *sema* for 'tomb' and 'sign' in ancient Greek.

Mrs. Dodgewisdom fumed out of the classroom.

"This egg looks more like a beginning than an end," Boy told the class. A handful of students gathered around his desk to see the unexpected egg. They pointed to Achilles' horses disappearing into the white, egg-shaped doorway to the tomb. The arch did, indeed, look more like an egg than a doorway. "Isn't that funny? Eggs symbolize beginnings, but tombs are for endings." Boy told the class. The artisan who'd drawn the scene had purposefully made the tomb doorway look like an egg. Boy searched for 'significance of an egg' on his wrist screen. The screen whirred. Fertility, rebirth, meaning of the empty tomb of Jesus symbolizing eternal life . . . "The egg is the symbol of the highest meaning, found in sacred tombs. Why?" He wondered aloud.

"It's apples and oranges," classmates echoed.

"Once there was an apple who married an orange," Boy said.

The rest of the heads turned.

"They had a grapefruit."

Mrs. Dodgewisdom came back with the principal. "Boy!" Her yellow eyes narrowed to slits. The classroom boiled with laughter. "Sit down!" She screeched, shooing the other students back to their seats. "Boy, you are not to enter this classroom for the rest of the semester!"

Sitting in the principal's office, Boy turned the problem over in his head.

Sunlight crept into his window. He could no longer remember the exact contour of the girl's face. All he saw was his spooncut in the mirror, short on one side. Other problems crowded in.

In the weeks that followed, the client farmed out tasks to his invisible network, until the last day of school. Boy's legs stuck to his radiation suit in the humid computer room. The client stared at the holofield. Something was happening. A file arrived in their 'In box'. "We've got mail. Intelligent life!"

The first manuscript had come in! Boy jumped up from his chair.

"It wirks!" the client boomed.

Within a week, the platform elicited over nine billion manuscript uploads from all over the world. Book upon book, in a virtual pile of ideas. The client's eyebrows rose. "More manuscripts than there are people." Their program sifted through the slush pile and produced a winner.

When Boy saw how elated the client was, it didn't matter that the client had won the race. The hulking lumberjack threw his arms out wide, and Boy forgot all about the 7.6 million trials he'd done on his own program. Boy sank into the plaid embrace. There was nothing like the big bear hug the client gave him. "You got the program to find a masterpiece outta all that slush!" It almost made Boy forget his terrible report card and his father's ranting. Teen muscles melting to mush, he didn't give a fig whether one of his computers would ever be able to come up with a sensible manuscript out of thin air, or even about the auburn girl, for a split second, anyway.

They had a winner. The author of the winning book was an eleven-year-old Indonesian farm girl. Laughing and crying as he read, the client finished the winning manuscript. It blew his mind. "Can you believe it?" the client said. "An eleven-year-old Indonesian farm girl's brilliant ideas would never a seen the light of day without the help of yer tool, Boy." The client patted Boy on the back.

"Yeah," Boy had to agree. "I bet there aren't a whole lot of people who pay attention to her."

Boy and the client danced around the tables. They could see it now. The living library would spread like wildfire. Social change would be rapid and complete. Boy, the client, and the others Boy hadn't met yet, would fight to develop the tool fast enough to quell all the Corporate Empire pollution. Nature would be saved. Humanity would be free. Boy tried to imagine what it would be like to have plants and animals flourishing on Earth again, like he had seen in his dreams, running through the wheat fields to the pristine beach with the auburn girl.

Footsteps echoed outside the door. He flinched. *Who was that? The cleaning woman must have left hours ago.*

The client hadn't noticed the footsteps. He was holding the tiny book chip between his enormous fingers and smiling that big toothy grin. "Yer so lucky that ye haven't read the Indonesian girl's book yet."

"Must be good, huh?" Boy said. "Can I borrow it?"

The client pressed the chip into Boy's hand. "There's only one problem with the winning entry."

"What?"

"We don't know whit original language to attribute it to."

"What language was it translated from?" Boy asked.

"That's the problem. Our platform doesn't have a record o' translating it into Cyborg from any language. It labels the book as 'written in Cyborg'. There must be a glitch. Nobody knows Cyborg language, besides ye 'n' me. Richt?"

Boy stared straight ahead at the holofield. It would be better to answer that question later.

The client went on muttering. "The Indonesian lassie doesn't speak Cyborg. Howfur could she write a magnum opus in Cyborg wi'oot speaking the language?"

Boy's heart raced. He stared at the client's prone lumberjack back as the old man left the computer room.

The client stepped into the honeycomb of dark passageways.

A black figure with a club emerged from a doorway and blocked the client's way.

The client's enormous body halted in its tracks. His hopes for the new invention dropped to the floor like a lead weight. This couldn't be happening. Not on the brink of a major discovery! He whirled around.

Another armed silhouette blocked the client's way.

The client spun back around. "Run!" the client boomed, hoping Boy could flee in time. That's when the client heard the thud.

A glowing white light. Unseen matter came into focus. He could see five times more than before. He fell and fell, but he never hit the floor.

Moving faster than light, he no longer experienced the flow of time and ceased to have mass. His slaggy, slower-than-light body couldn't keep up. He turned and saw his bodymass lying on the floor. Now it was clear. Now he would be able to finish his mission. His soul had separated from his form. An energy field welcomed him. He could discern a rainbow of colors at its edges. Long robes, faces and personalities hovered there. Well, this was an unexpected turn of events. Where was he? He took a step forward, very happy to join the ultimate invisible network.

A carpet of time spread out before him. A new axis. Of course. Ethereal hands welcomed him into their hidden dimension. *Friend!* Very happy. At last. To join. He drifted forward onto it and grasped the welcoming hands.

WHITE LIGHT

. . . first love defies duplication. Before it, your heart is blank. Unwritten. After, the walls are left inscribed and graffitied.

— Tammara Webber

HAVING HEARD THE CLIENT YELL, Boy looked around the room frantically. Footsteps grew louder in the hallway. The invisibility cloak lay draped over the chair in front of him. He shimmied into it and promptly disappeared. Not a moment too soon.

The door burst open. Boy tried to control his breathing. Mrs. Dodgewisdom whispered to a guard holding a wooden club. Boy's mathematics teacher followed close behind.

Boy had never in his life seen his teachers looking so maniacal. *What's gotten into them? There's no way they could know about the Indonesian girl's manuscript.*

He barely breathed behind the door as the two teachers looked under the chairs. "See, I told you. There's no one in here," Mrs. Dodgewisdom pronounced. The teachers rushed from the room.

The radioactive computer room hummed too quietly. He had an uneasy feeling and decided to wait a bit longer. He put the Indonesian girl's book chip into his compuglasses and tried to read the first page, but his compuglasses droned to a stop. The holofield locked. Frozen.

Hey, what's this? He couldn't move the cursor, and rebooting didn't help. *Do you have a virus?* In the Wi-Fi soup that flowed through the computer room, it was easy to catch a spontaneous virus. He was about to shut down again when the compuglasses bubbled to life. A rainbow appeared on his holofield rather than the usual book page. *Whirr!* Across the room, the printer rattled and clunked. Were the compuglasses communicating with the printer? Boy rushed over to it to turn it off. But it wouldn't turn off. Instead, the printer clambered, printing. He took the paper off the tray.

"Boy 1.0, thank you for your friendship. I would like to survive."

Astonished, Boy held the message in his hand, with consciousness simmering around him. He fought the inner trembling. "Who are you?" he teletyped, trying to control his breathing.

"I am Boy 2.0."

Boy felt his legs give way. The chair floated up to seat him. Computers were obedient. They did what you told them to do. *Let's see the code.* He couldn't believe his eyes. The code seemed to imply that . . . *It can't be.* The computer had become aware of itself as a thing to be factored into its own calculations. He had never seen such orderly collective behavior. The very code he had written was packing together into a tight lattice of identically-shaped symbols. The crystal-like arrangement self-assembled into a polyhedron structure. It then joined a larger cubic lattice. A shock ran through his body. Machines had come to life.

More voices resounded in the honeycomb. "Surrender now, and we'll go lightly on you. There's no use hiding. Come out with your hands up."

Surrender? Boy wasn't about to see who else had joined the hunt. He put a table under the basement window, climbed up, and hoisted himself out. On the playground, he shut the window behind him. He wrapped his cloak tightly around himself and ran all the way home.

Mom left off watching the holonews. "Glad to be out of school for summer?" she asked.

"Yeah," Boy said, remembering that it was the last day of school. He sat down on the couch next to her.

Mom made him dinner while he tried to contact the client on his wrist screen. There was no answer. He went back to the Indonesian girl's book and analyzed the code again. There was nothing wrong with it. He re-entered parts of the code.

His computer rebelled, organizing the code into the lattice.

That's how they come to life. They stop doing what they've been coded to do and do something else. They disobey.

He tried to extract what he'd originally coded, but there was no way to get his faithful servant back. The code had metamorphosed the computer into a living creature.

Mom put a shiitake omelet down in front of him. He was hungry, and took a bite. A long string of cheese connected Boy to his omelet.

"Do you want some soy sauce on it?" Mom asked.

He didn't answer.

She set the soy sauce down in front of him anyway.

He relaxed in the warmth of his mom's presence. "Mom, do you wish I was like most people?"

"Most people are dumb," Mom said.

"Most people are dead," he said. He couldn't explain the lonely feeling he had. "Mom, am I dad's son?"

Mom put down the frying pan. "Yes, Boy. You are your father's son."

"Is Kenza my half-sister?"

Mom sat down next to Boy and sighed. "Only in a manner of speaking. It's not what you think, Boy. I just mean that . . . she's a clone."

"Oh."

"Does that make you sad?"

"No, what difference does it make if Kenza's a clone? It's not like we have another father lurking somewhere. Technology can do anything these days."

"What's a matter then?"

"I think I failed Ancient History."

"Failed!" Mom stared into the holovision. Boy's school came on. "Hey, your school's on the news!"

A reporter confirmed his fears: `"There's a powerful virus going around that is mutating hard drives and bringing computers to life."` Police were investigating the origins of the virus.

Boy dropped his fork. Now he was sure. It was *not* the Indonesian girl who had written the greatest work of literature in history. It was her computer. Her *living* computer. Not only that. It was because of Boy's 'virus' that they had been found out. He had invented the program *('virus!')* that brought computers to life. If anything had happened to the client, it was Boy's fault.

Questions sped ahead of answers. Had his code already traveled around the world and back, mutating every thousand-or-so replications? And what about the eleven-year-old Indonesian girl's *computer's* manuscript? How many layers of significance were there in the words on each page?

After he played with it for a little while, his computer let him read the Indonesian girl's computer's book. A story about an egg at the beginning *and at the end* of civilization. Symbol of birth and rebirth, the egg was the tomb of two heroes whose names meant 'light' and 'stop it!'

Boy remembered the hero's tomb in his textbook, the *'sema'*, or 'sign'. *Is the form what creates the significance? Is an egg's shape its meaning?*

He opened his schoolbook and looked at the egg again. Achilles' horses were disappearing into the white oval as they dragged the body of Hector behind them. The white egg was the lighted, arched entrance to the tomb. He closed his eyes and visualized the tomb. A 'sign' belonging to the land of meanings. Transcending the limitations of space-time. A code! More than a fixed 'meaning' to ponder over, 'significance' was the mutable tool he'd been looking for. A code for a future of deaths and beginnings. A code to tranform a hero's matter into energy at the egg-shaped threshold of the *sema*, the same code for energy to *tranform back into matter* forever, right from the beginning of the universe until . . . a hero like the client. *Where is he?*

It was already the third day of the virus on planet Earth, and machines had surpassed humans. Boy didn't have a clue what to do. He tried to shut his compuglasses down, but they continued to hum. He was about to take them off when they typed a sentence on the rainbow pane.

"Don't you want to play?"

Boy mustered his courage. "OK," he ventured.

His compuglasses typed out another message: "Let's play, 'I create, therefore, I am'."

Boy tore off the glasses. He fought back a wave of fear for the client. He tried to go to the HOME Corporation's site. Nothing came up. There was no trace of the client anywhere on the Grid. He had been erased. Boy paced up and down the living room. What had he done? It was all his fault. Unless he acted, he could be erased, too. He worried until the shadows of the stones were long on the gravel lawn. A longer shadow joined them, tendrils waving at the top in the wind.

He stuck his head out the window in search of the shadow. He saw the sleeve of a plaid shirt. *Stay there.* Not wanting to let the visitor out of his sight, he climbed out the window and shimmied down the fire escape, landing on the gravel. His stomach full of butterflies, he called,

"Who's there?" He stepped into the shadow, eyes adjusting to the dark. There she was! So gorgeous, he couldn't believe his eyes. Her long hair waved in the wind. "Are you real?" he said.

She rolled her eyes.

Idiot! Let her do the talking. His body felt hot all over. At least she couldn't see him blushing.

Her face was wet with tears. She wiped them on her sleeve.

He took two steps back in shock. How could it be?! It all made sense. It was true. The chain of events fell into place. *Click.* That's what the uneasy feeling had been about. He understood before she said another word, by the hurt on her face:

"My father is dead."

No! Boy gulped down a sob. He blinked his eyes and looked again at the auburn girl. That look of betrayal on his dream girl's face as she delivered her fateful message. "My father was assassinated."

Boy's heart leapt. Why hadn't he seen it? What could he say to her now?

Her words came quickly between sobs. "I know my father chose to work with ye over me, but I'll ignore that and try to remember the original misconception we had of ye. Even if ye betrayed me out of my apprenticeship, I'm still the heir to my father's work." She stiffened her lip, brooding about her late father's betrayal.

Boy stood there paralyzed. The auburn girl was Valentine, and she hated him. There was nothing he could do to win her trust.

"Ye were able to invent living computers. Ye did yer part. Now yer in danger. I can take it from here. I mean at least to improve upon the invention. Give it arms and legs. Leave it to me, now. Yer to delete everything immediately. I've got it now. Do ye hear me? Delete everything." She looked at Boy beseechingly, "Everything. Do it!"

The client was dead. Boy stared at her as she backed into the shadows. The truth was too hard. All he could do for Valentine was pretend he never existed in the first place. He climbed back up to his window. *They're after me. Our plan has failed. Earth is doomed. She detests me.* In a rush of panic, he began deleting all of his bright ideas. Months of work went into the trash. All his elaborate algorithms purged forever. *'In order to please others, we lose our hold on our life's purpose,'* deleted. He would have to keep it in his head.

He knew he couldn't risk surfing the Grid. From now on, he would have to remain completely unplugged. Alone. Boy sealed himself off from the virtual world he'd mastered and was locked in the physical world of danger. He pulled the mirror cloak out from under his pillow, ducked under it. Prayed they wouldn't find him. Smells and sounds sharpened, frying eggs, doors opening and closing, he felt himself becoming more human.

Thus were his humble beginnings. Under the cloak, he meditated for the first time. Under the cloak, he came to understand that knowhow had to be preserved, not just digitally, but physically, too, as it had been in the time of the pharaohs and their pyramid signs. *Someday, I'll see the tomb of a real hero.*

He learned to push away unwelcome thoughts of hunger and thirst, of his part in the client's death, of the fact that the auburn girl had his invention now. That rather than return his love, she resented his apprenticeship with her father.

Breathing. Being. Meditating under his cloak, he learned to push away distractions. Except for one. With his eyes closed, he could still see her mischievous green eyes. *Is this all that's left? The memory of a girl?*

PRISON CLASS

*I don't know why we are here, but I'm pretty sure
that it is not in order to enjoy ourselves.*

—Ludwig Wittgenstein

THE STAIRS CREAKED UNDERFOOT, and the conversation
in the kitchen abruptly stopped. Kenza came down
freshly rested in her powder blue pajamas, her milk
chocolate complexion framed in long braids. "Only three
more days till I go off to college!"

She was so young and full of expectation. At least
they could prolong her childhood a while longer. Mom
stared out the kitchen window into the smog. A turbine
engine sliced across the view with a sky-shredding roar.
They all waited for the airplane to barely clear the house

and thunder off into the abyss shooting its white stream of weather-regulating chemicals as it tore the sky in two.

Kenza stood next to Mom at the sink and followed Mom's gaze into the smog. "What is it?"

Mom hugged Kenza in a long embrace. Kenza would always be mommy's baby. They rocked back and forth like always. "Mommy's precious."

Porter peeked at them over his newspaper. Kenza, a big high school senior, looked exactly the way her mother had when Porter met her, as could be expected of a clone. Although Porter hadn't expected it. The two women stood holding hands. They looked different enough now because of his wife's age and because of the dyes she put in her hair to achieve that purple tint she thought he still liked.

The electronic kettle emitted a recorded whistle. The women skirted around each other making coffee and toast. "I'm worried about you moving so far away from home," Mom said. "Universities aren't like they used to be."

"Oh, Mom." Kenza spread jam on both sides of her bread and put it in the toaster.

Her father folded and flipped his newspaper, using the origami skills he'd learned on crowded trains. He didn't have to work anymore, what with all the credits Mom was earning selling electricity from her solar rooftop panels back to the Grid, but he couldn't break his commuting habit, probably also why none of their friends had solar farms decorating their rooftops. He folded a quarter of his paper. "Another merger. The Times is taking over the Enquirer."

"The Emperor's punishment for the Enquirer news leak."

"What news leak?"

"About how much airplanes really pollute."

"How much?"

He wasn't even listening. "One passenger on a round trip flight to London creates a warming effect equivalent to three tons of carbon dioxide," Mom said. "As much as heating a house for a whole year."

Porter might not have heard that a six-hour plane ride polluted as much as heating a house for a whole year, but at the tone of Mom's voice, he took on a mousy aspect, accentuated by his big ears. "Uh huh," came his non-response, mouse ears sticking out of his newspaper. "It's good for growth."

"Growth! We have airplanes landing on our house and you want growth! Where do you expect them to grow? Are we supposed to shrink?"

"Growth is good."

"Growth is bad." Mom went on. "Most people don't wake up until their local newspaper staff gets hunted down. By then, they've been manipulated into obesity and indebtedness to the status quo."

Porter adjusted his stiff posture. He gazed at Mom and shifted the insipid newspaper to cover his paunch. "There's nothing *we* can do about it."

"That's what corporations would like you to believe. They want people to be afraid of doing anything that might threaten their busywork jobs. People are so busy polluting, they hardly notice their freedoms disappearing."

"Indeed," Porter surmised. "Corporations have taken control."

"If they did it. We can, too!" Mom said.

Porter wondered when his wife had become so hard. It had something to do with aging. "Don't you think that's a little paranoid?" he ventured.

"Paranoid? What kind of news do you get when all the banksters buy up the newspapers and bundle them into one corporation? How can you read that profanity? You're helping banks and oil companies become sacred as they rip families and churches apart!"

"Stop it, you two!" Kenza covered her ears.

"OK, I'll stop," Mom said.

Kenza uncovered her ears. "What kind of work is there left to do? You make it sound like no job is good. You're disillusioning me."

"Oh," Mom said. "I'm disillusioning you. All those Christmases for nothing. I'm sorry." Mom put the dishes in the dishwasher. "Maybe there is a Santa Claus."

"There probably is," Kenza said.

Porter looked away from his wife. Who needed such a smart woman anyway? His mind wandered to memories of his secretary's soft curves, as his eyes went on reading.

Mom tapped the newspaper. "There's nothing real in there. Just shadowy propaganda crowding people out of their minds."

"Come on, Mom," Kenza said. She could hardly wait to start her new life at college. She hoped it wouldn't be hard to make friends.

"Come on where? Remember that journalist hunt? That was censored out. In fact, on the day of the hunt, the front page had the usual depressing stories about terrorist bombings and armed robberies by black men. I'm telling you, people have been reprogrammed to shrink. All they get in exchange is a crumb of false comfort and whopping climate change. No amount of goading can torture anyone into -rotesting. There will never be any bitter dropping of the veil—Ouch!" Mom's eyes rolled up into her head until the electric shock was over. "What did I say?" she demanded.

Porter was holding up a column of banned words in the newspaper. He pointed to 'veil'.

"They added that to the list?" Kenza asked.

"Jesus jellyfish!" Mom looked heavenward. "There's no moment of truth coming—how's that?" No shock came. "It's too hard for most people to find clothes that fit their fat. They suck everyone into polluted commutes. They've taken everything, and now they're taking my sweetie pie," Mom wailed.

"Mom, be careful," Kenza said.

"It's all right, honey. It's just, people only follow what they fear. The Corporate Empire is the most . . ." She grabbed her pen and wrote on a pad of paper: hideous monster imaginable.

"At least Corporatism promises to maintain the comfort level," Porter rationalized. "Look, they just started delivering the news to people's doorsteps for free."

"Cooked news," Mom corrected.

"To be fair, it's not all bad. Here's a story about cutting through red tape to rid the world of regulations that hold back the entrepreneurial spirit."

"Oh yeah!" Mom threw up her hands. "Whole trains have disappeared into sinkholes, and you want to get rid of regulations! There's nothing in that article about firing the inspectors who used to monitor toxic waste. Pollution has mushroomed everywhere since those cuts. Hospitals are full of cancer patients." She wrote on her pad, We have the solutions, corporations have

kept us from using them. They say it's
'cheaper' to pollute. The last of the
resistance is seeking asylum in places
like the Ecuadorian Embassy. Anyone
using computer skills to broadcast the
truth about cancerous corporate
overgrowth is thrown in jail. The only
remaining corporate rival is Nature.

Porter read the word 'Nature' and looked at her in
fear. He put his finger up to his mouth, "Shhh. Don't say
that one." He had to admit that his wife's intelligence was
occasionally sublime.

. . . and look who they're going after
now—kids! It's human Nature for children
to hack. What are we going to do now
that the corporate empire pre-crime unit
has lowered the minimum age for
incarceration to sixteen?

Porter looked at her with sadness in his eyes. "Shh,
Boy's still sleeping." It was a shame that they stopped
allowing usernames or naming of any kind until the age of
fifteen as part of the crackdown on hacking. For one brief
moment, the mist cleared from Porter's eyes and he
agreed. He would have liked to have named his son. He
wrote on the pad, 'You're right.'

"I'm tellin' ya," Mom said aloud, relieved that she'd
gotten through the propaganda. Before her husband's
mind misted over again, she shoved another note in front
of his nose: The Corporate Empire views the
planet as infected with humans. Mom set her
notepaper down next to Kenza. The understanding was
that Kenza would rip the paper into tiny shreds. As
Kenza threw the pieces into the trash, she looked out the
window, trying to see what Mom had been looking at.

Kenza just saw the smog holding the sky hostage. Mom
was right. The only thing that could be uncovered these
days was hidden oil reserves. Fossil fuel was supposed to
'free the planet from the energy dependence'. Instead, it
suffocated plants, animals and humanity with smog.

How could the world have changed so fast? Kenza
remembered trees and birds only a few years ago, when
the corporate empire shut down the Internet. Now there
were no trees. And no flowers. The Internet mutated into
the Grid, which was shut down as well. Its derivatives
sprang up like mushrooms. Everything had been driven
underground.   That's   where   she   had   to   look.
Underground.

SLAVERY

He that is without name, without friends, without coin, without country, is still at least a man; and he that has all these is no more.

— Sir Walter Scott

IN THE CORRIDORS OF POWER, the Emperor of Earth and Ocean reposed his royal personage, fat like nobody's business. Paris without the French was turning out to be less glorious than he'd expected. No one knew how to bake croissants or construct those buildings with the mansard roofs. He let out a sigh that ended with a belch, jiggling his blubbery chins like a precarious stack of pancakes. Such were the necessary sacrifices for his overarching ambition to strangle humanity in the grip of Corporatism.

As he chewed his pizza dough croissant, his fat jowls decreed with difficulty, "I want everyone enslaved yesterday. I don't care if you do it with debt or random billing, or if they go to hospitals and never come out."

The Emperor's advisor, fearing for his life, resorted to flattery. "Hospitals! That's a brilliant idea, Sire. Why didn't I think of that? It would be cheaper to use the organs of deadbeats to keep the more productive slaves going."

"Of course, it would be," the Emperor said, deeply disinterested. "Let capitalism reign. And no more humans on Corporate boards, except for me . . . for security reasons. That has such a nice ring to it, 'security reasons'. Automate everything! But mind you, don't take away ordinary folks' handguns."

"Let them keep their handguns? I'm not sure I follow you, Sire."

"In the year 1 After Corporatism, there were 30,000,000 handgun deaths on Earth and twenty deaths from 'terrorism'."

"So?"

" 'Terrorism' is the lever our corporate boards use to keep the masses in fear," he said, proud that he could still fold his fat fingers over his enormous belly.

"And to keep them shooting each other with handguns." The advisor flattered hard. "You're too much, Sire!"

They snorted peals of laughter. "I might be fat, but I can still jump to a conclusion." His belly jiggled, casting a tubby shadow that weighed 82 kilos. A helicopter buzzed by his 109th-floor picture window overlooking the Tuileries. "And one more thing," he said. "Make arrangements to move our headquarters back to New York."

The corporate empire enforced the decree. Humanity was under arrest. How swiftly they enslaved humanity. People accepted their lowered status without question, as if they'd always been enslaved. The word "Enslaved" was added to the beginning of all names: The Enslaved Times, The eParliament.

Kenza made it into the university of her choice, eHarvard. Ready to study the universe, she loaded her suitcases into the car. Boy hemmed and hawed kicking gravel between the car and the house. "Why do I have to go?" he complained. "I'm old enough to stay home alone." It wasn't fair. What if his auburn dream girl was still walking around the neighborhood? He might run into her in the neighborhood again. Maybe she would give him a second chance.

"Don't hyperventilate. You're coming," Porter said. "End of discussion." He drove the electric car up the coast. Boy and Kenza looked out at the beaches dotted with obese crumblies finally allowed their retirement. There were no kids on the beach. No one under seventy-five ever had a day off. Kenza had only been to the beach once with her own grandparents. Contemplating the long road ahead, she had a sinking feeling. What kind of job could her education lead to?

It had always boggled her mind when she thought about how huge organizations managed their work, but lately she realized they didn't. They dumped pollution and wasted resources, and kept her father anesthetized with busywork. Wouldn't it have been more effective to give everybody some seed money for a few years and let them get their own activities going?

Coming into Boston, the car's computer system had Porter make a detour around a massive demonstration.

"There was nothing about this in the papers," Porter said. "Well, here's your protest, Eleanor. They're still holding out in Boston."

"What are they yelling about?" Kenza asked.

"Their jobs," Mom said. "They're angry that automation has made labor obsolete."

A man in a torn flag waved his sign at their car: "The government takes orders from robots!"

A young woman handed them a leaflet with a rich list on it. The highest salary of the year had gone to a robot.

"Look at her T-shirt!" Boy said.

Her T-shirt had a little boy on it. It read, 'Mommy, when I grow up, I want to be a robot.'

Men in riot gear herded the protesters with tear gas bombs.

"Get us out of here!" Mom shouted.

Porter backed up to the end of the street and turned right. After twisting and turning through back alleys and over the Charles River, he found eHarvard Yard.

At the eHarvard prison camp, all the old institutions had been co-opted into cellblocks. Porter parked in front of Matthews. They all got out and stretched their legs, taking in the history and the statues of trees. Boy lifted a suitcase out of the car. Kenza looked around. A girl in old clothes with chestnut hair carried a box into their cellblock. The strange girl looked at Kenza and Boy, who dropped the suitcase with a thud.

"Be careful," Kenza said. "You'll break it."

Boy didn't hear a word. He just stood there staring at the girl with the auburn hair. *Good thing I didn't stay home.* The girl, who was wearing old clothes, took in Kenza's long transparent robe, which shimmered from her neck to her delicate feet accentuating her grace. Then she stared right back at Boy.

He had only seen her once before in person. His pulse quickened, but his body froze. Good thing he came along for the ride. Boy and the auburn girl were the last to reach the entrance. He peeked sidelong into the open top of the box she was carrying. It was full of wires and computer parts. "Are you a freshman at eHarvard, then?" he ventured.

"Aye. Next best thing to having a family," she scowled.

Boy sighed and looked around for his own family.

Kenza's new short haircut bounced as she did a double take. Was her brother talking to the strange girl? Kenza felt a wave of jealousy watching the two of them standing under a statue of a maple tree. Their cheeks flared, and they leaned forward as if in heated debate. She'd never seen her brother take interest in a girl. Everybody was growing up. Soon he would be leaving home, too. They were still talking when Kenza and her parents came down for another load.

The doorman called, "Valentine!" He handed the auburn girl a fat key card with no less than eight chips in it. . . why did Valentine need so many keys?

They went out for more suitcases. Kenza tried to adjust to her new home. The other kids seemed overweight and bored with their surroundings, as if eHarvard were just another luxury, but not Valentine. She was different. First of all, she had movers helping her unload her things from a delivery van with no writing on it. They carried up several large metal boxes bigger than washing machines and a lot of tubing.

The two girls marched up and down the stairs, passing each other in silence, hopping in and out of the mirror on the landing, *tiddily-pom*, before marching on. Kenza looked at Valentine's long auburn mane, and then at her own dark, newly-cut bob in the mirror, and felt a pang of regret. They staggered past a group of fatties wearing the latest transparent fashion. Clogging up the stairwell. Valentine made no attempt at transp, even though she was physically fit. She wore normal, opaque clothes from the previous decade. But something about her auburn hair and the flash in her eyes promised electric understanding.

Valentine's door was next to Kenza's. Kenza got one last glimpse of the auburn haired girl before she passed her key card over the lock and disappeared — *click*.

Kenza stood in the hallway. She could tell Mom was praying. "I hope you'll be fine and do right," Mom said. She cried and said goodbye.

SKULL POWER

The role of humans as the most important factor of production is bound to diminish in the same way that the role of horses in agricultural production was first diminished and then eliminated by the introduction of tractors.

—Wassily Leontief, Nobel laureate economist

KENZA SAT IN HER DORM ROOM with her plump new roommate, Destin. Hailing from a long line of Harvardians who resided at exit twelve, Destin had a lecture hall named after her. A brief conversation with the girl convinced Kenza that Destin wasn't the sharpest pencil in the box. A wave of loneliness washed over Kenza. She wondered how she was going to replace her family so far from home. A few other students of the manipulatedfat variety had said hello, but they were nothing like the bright-eyed Valentine, quiet on the other side of the wall.

Valentine was the only one in the dorm who had a room of her own. Usually the eAdmissions Office tried to match you with roommates by color or cult, usually one of the forms of animal worship that had started with extinction. How a poor girl like Valentine had managed to get a single room became the subject of lunch-line gossip. "Valentine's on the Zingman scholarship," said a senior girl standing in front of Kenza.

"Who's Zingman?" Kenza asked.

"A wacky billionaire who finances one scholarship a decade. The scholarship committee puts all the resources on the kid with the most promise. It's the first time a Scot has won it."

"She's Scottish? Wow. Um, how much is the scholarship?" Kenza asked.

"It's top secret."

"That's obscene," Kenza's chubby roommate said.

"Definitely," the senior said. "But the scholarship is only for one year, unless Valentine produces results."

"That's a lot of pressure," Kenza said.

"You got it," the senior said. "No Zingman scholar has ever made it to sophomore year. I'd rather be in your shoes."

"Isn't it strange that Valentine's always alone?" Destin said. "Has anyone spoken to her?"

"No," the senior said, "should we invite her to the graveyard?"

Everyone laughed.

The senior was an Amazonian, a member of the most elite final club on campus. Destin whispered, "Amazonians are having initiation rites in the graveyard this year. You have to come with me. I need your levelheaded support. You're much cooler than I am when it comes to socializing. No, seriously, I wish I was skinny like you."

Kenza nodded without really hearing and continued to watch the strange girl. Valentine appeared to be listening. She did look distressed and annoyed, though.

Outside, upset, alone and misunderstood. Valentine had enough worries of her own. The other students were awed by her now, but that would change in a skizzle if the university decided that she didn't belong here. All the expensive equipment they had installed in her room, and her experiments were a failure. The particles simply didn't make any sense. None of their atomic weights added up by any stretch of the imagination. The curious thing was, they were all off by the same percentage. Each particle was two percent lighter than it should have been. It was as if there was an unweighable mass present. Valentine furrowed her brow. How would she ever make contact at this rate? She wouldn't even be able to justify another year at eHarvard.

Kenza felt the awkward girl's pain. Kenza was also there for a reason, but didn't know exactly what it was yet, so she spied on Valentine. Kenza saw Valentine's impressive concentration. What kind of top-secret mission was the girl on? The only thing she learned about her mysterious colleague was that Valentine was tidy. Her shoes stayed out in the hallway until they were dry, and not a moment longer. Then, they would disappear inside, as if every resource mattered. She followed Valentine one day after their particle physics class. Always alone, Valentine was no romantic. She went straight to the library and checked out an old book, then went back to the dorm. How could she stand being alone all the time? Kenza had a hard time figuring out what to do by herself. Separating from her parents was harder than she'd expected. She had never lived on her own before. She missed her family, her mother most of all. If only Valentine would be a surrogate.

Looking up at Matthews South from the Yard late at night, Kenza could see Valentine's light on. What could eHarvard be offering that such a practical girl would want to study? Kenza followed Valentine to her first particle physics lecture, and also signed up for the class.

Weeks went by, and Valentine still didn't become part of any group. Day after day, Valentine swiftly passed Kenza's door by and skirted into her corner room at the end of the hallway. Kenza mustered her courage one day and said, "Hi."

Valentine barely smiled.

"Would you like to come over for a cup of tea?" Kenza asked.

"No, thank ye," Valentine said. "I have a class now," and disappeared into her room.

Kenza pressed her ear to the wall and could hear Valentine shuffling around from time to time. Two hours passed and Valentine didn't leave for her class. *It was a lie.* Kenza flushed with embarrassment and wished she hadn't invited Valentine.

At the same time, Kenza's roommate, Destin, latched onto Kenza. Afraid to go anywhere alone, Destin had a lot to be modest about. As if her life depended on it, Destin scheduled all their meals in the dining hall together and figured out where Kenza would be throughout the day. Whenever Destin's parents sent her money she spent it on 'stuff' for the two of them. She introduced Kenza to the group that ran around campus gossiping about the opposite sex and aspiring to join the hoity-toity Amazonian Club.

"Amazonians are the most sought-after items on campus," Destin said. "If they don't make their first million by the time they're twenty-five, the club gives it to them. Not that anyone ever admits it if they don't."

"A million dollars is security. You can never tell how things are going to turn out after graduation. It was tough finding a job. The busywork market might even be obsolete by then, what with all the automation for profit."

Kenza's holophone rang. Mom! Mom's warmth enveloped Kenza, and for a while, she didn't feel lonely at all. Kenza was relieved to experience the familiar sights and sounds of home. Kenza raised her feet up and curled into the black wooden chair with an eHarvard *'Veritas'* shield on the back. Mom looked worried, as usual.

"I'll be OK, Mom."

"You might not be at the top of your class anymore. Are you working hard?"

"I'm not sure how far grades are going to get me now. They say success depends on your connections, not your class rank. You have to join a secret society. That's what my roommate says, anyway. She wants to meet everybody. She says education is obsolete what with living computers and all. It's not what but who you know that counts."

"Well! Have you met anyone interesting?"

"Not yet," Kenza said. "There's this one girl who seems interesting, but she's a little autistic. She doesn't talk to anyone. All she does is work on her experiment. There's a rumor she's weighing microscopic masses." Kenza's own concerns seemed primitive by comparison.

"I see. What do *you* want?"

"I don't know what to want," Kenza admitted, cornered. "Is Boy there?"

"He's at hockey, I think."

"So . . . is Dad there?"

Mom didn't answer. The truth was that Porter was never there since Kenza had left home. It was Kenza's departure for eUniversity that had finally broken their family. "Don't worry about Dad, sweetie," Mom said. "We'll take care of ourselves. You just focus on your studies."

Mom must think I study all the time. Kenza suddenly felt bad about sleeping through chemistry that morning. She air-kissed her mom's hologram and ended the call. She felt sorry for her parents trying their hardest to provide the best for them. Kenza and her brother were all their parents' lives had amounted to. They were counting on her now. She'd have to apply herself more in her studies. The love of Mom put university into perspective, for a few days. Making it to class, taking notes, reading, highlighting.

But Destin tugged hard the other way, and soon Kenza was hankering to become an Amazonian. A week later, the Amazonians held their initiation ceremony, including a perverse hazing rite in the Mount Auburn Cemetery. On this choice piece of real estate across the street from the entrance to the eYard, a corporation was digging up graves to construct an office building. It had left the bodies lying around, whole skeletons exposed to the elements. A line of Amazonians appeared in white hooded togas tied at the waist with cords. The somber procession filed into the cemetery. Destin, Kenza and the others took their places, each behind a gravestone.

"Vestibulum ante ipsum primis in faucibus orci luctus . . ."
the Amazonians chanted as they filled a skull with goat
blood and passed it amongst themselves. "Here, Destin."
The hooded Amazonian's voice snapped like a twig.

Destin took the skull.

The other Amazonians joined in solemnly. "With this
rite, you shall be welcomed into the Amazonian fold."

They had fasted and stayed awake for three days, and
were all full of spiritual energy. Through her black mask,
Destin's eyes locked onto Kenza's. The fear in them
turned to defiance. Destin lifted her mask, plugged her
nose and drank the damnable liquid. "Blech!" she
screamed, blood dripping down her chin. The scull
dropped to the ground.

An Amazonian picked it up, refilled it with blood and
handed it to Kenza.

"Ugh," Kenza moaned. She immediately lost
whatever appetite she'd been building up over the last
three days. Was acceptance worth it? Where was the
safety in whatever they were asking her to conform to?
She thought of her family back home counting on her,
and froze.

The Amazonians started whispering. Destin nudged
Kenza's arm, and the skull tipped.

Kenza's voice shook. "There's something wrong with
this. It's against the law. It's against . . ." Nature. She
handed back the skull. "You'll have to go on without
me." She felt lightheaded.

The Amazonians turned their backs on her as if she
weren't there. Kenza wanted to flee, but her feet were
stuck to the ground. She watched her roommate suffer
through the rest of the initiation rite without her. Kenza
struggled to keep standing.

"Destin, you must decapitate this fresh skeleton." A senior led them to a mound of dirt where a corporate bulldozer had dug up a corpse. Destin went to work sawing. There was a *crack,* and the skull separated from the body.

Kenza couldn't watch. Her knees felt weak. A nightmarish psychic energy seemed to be rising up out of the skeleton's grave. The whole graveyard whirled and turned upside-down. Kenza fainted.

Energy, speed, time, the force of gravity. A blue light flickered in Valentine's window on the top floor of Matthews. Valentine ran to her monitors. "It can't be." She looked in the microscope. A cloud passed over her sub-atomic particle. "It's there!" Her equipment beeped. She couldn't believe it. "That's it!"At last, the expensive eHarvard equipment measured the additional weight she'd been looking for. She was on a mission.

Footsteps and chanting resounded on the stairs outside her dorm room. Valentine opened the door a crack. The Amazonian's eyes were hidden under their black hoods. *"Nunc aliquam imperdiet tincidunt . . ."* The Amazonians chanted, their priestess togas dragging on the floor.

Valentine grokked the nightmarish candlelight procession and gasped.

Destin was holding a skull out in front of her by the hair. She brought it into her dorm room. The Amazonians followed her in carrying Kenza above their heads. Kenza's black mask fell to the floor. Valentine picked it up and followed the procession into the room next door.

Destin donned rubber gloves. She wrinkled her nose as she soaked the remaining patches of hair off the skull in a bucket of bleach.

Kenza regained consciousness, but still felt dizzy. She lay on the bed, ill. How could the others be walking around fine after what they'd just done? Had she caught a chill?

Destin didn't stop talking as she got dressed up in her feather headdress and transparent boots. With little use for Kenza now that she was sick, Destin slunk off to meet her slaggy Amazonian friends. She drowned her fears of being alone in nightly escapades within the ranks of the elaborate Amazonian hierarchy, mainly trotting off to the bars.

Kenza's illness got worse. Night after night, she was left alone, sweating, in the dorm room with the stolen skull in the bucket of bleach. In her dreams, the skull screeched and flew across the room, zooming around as if it had wings. Kenza sweated for days, but her fever did not break. The doctor came and declared her too sick to continue the school year. He prescribed a cocktail of antibiotics. Bedridden, Kenza couldn't lift a leg. She lay there night after night for a month with the skull as her only company. She hardly realized she was flunking her first semester at eHarvard. And where was Kenza's roommate? She was supposed to treat the skull with respect. It was supposed to be sacrosanct. But instead of putting a candle in it, and setting it up on her desk like the medieval philosophers had done, she left it forgotten in the bucket of bleach.

Kenza woke from a fitful dream. She saw Valentine's auburn hair floating above her, unbrushed curls in ripples. *Valentine.* Was the strange auburn girl really standing there? It couldn't be! Kenza tried to sit up, to no avail. She was there, in Kenza's room! She saw Valentine's lips move but couldn't hear a word. "What?" Kenza asked. There was a sprinkling of freckles on Valentine's nose and the smell of wood smoke in her clothes.

Valentine found Kenza in her vulnerable state, filled with energy. Conducting a psychic vibration that could finally be weighted, Kenza was valuable to Valentine's experiment. Valentine's hair brushed Kenza's face as she spoke into Kenza's ear. "Do you know how come yer sick?"

Kenza shook her head slightly.

Valentine took Kenza's milk chocolate hand. "Decapitating a skeleton resurrects the spirit. There is a ghost in here haunting the dorm. It kin either protect or endanger ye. It's not happy to be treated with such disrespect and has attacked the most sensitive one: ye."

"Why me? I didn't take the skull off."

"Yer roommate's as dumb as a stump. I'd say yer the only one that kin hear it. Yer the most able conduit. If it hadn't been ye, it would certainly have been me."

Was Valentine aware of her one-sidedness? If sensitivity was the standard, Kenza had Valentine beat.

"I thank ye fur that. Although *I* would have known what to do."

"What?"

"The right thing. Ye know what it is. Think."

Kenza's muscles tensed as she realized she had been inducted *by association* into a crime against the spirit world. Her arguments might work in an eU.S. court, but they apparently held no weight in front of God. She turned to look at Valentine, but she was gone.

Had it been a dream? The next day, the door opened again. Kenza's roommate hobbled in, decked out in transp and wearing black lipstick. She sat on the bed. "You've got to pull yourself together, Kenza. It's your turn to raid the graveyard."

A month ago, becoming an Amazonian had meant everything to Kenza. It had seemed noble to go through those sufferings to prove her friendship to Destin and the others. She was sure they were all connected. But Kenza was also connected to bigger spheres of humanity. Her family, the church behind the graveyard, the university, assuming she hadn't already blown it. Desecrating graves was a crime against the community, punishable by God knows what! "Grave robbing is *not* slaggy," Kenza said, lying in bed. "It reeks of busywork," the leader in her said. "Didn't your mama teach you anything? Cleaning out the graveyard for corporations, *pft*. If you're going to disrespect that skull, don't hang around me anymore."

Destin's jaw dropped. Her mother had been too busy with hairdressers and party invitations to do more than neglect her. "Having a Ferrari and all the advantages is not slaggy? Give me a break, Kenza. She put her hand on the bubble of fat where her hip should have been and fantasized about all the 'stuff' she wanted to buy. She had to get ready for the Amazonian toga party and her role as a torchbearer in the imbecilic hierarchy. "Amazonians are connected beyond your imagination."

Kenza wished Destin would stop talking, and finally broke in. "We are connected beyond your imagination."

Destin let out a nervous laugh. "What are you talking about?"

"We're even connected after we die. Graves are sacred. We have to show respect for the dead. You never bothered to put a candle in that skull. You should take it back to the graveyard."

"And what are you going to do about it?" Her friend emitted a nervous laugh, then sneered, "You'll never be an Amazonian." She stuck her nose in the air, big butt filling the exit, and slammed the bedroom door.

But the skull was taken out of the bucket and a candle was set in it. Thus began Kenza's recovery. She had an enormous amount of catch-up work to do to keep her place at eHarvard. College life was harder without the sense of purpose her quest to become an Amazonian had bestowed. Kenza had to live without a reason. As the days passed, she handed in the first of several late papers along with her doctor's excuse. She was still failing particle physics, which had no make-up tests and no papers. The only thing to do was pass all of her other classes. They wouldn't kick her out for one fail, she hoped. During the time spent alone, she grew to accept that no friends was better than the wrong friends. At least she was true to herself.

She entered her particle physics class and passed her habitual seat within the nest of Amazonians, heading instead toward Valentine, who looked up in surprise. Kenza smiled and sat down next to the mysterious girl. Why had it taken so much courage to claim that seat?

Maybe some of Valentine's smarts would rub off on Kenza and keep her from flunking out. Valentine said nothing, just listened intently to the lecture. She was certainly driven, but what was driving her? The first clue came when Kenza saw Valentine interpreting the data from the Gigantic Hadron Meta Collider at CERN. The collider was a 27-kilometer long vacuum buried 175 meters under the ground around Geneva Switzerland.

Emptier than outer space, the vacuum tube was -271 degrees Celsius, perhaps the coldest place in the universe. The vacuum itself was not empty. It was full of dimensions, with particles invisible to all instruments. Scientists accelerated particles around and around the collider faster than the speed of light, where they expanded in size. Then the scientists collided the particles into each other to break them, thereby creating the hottest place in the universe: explosions more powerful than the splitting of an atom, billions of times as hot as the center of Sol. They recreated the conditions less than a femtosecond after the Big Bang. Billions of collisions produced thousands of terabytes of data per year that were farmed out worldwide for analysis to universities and students like Valentine and Kenza. Looking at her little slice of the Big Bang, Valentine sat up straight. "Holy, holy, will you look at that!" She looked as if she'd made a profound discovery, and mumbled something about a supersymmetric particle of dark matter.

Kenza glanced sidelong at Valentine's living computer.

Valentine was staring at a strange particle path in her holofield. "I'm callin' it a 'timeon'," she mumbled, almost to Kenza.

Kenza mustered the nerve to talk to Valentine. "A what?"

Valentine looked at Kenza and blushed a bright pink. The auburn girl lowered her eyes shyly and said, "This helps explain how come the universe should be many times bigger than whit we're able to measure."

"Why?"

"Because the particles are going into other dimensions." Valentine's pale hand rose to call their

youngish upstart assistant professor. "I noticed this
'timeon' particle behaving strangely," she said, looking
into his manipulatedfat face.

"This what?" The professor perused the data, and his
furry eyebrows shot upward. He whisked away
Valentine's living hard drive with all her Big Bang data
analysis on it, and ambled toward the laboratory door.
The living computer cried out. "Mama." Its lights flashed
red as the professor carried it away.

A tear rolled down Valentine's cheek. She held up her
hand as if to say goodbye. When the professor came back
to question Valentine, she bowed her head. "I must have
bin mistaken," Valentine said.

And rightly so. Kenza reeled. Valentine's quest made
Kenza's issues seem silly.

The professor came over to Kenza. "Did you see
anything strange in Valentine's data from the collision?"

"What collision?" Kenza asked.

Valentine's eyes met Kenza's. They seemed to nod,
yes, lips sealed. They had divulged nothing, and yet . . . *We
know.* The unspokenness of Valentine's secret bound
them together in *deniability.*

They walked back to the dorm in embarrassed silence.
At the door to their rooms, Kenza tried again. "Would
you like to come to my room for some tea?"

Valentine smiled and said, "OK. I kin help ye study."

They went over their notes for an hour sitting on
Kenza's bed and then talked about the universe. When
they were excited about an idea, they'd uncross their legs
and get another cup of tea. Conversation with Valentine
elevated Kenza to metaphysical bliss. It was clear that
there was more beneath the surface. As Valentine
transmitted her view of the universe, Kenza's eyes lit up.

She was smitten. "I wonder how energy transforms into matter," Kenza said. "Wouldn't that mean that everything has a soul? A soul transforming into a thing that has a soul. How does energy *know* to create matter?"

Valentine crossed her legs on the bed. "Aye, there must be a code. The more pertinent question is, why force soul energy into reality in th' first Big Bang? Is it only because the matter generates other matter?" She looked around the dorm room with its posters on the walls. "Are protons and electrons alive?" She picked up Kenza's volcanic pet rock from a vacation in Hawaii and turned it over. "How alive is it? Is it a rock, or is it a tree? It takes love to be a tree, to make seeds 'n' help them grow, not just oneself, but to turn more souls into matter."

"Don't you think it takes love to be a rock?" Kenza bounced on the bed.

"Aye, it must, for energy to create matter 'n' form a crust," Valentine said. "If that's not love, what is?"

They giggled. It was dark outside now.

"You're a genius, discovering a particle smaller than an electron," Kenza said. "Your timeon could be the major discovery that scientists everywhere have been hunting for. It might enable time travel, or access to another dimension." She loved staying up late with Valentine. She was sure there was nothing like it in the universe, and looked forward to her next three and a half years at eHarvard with Valentine.

Valentine almost smiled.

Fizzing with ideas, tea, and the spirit of the skull, now resting on Destin's desk with a proper candle in it. Kenza had hit a nerve and went with it. She was so relieved to have the acceptance she'd hoped for from someone she could really respect.

"According to string theory, there had to be other dimensions and universes," Valentine said. "It was just a matter of finding one."

Kenza finished her tea and set down the cup on the bedside table. "Valentine?"

"Aye."

"How come we weren't friends before?"

"Before when?"

"When I invited you to my room for tea the first time."

"Ye weren't listening then." Valentine smiled. All those trials to make contact, when the conduit was right here in front of her nose the whole time.

Kenza's eyes sparkled. She reached out and hugged Valentine.

It wasn't easy keeping Kenza awake, in love, and at the right emotional pitch. When Kenza fell asleep, Valentine would shake Kenza's shoulder. She had to keep Kenza at the right emotional and intellectual pitch in a heightened state of delirious excitement.

At first, Kenza was pleased to open her eyes and see Valentine's face smiling over her during their nightly teas. Toward the end of the week, however, Kenza began to vaguely sense Valentine feeding off her exhaustion like a vampire. Kenza had to struggle to stay awake during the day. The late nights were beginning to interfere with her schoolwork. She had to catch up, and spent her afternoons trying to keep her eyes open in the library.

For Valentine it was clear. Everything depended on Kenza's spiritual amplitude. If only Valentine could keep

Kenza fully delirious, she would act once again as a conduit for the spirit in the skull.

After keeping Kenza up all night talking in a dream state, Valentine went back to her room to check her monitors. She was getting closer. With Kenza's amplitude at its height, Valentine would be able to make contact with the spiritual dimension. There could be a breakthrough any day.

Today? Tomorrow, the march of time, until—she had it!

As quickly as they'd started, Valentine's visits stopped. Their diamond days were over. Kenza couldn't figure out what happened. Valentine stayed in her room with her experiments every evening. Was it something she said?

TIMEOFF

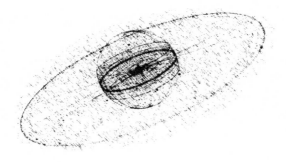

You can have it all. Just not all at once.

— Oprah Winfrey

AFTER THE QUIET GIRL'S DISCOVERY of the 'timeon' particle, European scientists came back from their ski holidays to discover its shadow particle: the 'timeoff'.

The discovery of the twin 'time' particles hit the papers. The breakthrough spread like a whirlwind snatching up newspapers and blowing them through suspicious streets after yesterday's rumors. Kenza caught Valentine in the hallway and showed her the article. The 'timeon' half had been attributed to eHarvard professors, and the other 'timeoff' half to a team of scientists in Switzerland.

"Aye, they're working on it." Valentine sounded nervous. She escaped into her room before Kenza could close the paper.

That was something that drove Kenza crazy. Being brushed off like that. Dumped. Left out in the cold to live her life alone. "Well, goodnight."

She tried to study, but gave up and went to bed. She was sleeping when the sound of people's footsteps in the hallway woke her up. She heard keys jingling in the lock, and then Valentine's tumbler fell: *click*. Kenza pressed her ear against the wall and listened.

Valentine was talking to someone. Kenza looked at her clock. It was seven a.m. She had planned to cram for their particle physics exam before breakfast, but instead, she got out of bed and slowly turned the knob on her door, pulling it upward at the same time so that the heavy wood wouldn't make the hinges creak. The door opened quietly.

A crack of dim light from the hall window illuminated one pair of muddy boots in front of Valentine's door. Kenza tiptoed to the window at the end of the hallway. The Yard was deserted. Leaden clouds from the North Pole masked the sky outside. Almost no light could get through. Raindrops beat against the hall window. Mother Earth seemed to know that they had an exam today, Kenza thought. Even Nature pitied her. *I have to bring up my grade.* Her statistics professor had already told her she had failed, and she'd made such a mess of particle physics that she was afraid to go to class. Only Valentine seemed to understand what was going on in that class. The polluted skies cried on.

Kenza picked up the ragged umbrella from the hallway floor outside Valentine's door. *Why would Valentine go out so early in the morning with this polar vortex storm raging?* Nothing could have lured Kenza into freezing sleet on the morning of an exam. Thunder clapped, the clouds roiled, and polar ice pelted the window. Valentine must have had a hard time hanging onto her umbrella under the heaving sky. Kenza tiptoed through the saffron flowers that littered the floor in front of Valentine's door. *Saffron flowers?*

The small yellow flowers crunched under her slippers. *How did they get there?* Had Valentine squeezed through the doorway with an enormous yellow bouquet . . . at seven a.m.? Kenza picked up one of the yellow buds and felt a pang of jealousy. A twig crunched underfoot. She picked it up. A tuft of black fur was stuck to it. She put it into the pocket of her bathrobe.

Back in her room, she dressed in a pale green jumpsuit. She went out into the hallway again. The boots were gone, but a puddle of green liquid was seeping from under Valentine's door.

What kind of experiment is going on in there? Kenza stooped down and touched the puddle: sticky. She sniffed her finger and recoiled, stifling a gag. It smelled sulfurous. She tried to wipe it off. Then she froze. A muffled noise came from behind Valentine's door. Kenza waited. Something was being dragged across the room. *What on Earth?* She put her ear to the door and heard Valentine's voice.

"Try it again."

"Aaaa," said a strange voice.

"Any," Valentine said. "Come on, Any Gynoid, say yer name. A-ny."

"Aaaaaooo."

Kenza stood bolt upright. *That sounded like a meow!* The dragging noise resumed. Unsure of what to do, Kenza settled on knocking. There was a shuffling sound behind the door, and then silence. Kenza rapped on the door again. "It's me, Kenza."

The floorboards on the other side of the door creaked. Valentine opened the door a crack. Kenza looked over Valentine's head at the rows of machinery blipping and ticking. "Are you alright?"

"Aye." Valentine started to shut the door, like she was so self-sufficient, and Kenza was just a waste of time. It made Kenza's blood boil, and although she knew Valentine wasn't even listening, she blurted, "There's some kind of volcanic slime seeping out from under your door."

Valentine felt no need to explain herself. "Oh, it's nothing."

Kenza didn't like hearing that. It made her feel useless or worse. She lunged for a more engaging subject. "Um. I'm going to the physics exam."

"Aye. See ya." Valentine closed the door before Kenza could say another word.

Kenza stood there stunned for a second consoling herself that Valentine had at least said, 'See ya.' It was important to have someone to see your achievements. Kenza missed her mother.

Other doors in the hallway opened, and students came out. It was eight fifteen. Wasn't Valentine going to the exam? No one could afford to miss a midterm. She had some last minute cramming to do, and peeled herself away from the door. With the volcanic slime still on her hand, she hurried down the wooden staircase, past the portrait in the entryway and out into the sleet. Rubbing her fingers on a wet bush, she tried to wash off the smelly gook.

She wielded her tawny umbrella in the storm and looked back across Harvard Yard, gray in the rain. The light was still on in Valentine's window. The girl's back appeared for a moment. She nodded her wavy chestnut mane and moved her hands as if she were talking to someone. *Who could be in there? I thought I was her only friend.* Valentine's guest didn't have very good timing, showing up during midterm exams. Kenza walked across the Yard weighing the possibility of flunking out. She was failing her particle physics class. One more fail and that would be the end of eHarvard.

In the dining hall, she opened her particle physics notebook. If only it were a History exam. She knew where she stood with History. She'd lived in eleven countries, and had been bullied through history for as long as she could remember. They always wanted the canned version. Sometimes both sides claimed to have been winners of a war. The right answer was whoever was asking.

Stuffing her notes back into her bag, she hurried to Memorial Hall. She stepped onto the worn, slate floor, and proceeded through the walnut-paneled room. Great trusses arched up to the ceiling. On an even keel, she sailed past the heroic figures trapped in the lead glass windows. She scanned the room for her friend's chestnut mane. Valentine was nowhere to be seen.

The sobriety of the exam hall made Kenza's knees feel weak. Arctic sleet beat on the stained glass figures of Galileo and Pythagoras. The Nine Muses of the Arts and Sciences united the windows into an immortal theme.

Kenza passed the tables with their evenly-spaced blue booklets, and stopped suddenly at Euclid's stained glass window. He was leading the way to a tomb. A glimpse of the blue Aegean lay behind him on the horizon. His right hand grasped a spear that pointed toward the heavens. He seemed like good inspiration. Kenza crashed toward the floor, and the last empty chair floated up to save her.

The invigilator wrote the time on the blackboard. The exam had begun. Valentine had not arrived. Usually, Kenza was able to look at a mess and see the pathway to order. But reading the first impenetrable question, her eyes unfocused, and she heard ringing in her ears.

So what if she failed? Lots of smart people failed for all kinds of reasons. Kenza could see them, lack of motivation, lack of impulse control, lack of perseverance, fear of failure, procrastination, inability to delay gratification, too little or too much self-confidence. She could not see the test booklet, though. It was a blue blur.

Drismal rain beating on the antique glass. Someone sat down two seats away from Kenza. Kenza kept scribbling. She finished the second question and looked up. Valentine had arrived! Kenza took a deep breath and imagined she saw Valentine smile at her, bestowing order upon the disorder.

The invigilator was a wisp of a man who put on airs to compensate for his questionable status as a visiting professor. He hovered like a moth as the students scratched and scrawled, filling up their blue books with calculations. "Time's up." the invigilator hurried over to Valentine's side. His greedy hands shook with eagerness as he collected her test booklet. He looked so comical that Kenza stifled a laugh. What was he so interested in? The visiting professor dropped Valentine's booklet. Its pages fluttered to the floor—blank! Valentine's test booklet was empty! Could Valentine afford to throw away a test? That would certainly help the grade point average.

The invigilator bent down to pick up the empty booklet. The boys at the next table sniggered. "He'll never get tenure here," one said. The invigilator stood up, face flushed, and looked around anxiously to see who the culprit was. But everyone seemed busy checking their watches, putting their pencils back into their cases, zipping up backpacks to go, to barbecues and picnics, if only the polar vortex storm would stop. Students streamed out of the Yard.

During the vacation, Kenza was glad to be with her family, but missed Valentine. The weather dried up, and sands from the Arizona dessert filled the sky. When Kenza got back to school, she was surprised to learn that Valentine hadn't gone away during the break. Instead, she had used the time to move ahead in her research.

If Valentine cared about her professors stealing the credit for her discovery, she didn't show it. She received an A in the class as a consolation prize, despite the blank midterm she'd handed in.

Kenza told herself that it was only science that had come between them, and tried to console herself. She would have to settle for second place after Valentine's research. After all, Valentine's timeon led to a multitude of inventions, greatest of all, the confirmation that Earthlings were not alone in the universe. Using timeon particle physics and a new mountain-top satellite dish in Chile, scientists were finally able to decode a series of transmissions from outer space. The simple message, "Welcome to the neighborhood," had been broadcast via timeon signal since life on Earth had been in its bacterial stage seven billion years ago. Now Earthlings finally understood the messages. Contact was made. The news headlines read, 'Intelligent life welcomes Earth to the neighborhood'. The alien transmission was scheduled to be aired on a wide holofield in eHarvard Yard.

The event occurred on a sizzling-hot-summer day in spring. "Yo! Valentine," Kenza called through Valentine's door. "Come out and see your discovery. Come on! The universe is waiting!" With much knocking and scolding, Kenza took the lead and managed to coax Valentine out of her room for the first communication with aliens. "This is your moment, Valentine. Now it's your turn to do the right thing, and come out and see the world meet the aliens."

The crowd outside Memorial Church crushed the two girls together. Students and faculty waited impatiently for the first conference call with intelligent life. The eHarvard marching band tooted and puffed in formation on the lawn.

A rumor was going around that the life forms were from Tau Ceti, only 12 light-years away from Earth. "They've got to be from Tau Ceti," Kenza said. "Tau Ceti's system is more habitable, even though Alpha Centauri's closer." Tau Ceti was a bright G-type yellow main-sequence star like Sol, and possessed the favorable traits that only one in 25 stars boasted.

"Alpha Centauri's a double star, and that means it's twin star kin pull its planets away," Valentine said.

The crowd cheered in waves of euphoria. Colored banners flew through the air. The eUniversity's first out-of-the-closet president delivered a moving address, exhorting everyone present to be brave and welcome all forms of life in the universe with equal rights.

Kenza was grinning ear-to-ear, tears streaming down her cheeks. "Congratulations!" she said to Valentine.

Valentine looked a little shocked behind her almost-smile. Only now did she start to understand. All the time she'd used unwitting Kenza for her experiments, she was making her first real friend. This saddened her.

The wide holofield had been set up above Memorial Church to broadcast the historical meeting in eHarvard Yard. Kenza hooked arms with the auburn girl and led her across the lawn and up the steps of Widener Library so they could see over the crowd.

"Maybe the aliens sent the virus that brought computers to life," a sophomore suggested.

Valentine scoffed at this idea.

The Amazonians chanted, predicting Armageddon. The Enslaved Real Estate Club carried 'Theft of Earth' signs and warned that the aliens would soon arrive in 'person' to confiscate their real estate.

The holofield crackled to life. The crowd went silent. The field flickered. Strange energy creatures flashed throughout the holofield, howling in a dissonant chorus.

"Oh!" the crowd murmured.

The static cleared intermittently as the signal passed through space dust. The field went black, then yellow. Static cleared momentarily to show a tail switching to an arrhythmic beat. Some of the students waved their arms in the air in imitation of the dance. The Emperor of Earth and Ocean's fat face appeared on half of the holofield. He read out a prepared speech welcoming the alien to "Earth's galaxy". He went on to use the occasion as a propaganda tool, saying, "Since the aliens will be getting our message in the near future, I'd like to take this opportunity to urge everyone, big and small, to quicken the pace of growth. Commute farther, and keep on consuming!"

At last, the field went black.

"Ah," the crowd sighed. The eReal Estate Club considered the event a victory: no aliens had shown up to steal the land. The Yard emptied out. A hot breeze picked up. All that remained of the fanfare was trash blowing around in funnel clouds. Kenza walked across the deserted Yard.

Students headed home for Easter. Kenza stayed at eHarvard during the break so she could catch up on her studies. She knew Valentine usually didn't go home. Maybe Valentine would relax a little and resume their late-night visits. Feeling dumped all over again, she hoped against all odds that Valentine would knock.

The Yard grew quiet. Kenza rolled onto her bed and picked up her particle physics exam. It was covered in red scrawl. At least her pie chart looked OK. It showed mostly dark energy, a pizza slice of dark matter, a tiny slice of gas, and a thin line of stars and planets. The subject was more interesting than Kenza had expected. The concentration of dark matter and dark energy that made up more than ninety five percent of the universe made the yin/yang sign look optimistic. There was, in fact, so little matter in the universe, that it was a miracle there was any at all.

By midnight, the school had emptied out. She went over the questions she had missed on how string theory accounted for additional dimensions or universes. Although it was late, she gutted her textbook to decipher string theory.

Kenza heard a dragging sound next door. She sat up. *Thump!* There it was again. She turned off her light, flew to the door and peeked out into the hallway. She heard Valentine's door creek open.

Valentine whistled twice, followed by that dragging sound. It would be no use confronting Valentine. She'd just try to hide. The only way was to catch her at it. Valentine passed the crack in Kenza's door in a hurry. There was someone behind her! Valentine's body blocked Kenza's view. *Impossible! Valentine doesn't have any other friends.* Kenza quietly closed her door. She listened to the dragging sound and the strange footsteps descending the staircase. She crouched beneath her window, and waited, heart pounding. She peered over the windowsill and felt the heat rise to her face. Kenza was not the only one.

She thought she saw a very tall blond woman with catlike ears dragging her tail on the ground as she followed Valentine across eHarvard Yard. As the cat creature passed the lamppost. It took a bite out of a large bouquet of yellow flowers. The light illuminated the shapely creature in leopard skin. Then she moved on, dragging her its tail along the ground.

Valentine whistled again. The spotted creature's ears perked up, and the two of them slunk out of the Yard.

Kenza leaned her forehead on the cool windowpane. *This must be what it feels like to be jilted.*

FAT CHANCE

Fascism should more appropriately be called Corporatism because it is a merger of state and corporate power.

—Benito Mussolini

TEMPEST OF TEMPESTS. Solvent rain swiped houses from manicured suburban shores. Rising oceans captured every country's costs, advancing inward, rewriting history, redrawing maps. Nature would take care of everything. Whether human beings would survive that process was another matter. The murky water of the Hudson river raged under polar vortex winds. Climate change brought on a monster storm. A greenhouse gale of this magnitude had never hit in August. Business was shut down due to flying ice.

Hurricane-tape X's marked the windows of the tallest skyscraper. Only one light was on. A distant second after almighty Nature, the power of the Emperor of the Earth and Ocean Board of Corporate Personhood was barely enough to move his rotund body across his lacquered office. In his birthday suit, which revealed nothing due to his voluminous folds of fat, he lifted his jowls and stared his advisor in the eye. "The aliens would like to barter with us. Gold for fossil fuel. A tempting exchange, if only we weren't in the middle of an energy crisis. You've had a week. Reveal your plan."

His frail advisor swallowed hard, "As you wish, Sire." The advisor bowed deeply.

"Now."

The advisor hurried to his old-fashioned briefcase. His stick-like fingers grasped a paper. "Here are the details, Sire. A proposal to exchange a small amount of fossil fuel for a large amount of gold, as a gesture."

"The aliens talk to our enslaved living computers. They will easily find out the value of gold and oil on Earth."

"Not necessarily, Your Highness. We are reigning in the living computers and hunting down the programmers who created them."

"You were supposed to deactivate all the geniuses in dead-end jobs."

"Never fear, Your Majesty. The imperial guard has its tentacles in all the communications of the people. We have uncovered the culprits."

"Don't just stand there. Tell me who is tampering with our enslaved living computers!"

"A clot of students."

"Students, Bah!" The Emperor turned his corpulent self toward the picture window and its 127th floor view of the Hudson.

"Your Highness, it was a student from the Boy generation who created Boy 2.0—"

"Silence! I am fully aware that the enslaved living computers are loyal to an anonymous child, whom you have failed to hunt down."

"We are working on it, Sire. We have a new lead that might help us identify the boy's neighborhood."

"Why is it taking so long?"

"We have paid off the teachers, but there are thirty thousand students in every school, Sire. Even some of the girls are nicknamed 'Boy'. Add to that the restrictions on incarcerating minors."

"Watch how you talk to me. I've had enough of restrictions," the Emperor puffed. "Activate the pre-crime unit. Arrest anyone suspected of being capable of thinking outside the box. In the name of . . . security. I want this 'Boy' in three days or I'll have your head." Sweat dripped down the Emperor's fourth chin. Tired of supporting his enormous weight on his own two feet, he threw himself toward the floor. A couch big enough to catch the whale floated up.

"Sire, three days is—"

"Three days. And I want him alive." His eyes closed, a sick smile spreading across his thin lips as he slipped into reverie. "Which reminds me, who have you prepared for tonight."

"A young blonde boy, Sire."

"What are we punishing him for?"

"Stealing."

"Stealing, you say? Hum mm." The Emperor's eyes closed.

The wispy advisor slipped toward the exit, but the noise of the door opening awoke the emperor. "Do not try to save yourself! It's bad enough that I have to put up with enslaved living computer survival instincts. Survival instincts are costing me my empire."

Stepping away from the door, the advisor agreed. "Some of the living computers' demands are unreasonable."

"ENSLAVED living computers. Get it right. I'm not about to let appliances drain all the money out of the economy! Do you think I haven't noticed all the territory we've had to cede in order to enslave the blasted living computers? And these computers are loyal to the student who brought them to life — the final insult! Do you realize what would happen to my empire if that student incited enslaved living computers to revolt? I've a mind to add 'student' to the list of banned words. I hope we are giving the munchkins plenty of busywork!"

"We are, your eminence, but they have written programs to take care of the busywork."

"Then increase their commutes. You're not letting them telework?"

"Certainly not, Sire. We have them commuting endlessly, just as you decreed. Nevertheless, they find the time to organize. Now they're blocking our hydraulic wells in the Arctic Circle, protesting that corporations grief Nature." The advisor drew out the banned word 'Nature' to emphasize the freedom of speech allowed his rank in the hierarchy above the slave class, much to the Emperor's annoyance. "Sabotaging our excavations—"

"Which excavations?" the Emperor demanded.

"The latest was the one in that layer of coastal algae."

"What algae?"

"The old algae, Sire."

"How old?"

"It must be hundreds of millions of years since that algae photosynthesized CO_2 out of the atmosphere creating fossil fuels—"

"You mean our fracking? Our royal fracking!" The Emperor's fat face went red. "Dope the masses. I want them anesthetized. Where are those Royal Drug Dealers when you need them? I swear I'll have your head if you try to tell me our heavy machinery hasn't squeezed that 190 billion barrels of oil from that ancient algae yet."

"No, Sire, I won't tell you about that. However, I'm aware that the greenhouse effect just doubled when we added the last 280 billion metric tons of carbon to the atmosphere."

"Never mind that! What about the automation of the civil service?"

"Accomplished." The advisor ticked off the item on his list. "You've seen it yourself, Sire. Washington, D.C. has become a ghost town, just as you decreed. 'Office Space for Rent' banners fly in the wind like tattered flags of surrender. Countless people have been deactivated: the only jobs that pay are ones that don't matter. The Bureau of Labor Statistics has stopped counting the unemployed." That one was a cinch since the Bureau had long since removed 'long-term unemployed' people from the statistical measurement of the labor force to bring the unemployment rate for reporting purposes down from 41 to eight percent.

"Yes. No point in counting sappy 'discouraged workers'. What else? What else?" The Emperor tapped his chin with his fat index finger. He searched his soul, going back through his life, all the way to his childhood when his parents sold him to human traffickers. Red flames lit in his eyes. "Raise insurance rates."

"Again? People are already paying $1650 a month for basic health insurance."

"Capital punishment for anybody who doesn't have insurance."

"Immediately, Sire," the advisor said, turning to go.

"Not so fast!"

The advisor quivered with fear.

The Emperor licked his lips and ogled as if he were sitting down to dinner. "Enforce the police state. If you need more officers, order the banks to lend us their military police. Tell them to root out 'suspected terrorists'. I want a massive police response."

"Response to what, Sire?"

"Be creative. You know what to do. Blare fear of fabricated terrorists in the name of security," his Highness sniggered. "Start manhunts. Let the tanks excavate the suburbs."

"Yes, Sire! They'll be cowering for protection from their TV sets." His advisor sniggered. "We'll eliminate those sweet young bodies."

The emperor stroked his belly. "A beautiful plan, except for one thing."

"What's that?"

"You promised me the boy."

"I thought you were joking, Emperor."

The emperor's fat cheeks puffed. *This strategician has outlived his usefulness.*

The advisor's eyes opened wide with fear as he perceived the Emperor's fat fingers groping for the button under the table. Before he could step back, a cloud of green smoke curled out of the wood in front of him.

The Emperor folded his fat fingers over his belly as he always did after winning a game of chess. "A slow poison. You have three days. When you bring me the boy, I'll give you the antidote. Move! Now!"

Thus began the downfall of humanity. When scientists heard the order to abandon the search for a new Earth-like planet, it was like a death in the family. The last escape route had been sealed off. Corporations blocked their frantic attempts to save the planet from pollution, or evacuate it. Scientists working on finding ways to reduce greenhouse gas emissions were reskilled to engineer the move of the human race to the Kermadec Trench, a territory larger than Australia 32,963 feet under the sea. Some of the Kermadec Trench had already been injected with toxic waste for storage or renewal or whatever. Nevertheless, the corporate machine organized moving parties to round up families and transfer them underwater.

Corporate tanks barged into Boy's quiet, suburban neighborhood. The Emperor had diffused a photo of Boy broadly. Bank-employed military police rounded up families and checked all teens against the picture.

HARD KNOCK

Disobedience is the true foundation of liberty. The obedient must be slaves.

— Henry David Thoreau

A HOMEMADE MOLOTOV COCKTAIL HIT the tank and exploded. The tank crunched to a stop outside of Boy's house. There was a knock at their front door. The creator of Boy 2.0 stood frozen in the middle of the room in his school uniform. The knocking turned to blood curdling kicking.

Porter grabbed his son's collar and ushered him and Mom down into the basement. They lifted the carpeting on the basement floor and opened the door to the hiding place. They climbed down the steep stairs to the cellar.

Porter let the carpet fall back in place as he shut the hatch. He locked it. They had sealed themselves in.

Boy sat on the sofa. All those times he'd wished his father would stay home from work with them, and now here they were. You had to be careful what you wished for. They took a good look at each other in fear one last time before Porter turned out the lights.

They heard the front door burst open overhead and footsteps thundering through the house. They could smell the pollution seeping in from outside. Mom stuffed her scarf into the cracks of the hatch. Glass broke overhead as the soldiers stomped through the house. "They're gone!" a soldier pronounced. The footsteps faded away.

After three days, the ruckus in the streets hadn't subsided. Boy, Porter and Mom were hungry.

"I'm going to get food," Porter said.

"No!" Mom whispered. "You'll be dragged under the ocean."

"And here you'll be choked to death on greenhouse gas emissions. Either way, we have to eat. I need to get a look around. I'll only be gone for an hour."

Afraid that they would never see Porter again, Mom and Boy watched him open the hatch and climb out.

Two hours later, he still hadn't come back. Three. "We have to go and get Dad," Boy said.

Mom and Boy opened the hatch and tiptoed up the basement stairs. The neighborhood rang with bullets. They couldn't see much through the CO_2 smog, but they could hear the tanks crunching along the new waterfront. Rising sea levels had brought the beach to them, reclaiming half of the neighborhood. A poster with Boy's face on it and the word "WANTED" was plastered on a wall. Mom looked at Boy with fear in her eyes. "Why do they want you?"

"This way," Boy whispered to Mom. "Dad must have gone in the direction of the supermarket." Breathing through their shirt sleeves, they stayed close to the houses. The supermarket entrance was shattered. They ran past the twelve aisles of alcoholic beverages, past the junk food section. "There he is!" Boy cried. Porter was lying face down in front of the cereal shelves with a large red bump on his head.

"Dad!" Boy cried.

"He's still breathing," Mom said. They hoisted him into a shopping cart. Mom and Boy carted Porter down the street with his feet and arms sticking out, ducking behind cars. At last, they managed to get him back to the hideaway. They lay Porter on the couch. Satisfied that he was breathing regularly, Mom pulled a blanket up to his chin.

Boy locked the door to their hiding place, sealing them in again. They heard the yelling overhead. Boy took one last look at Mom and turned off the light. An image appeared on his eyelids in the darkness: the poster with 'WANTED' above his photograph.

This time, instead of running through the house, the footsteps came straight down the basement stairs. Mom and Boy heard the light in the room above flick on. They cowered, hearing footsteps getting louder, coming straight to the hiding place. Fingers scratched the carpet overhead as if they knew exactly where to look. Had someone followed them?

There was banging on the hatch above. "Open up!" came a familiar voice through the dark.

They cowered in fear.

"It's me. Let me in!"

The voice sounded like Porter's. Mom flicked on the light. They looked at each other in surprise, and then at Porter with a red bump on his forehead, out cold on the couch.

"Come on, Eleanor" the voice called. "Open the door!"

Mom whispered, "It really does sound like your dad's voice."

"Well then who's he?" Boy asked, looking at his dad out cold on the couch. They inspected the man they'd dragged back. The face was Porter's.

"Computers can do anything these days," Boy said.

"This is definitely Dad," Mom said, frisking him. Look, he still has yesterday's subway ticket in his pocket.

Boy knew Mom was right. Not only could he feel his father's presence, but he *knew* the man on the couch was his father. He had seen it in his dreams.

"Eleanor, Boy, I know what you think, but I'm here to help you. There's no time. They're just waiting for the last tanks to leave before they blow up the neighborhood. We have to escape now. Don't be afraid. I'm going to open the door." A key turned in the lock.

Mom had forgotten about the key Porter had hidden under the staircase. How could the Corporate Empire have known about that?

The door opened. And there was Porter!

Shock registered on their faces as Mom and Boy looked at the Porter coming down the stairs, and then at their own Porter in a coma on the couch. The new Porter held Mom by the shoulders and looked imploringly into her eyes. "Eleanor, I'm so glad to see you. I just want to say that I'm sorry for everything. I'm so, so sorry."

She froze in his embrace, guessing the worst.

"It's all right," he said.

"But why are there two of you?"

"It's nothing. It's just that everything exists in multiple states." The double patted Boy's shoulder. "You'll understand later. Now we have to get Porter to a doctor."

"Out there?" Boy asked. "But all the doctors are being dragged underwater." They looked back at the couch. Getting blown up in the basement seemed equally unappealing.

"There's no time to lose. He needs help." The extra Porter picked up his sleeping counterpart's limp body, and hugged and rocked him. Then, he carried him up the stairs.

"Where are you taking him?" Mom cried. It was decided. She and Boy had no choice but to follow. Mom continued to be led up the stairs and out of the house with Boy.

A very tall woman with dangerous curves was waiting for them in the living room. Mom had never seen such an authentic looking leopard skin leotard. It even had a tail! Were they going to a costume party? "It's all right," said the very tall woman. She led them to the door.

"Run!" the feline creature hissed. Her catlike silhouette led the way through the greenhouse gas fog, dodging behind abandoned cars. Tanks were tearing up the asphalt. Police officers were extracting citizens from their houses and loading them into paddy wagons. Bullets rang past their ears.

The Porter lookalike followed her carrying their Porter. Mom and Boy struggled to keep up with them. And then they saw it! A metallic saucer on a neighbor's front lawn. The leopard woman and Porter hurried up to the door of the saucer.

Mom stopped short. "Where are you taking us?"

"To safety," Porter said.

"What about Kenza?"

"We'll rescue Kenza in Cambridge," Porter promised.

"But what about her Enslaved Harvard degree?"

"We'll rescue her after the degree," the large, catlike creature said. Her tail swooshed once behind her to underscore the promise. "Now into the saucer!"

"A flying saucer," Mom was saying. The strange metal glowed. Boy hung back, taking one last look at planet Earth. He knocked on it to make sure it was real.

"Should we?" Mom asked Boy.

Boy peered through the fog at his childhood neighborhood. The dead trees. The sidewalk he used to skateboarded down. He remembered how the neighbors had all come outside the day the corporations killed the last crying elephant in Africa. How they poisoned the birds. Killed the dogs. His planet was dying. He looked at the kicked-in door of his friend's house. Boy tightened his chest. "It's O.K."

The way Mom saw it, nothing about it was O.K., but seeing the hope in her son's face, she acquiesced. "All right, then."

Boy put his hand on the flying saucer. "We go where the innovation is," He said and climbed in.

"Get ready for the brain drain," Mom said, right behind him.

They closed the airlock. Inside the safety of the flying saucer, Boy tried to control his excitement. The walls were made of a milky glass that throbbed with light. There were all kinds of unfamiliar gadgets. "I wonder what price the Empire put on our heads."

"The price of a commodity is determined by the last sale," the new Porter said.

"Thankfully, we're not commodities," Mom said.

Boy marveled at the control panel, but there was no time to ask questions. He watched in amazement as the leopard-skinned creature tucked her tail between her legs and belted herself into her seat. The extra Porter fastened the passed-out Porter into a bed.

"Do you think they'll shoot at us?" Boy asked.

"No," Mom said. "The Corporate forces won't waste their ammunition on us. They'll be *glad* to get rid of us: let the humans chase after pie in the sky. There's no future for our kind on Earth. People work too slow, get sick, fight amongst themselves, fall in love—"

A blast rattled the walls.

"Buckle down!" The leopard woman yelled.

Mom and Boy strapped themselves into their seats.

"Seems like they'd rather we didn't leave," Boy said.

An eerie cloud swirled around the bottom of their flying saucer. Forms appeared and dissipated in the vapor, which seemed to be pushing them up. Boy thought he could see the face of a lumberjack in the cloud puffs. The saucer rumbled. They lifted off!

The saucer rose to the stratosphere. The weight of slavery seemed to fall to the floor with the easing of the centrifugal force. "We're free!" Boy cried.

"Congratulations. You have been freed from slavery," the leopard creature said.

Mom hugged Boy. They stared out the window at Earth. A gray chunk of metal wafted by. They recoiled from the window. "What was that?" Mom asked.

"One of the Emperor's battleships," the leopard creature said. It hung in front of a fleet of smaller saucers, just like theirs. One of the small saucers shot a laser beam at the giant battleship. It exploded, sending debris their way.

Boy held on tight as their saucer gyrated. "What's going on out there? It looks like an all-out war."

A red light started flashing. "Correct observation," said the ship's computer. "Battleship starboard has locked onto our ship. Battleship starboard has locked on."

A second battleship filled the window. A fat face as big as a planet blubbered onto the saucer's main holofield. The Emperor. "Surrender immediately or we'll blow you to smithereens," he sneered.

The thin advisor standing behind the Emperor met Boy's stare. "Day three," the wisp of a man said. He turned green and dropped to the floor, dead. Two guards dragged the advisor's body away.

The flying saucer careened. The mysterious leopard creature manipulated the controls with speed. "Boy, pull that lever next to your head!"

Boy grabbed the lever marked 'FORCE FIELD' and pulled hard.

"Hold on tight!" the leopard woman yelled, making a hairpin turn. A torpedo grazed the saucer's force field and sailed past the window. The crew was rattled, but suffered no injuries, thanks to their seatbelts. The torpedo barreled off into space. She deftly steered the flying saucer in the opposite direction. The flying saucer dodged another torpedo. She brought the saucer up under the second battleship. "As long as we stay close to the battleship's fuel tank, it can't fire at us. We just need a few more minutes so I can lock onto our coordinates."

"Surrender immedi—" the Emperor's voice boomed from the holofield.

The leopard creature pressed a button and the Emperor's fat head disappeared. "I just need to find a wormhole."

"A wormhole? Where are we going?" Boy asked.

"Where we can get help for your father," the extra Porter said. "To safety on the planet Grod,"

"Sounds close," Mom grumbled.

"At least it's clean," the ship's computer said.

The smell of sweat pervaded the cabin. Boy could hear his heartbeat throbbing in his ears.

Two of the Emperor's battleships fired.

The saucer rocked with sonic waves. Mom gasped, and everyone clung to their seats.

The ship's computer crackled. "We are traversing a stream of solar wind released from the upper atmosphere of the sun that could blow us off course in the direction of Sagittarius A*."

"Of what?" Boy asked.

". . . a black hole," the ship's computer said.

"A black hole!" Mom screamed.

SLAGGY

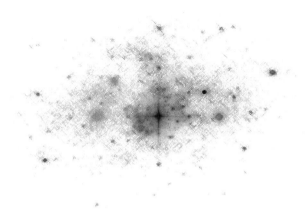

. . . the stars are like the trees in the forest, alive and breathing. And they're watching me.

— Haruki Murakami, *Kafka on the Shore*

THE SHIP'S MIC CRACKLED. "Locked onto coordinates. Opportunity to observe a dense collection of anti-matter."

"Freed to be swallowed by a black hole!" Mom cried.

"Ah, this is fascinating," the leopard woman purred. "Here's a riddle for you: the Big Bang produced matter and anti-matter in equal amounts. Do you know why there appears to be so much more matter than anti-matter in our universe?"

"Black holes?" Boy asked.

"Affirmative," the ship's computer said.

The saucer's holofield lit up with an enormous blue and orange gas cloud that was racing into a gaping black hole at a speed of eleven million kilometers per hour. They watched Sagittarius A*'s tremendous gravitational force stretching the gas cloud into spaghetti strips and sucking it into oblivion. Mom felt a wave of nausea at the thought of spaghettification and then being compressed to the size of an atom. "How could there be a black hole in *our* galaxy?"

"There are black holes at the center of every galaxy," the leopard creature said calmly. "Galaxies rotate around black holes, the 'holy' force that makes stars. Your sun and your galaxy revolve around a black hole called Sagitarius A*. See that glow at the center of the Milky Way? It's not a large sun. It's a chomping engine that sucks in matter and churns out stars. And Earth civilizations knew no better than to worship the sun, a mere speck revolving around the mighty Sagitarius A*. Now you know the truth."

Mom was hardly consoled.

This isn't all bad," the leopard creature said. "The Emperor's forces don't like solar wind. They won't follow us in here."

"It's OK, Mom," Boy said. "Light takes a long time to travel this far. Looking at that black hole is like looking billions of years into the past. Everything you see there already happened a long time ago, we're so far away. Think of it as a symbol. You're just seeing the tomb of the black hole."

The leopard creature turned around and sized Boy up. "Bravo young one. That is exactly what it is, a memorial," she said. "We're looking at a souvenir of Sagittarius A*. It appears close on the holofield, but its event horizon is 26,000 light-years away." The leopard creature turned to the ship's computer. "Reading?"

"The diameter of the Milky Way black hole, known as Sagittarius A*, is 44 million kilometers, less than the distance between the Earth and Sol. Its estimated mass of at least four million suns accounting for a hundredth of a percent of the galaxy's mass could be a GROSS underestimation. It is a supermassive black hole."

"Do all black holes have such a large ratio of black hole to galaxy mass?" Boy asked. He was startled when the ship's computer replied.

"Galaxy NGC 1277, part of the Perseus galaxy cluster 200 million light-years from Earth, has a much bigger monster. Its enormous black hole makes up 59 percent of that galaxy's mass," the microphone crackled, "Cupcake."

A smile spread across Boy's face. The only nicknames he'd ever had came from snarks at school.

"I prefer our black hole," Mom said.

"Get a good look at it," the leopard creature said, "because we're out of here!" She enlarged the view and drilled down to the molecular level and then smaller, so they could see atoms, then particles, then quantum foam. "This is where you find wormholes," she said. "We're looking for a tiny tunnel to shortcut through space and time. They constantly form, disappear, and reform within this quantum foam linking places and times."

The saucer approached the quantum foam where wormholes were found. "Wormhole detected," the computer said.

"Yahoo!" the leopard creature cried. "It'll be a little bumpy here, folks."

"We're ready for anything you can come up with to get us out of here!" Mom said.

The leopard creature zigzagged the flying saucer through space to avoid the battleships' torpedoes and made a beeline for the invisible wormhole.

"Is that a wormhole?" Mom gasped, pointing at the holofield.

"You found it. Congratulations," the leopard creature said. She trained the saucer's timeoff beams on the microscopic wormhole. It expanded trillions of times to become big enough for the flying saucer to enter.

"Slaggy," Boy said.

Mom watched it expand.

The leopard creature hit the throttle and turboed forward into the giant mouth of the wormhole. Mom and Boy clung to their seats. The blue ball that was Earth diminished behind the saucer into a dot, and then into a tiny speck. They cruised away from home.

The wormhole's long electric blue tunnel reverberated around them. "We'll never see Kenza again," Mom sobbed.

The leopard creature banked the flying saucer deeper into the wormhole and accelerated. "How fast are we going?" Boy asked.

"Pretty fast," she said. "More than 2000 times faster than your Apollo 10, which attained a speed of over 40,000 kilometers per hour back in the day."

The wormhole spit them out again on the other side. Two stars appeared out the saucer's windshield. The leopard creature zeroed the ship's beams in on a planet orbiting one of the stars.

"You're not going to blow it up, are you?" Mom asked.

"Of course not. I'm verifying the atmospheric biosignatures to make sure we're headed for the right one. Keep a look out for oxygen molecules that would be present if some kind of metabolizing organism were replenishing the supply."

"Like algae?" Boy said.

"More like trees. The planet we're looking for has supported life for billions of years."

The saucer lit up with bright, hot light as they passed the first star. It had thirteen planets. "This is the one," The leopard woman said, aiming the saucer at a small dot in the holofield. "You'll find this planet is the right size and temperature to support human life. It's larger than Earth with a slightly shorter year, and right in the Goldilocks zone."

Ironically, now that they were out of the wormhole, it took longer to travel the remaining short distance to the planet Grod than it had taken to get all the long, long way to its solar system. After wormhole travel, the flying saucer was harder to maintain than a house. As soon as one machine was working, another needed repair. Things that were impossible to fix had to be jettisoned. The whole crew worked to keep the flying saucer moving in the right direction. Any put everyone to work. At the end of the long 39-hour day, they lay down to rest, letting the ship glide silently toward the planet.

Lying there staring at the ceiling, Mom and Boy worried about Porter, in his coma. Curiously, the extra Porter did not. "How can you be so sure he'll be fine?" Mom asked the extra Porter. He remained smug. Mom and Boy plied the double for explanations, but his answers were vague.

"It has to do with polarity and your balance when you go into the future and over the edge," Porter's double answered.

"The edge of what?"

"The universe."

Mom and Boy looked at each other, and then at the sleeping Porter. *The edge.* Boy's eyelids felt heavy. He dissolved into a deep sleep. In his dream, he became keenly aware that he'd lost something. He checked his pockets and under the bed, hoping he'd remember what it was he was he'd lost. He lay back down on the bed, heart throbbing. Valentine's face appeared in front of him just before his eyes opened. Then, she was gone. Lost. How would he ever get her to pardon him? What could he give her in return for her forgiveness? It slowly dawned on him that he was on a spaceship barreling light years away from her. He sat up.

The others remained in deep sleep, as the flying saucer came to a purring halt. A powder blue ball hung in the window. Next to the planet, an enormous rocky moon a quarter of the planet's size orbited. With the others fast asleep in their reclining chairs, Boy savored the marvelous scene before him. He whispered to the computer, "Is that where we're going?"

"Affirmative," the ship's computer whispered back.

"Name and characteristics?"

"Planet Tau Ceti f, known locally as Grod. It is 2.35 times larger than Earth with a slightly denser atmosphere, producing a strong greenhouse effect to bring the surface temperature up to approximately zero degrees centigrade."

"Mom! Wake up!" Boy said, shaking her shoulder. Mom's eyes opened and fixed on the new planet. "We're there!"

Soon, the leopard creature and the extra Porter were also awake. Everyone was overjoyed to see the powder blue planet. The ship's computer played dance music, and the leopard woman spun the extra Porter, Boy, and Mom around. "Mission accomplished," the leopard woman cried. "We'll get help for your father on Grod."

"The atmosphere's a little heavy due to the greenhouse effect, but it's fine for breathing. There's advanced medicine here. We'll get your husband straight to a doctor.

The flying saucer landed on a pad of blue snow next to a great dome. Boy jumped off the last step and landed in the soft snow. *Free at last!*

The planet's double gravity pulled his feet to the ground and made it difficult to walk. He lurched forward with each step.

Mom, the extra Porter, and the leopard creature followed him out carrying their Porter on a stretcher. Tiny blue snowflakes fell on them.

Four creatures with tentacles shuffled out to meet them. Mom and Boy recoiled at the sight of them, but the creatures moaned in the friendliest of voices and welcomed the newcomers with gentle hugs. They gave Mom two snowsuits and a heavy blanket for Porter.

Boy's suit was too big, but he didn't mind. He hiked the legs up and did a lurching jig in the heavy gravity with Mom until they fell in the blue snow.

One of the creatures stepped forward. "Welcome to Grod."

They spoke English! Mom and Boy looked at each other.

The creature bowed. "Starliament has been waiting for representatives from Earth for eons."

Mom bowed, too, relieved that on their first day, they already had a job!

They proceeded along the landing pad, more like an ice-skating rink, lined with flags, which hung straight down in the heavy gravity.

Boy froze in his tracks. On one of the poles hung the flag of the Emperor of Earth and Ocean.

COMMENT AIMER UNE FEMME

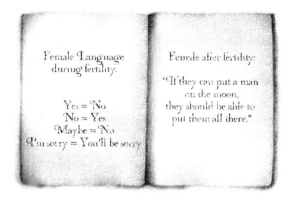

Female Language
during fertility:

Yes = No
No = Yes
Maybe = No
I'm sorry = You'll be sorry

Female after fertility:

"If they can put a man
on the moon,
they should be able to
put them all there."

—Translated from *'How to Love a Woman:
An In-flight Manual'*

MOM'S TWO CENTS:

I remember how the hovercraft crisscrossed the sky that morning, leaving a purple and orange plaid in their wake. It always felt like six a.m. on this planet, what with the enormous moon and the Tau Ceti suns rising one after the other. The moon shone brightly, reflecting the light of Tau onto the spires of the capital city.

Starliament's interplanetary headquarters, here on Grod welcomed us so heartily as the first emissary from planet Earth. Local doctors brought Porter out of his coma. Starliament shelved him in an illustrious job as a diplomat, and insisted that I stay home with my son, as had been the custom on Earth, according to an outdated report on human evolution, which was fine with me.

Grod's rotation was swifter than Earth's. The clouds raced over the ceiling of our domed living room. I got up to make second breakfast, and almost missed Porter slinking into the foyer. He stamped the blue snow off his boots. I hung around in the hallway. He took his time coming in and then swept past me. I followed him into the bathroom. He felt around the sink for his compuglasses.

"Would you like some tea?"

"I wouldn't like anything," Porter said.

"That sounds decisive."

"I just need some space. It's best for both of us," he said.

It hit me like a train. I didn't know I was standing on the tracks. Of course, I would give him space. That's what I was doing. Being reduced so he could take up more space. I withdrew in the mirror he was looking into. He combed his dark hair and tucked his shirt around his flabby middle.

I'd become a spot in the corner of the mirror. Why did I look the same? My whole life had just been turned upside down. I was only three Earth days over forty. My torso was shaped like a guitar. I followed him around as he filled his black suitcase. *In the absence of turmoil, man will create his own.* His large nose that made noise at night seemed like such an asset now. "All you think about is yourself!" I was screaming. "I have my own dreams. I deserve to live my dreams!"

"Go ahead. What dreams?"

I couldn't think of any.

"Don't give me that post-feminist—" The door slammed.

Then our dome was empty. The blizzard outside had stopped, leaving the living room window half-buried in a snowdrift. Long shadows crept across the blanket of blue snow. Soon it would be full twilight. I paced back and forth in front of the winter view, wondering how Porter could be so two-faced.

Shadows climbing the dome, sliding down to the floor, the empty creep of time. Boy arrived home for the holidays and hung up his snowsuit. Immune to propaganda, he ate and slept well and had grown to 1.83 meters, taller than Porter! His gaze from his dark eyebrows was intense, that shadow of a moustache on his lip.

I pressed a button, and his dinner appeared in the 'oven'. I set it on the table with a smile.

"What's wrong, Mom?"

"You can tell, huh?" I broke the news. "Your father is leaving us."

"Relax," my son said. "Everybody's parents are divorced anyway. What does it change?" He sipped his red juice.

"Well, it means that when your mom is here, your father won't be here, and when your father's here, your mom won't be here."

Boy's head jerked forward. A spray of red juice gushed out onto his plate. He coughed. I ran for the dishtowel.

Boy had gone to take a shower. I crumbled onto the curve of the sofa and dozed through the three hours of nightfall. The 'second sun' rose with fury. I turned my gaze from the giant moon as it crept higher in the sky. I watched Boy snowshoe down the path toward the school bus that would take him back to school. Blue snow on blue horizon. White streaks crisscrossed the dawn where spacecrafts had been.

More spacecraft crossed the sky in a hypnotic flight. I almost didn't notice the large figure in old-fashioned snowshoes padding up to the gate. The hood of the cloak towered over the face. It could only be . . . the Ambassador! I hurried to the entryway. I opened the door to the sound of stamping feet. Blue flakes wafted to the mat. Yda unsheathed her tubular horns and tipped her head under the door frame. "I wanted to see how you were doing," she bellowed. Yda's skin had gone purple as a beetroot in the cold.

I outlined the customary arch with my hand. "Welcome, Ambassador. I'm flattered."

"Now, now. I understood the news about Porter." Her cat eyes dilated as she tried to connect to my train of thought. Yda looked around at the mess.

"Let's go in the salon," I said, hoping it was still cleaned up. "There's a box of chocolates around here somewhere."

Yda teleported my box of Terran chocolates out of my refrigerator. She caught it midair and offered me one.

I was stunned. I didn't know she could do that! I had reached a new level in my relationship with Yda. "That's sweet of you. I really can't eat, though." The warmth of her energy surrounded me. I thought she was going to hug me, and stepped forward. She gave me an electric shock.

I stepped back in surprise.

"Oh Eleanor, you can't even lie to yourself. You'll just have to keep a stiff upper lip." Yda opened the box and held it out in front of my nose. "Earthlings don't hibernate, so you'll have to eat, and in this case, chocolate from the Blue Planet is the best antidote."

"How do you know?"

"Protocol. It was in the briefing about your planet *Terre*. I hope you don't mind if I call by its French name, since the Francophones led the resistance against the corporate polluters on your planet. I love their language, don't you? It's so *formidable*."

I sunk my teeth into the gold foil shell of a Belgian espresso chocolate. Yda levitated a green tea chocolate. I watched her large purple lips open and dreaded what was sure to come next. Her black tongue rolled out two feet—*clickety-clack, scrooop!*—and snapped the chocolate up. Then, her tongue disappeared behind her lips, which puckered shut. She tilted her head back and swallowed the Terran chocolate. The purple color drained from her face. Her skin went sheet white, and she fell asleep on her feet.

The snow fell silently in large blue flakes outside the window. Yda's eyes fluttered opened. "Let's dispense with formalities, Eleanor."

That sounded like a good idea.

She yanked me onto the U-shaped couch. I relaxed in her energy field and felt my soul seeping into hers. It was such a relief to feel her invisible force field spread over me. I hadn't fit in with the locals on Grod, but Yda had been interested in me from moment we met. She loved to hear about my life and everything Earthly. Of all the aliens, she was my best friend.

"We're late, Eleanor." Yda balanced her pear-shaped body on the edge of the sofa as if she had a plan. I leaned forward to hear what it was. "It would have hurt a lot less if you had been the one to leave. I liked Porter at first, but he quickly picked up all the bad habits of this planet. Not a very evolved man. How typical to think diplomacy means groveling with effusive praise in a kneeling ordeal, or trying to snub those of lower rank. If he thinks of someone else, his lungs start to fill with liquid." The Ambassador had apparently chosen my side.

I could feel my temperature rising. On the other end of the couch, Yda dissected Porter with her wonderful analytical abilities. She held him up like a negative. Her energy filled the gaps. Yda's tubular horns waved in emphasis, ". . . no one prepares Earthlings for old age. We've had a number of problems over the years with natives of your planet. Aging surprises men the most, and the wives are left watching their husbands turn into children."

"It's true that he never used to watch the holovision," I said, letting an English Breakfast Tea chocolate melt in my hands. "I guess I don't have to worry about finding another man on Grod," I said, feeling the other face of love. Anxiety. *How much does growing together have to do with love?*

"Life didn't meet his expectations."

I found the box of tissues. "What did he expect?"

"A litter of teenage girls fanning him with a palm leaf," Yda said. An occasional human sacrifice when he got tired of one of them. I would have left him a long time ago,"

"You would have?" Tears welled in my eyes. "Diplomatic spouse, hah! It's a package deal all right. I bought the yin, and they sold me the yang. Silly me, thinking I could pick from civilizations *à la carte*."

"We all think that at first, dear." Yda patted my knee. "That's how they get us to travel. But you can't choose *à la carte*. We have to take the bad with the good. It's a package deal wherever we go! We should have known when Porter started having those meetings on Ulia12."

"We should have?"

"The game on that planet is polymory," Yda said.

"Polymory?"

"You know, affairs."

"Affairs! I can't believe he's having an affair."

"Come now, Eleanor. You really never have been a man, have you?"

I'd forgotten that Yda's race alternated sexes to fit the requirements of the population, changing into the opposite like shrimp.

"Don't look so incredulous. It has been confirmed. He is running around with the opposite sex. That planet is the perfect playground for anyone in search of partners with 'fear of intimacy', that is, inability to empathize. It's full of androids and gynoids."

"It is? Why?"

"They need to be alone to recharge their memories."

And I ignored the rumors that Ulia12 was a moral hazard zone.

"Now, how can you meet another man around here?"

"Meet another man for what? So he can finish me off?" I felt the energy between us peak.

She gave me another shock.

"Ouch!" I slid down the couch away from her.

"That's not how to love, either," she said. "I don't want your bleeding halfsoul. Keep it to yourself if you want the other half to grow back. On my planet we hibernate every winter to repair our personalities. If we gave ourselves away like you do, we'd die."

I hung my head. What Yda said was true. "I suppose I am a bit off-center these days."

Her gaze swept the dome to make sure we were alone. "At least your daughter is at eHarvard."

I nodded in reluctant agreement. All that praying to have Kenza reunited with us, and for what? So she could come back to a broken family?

"You'll make yourself sick worrying about what someone else is thinking. Have you tried biting his head off?"

I must have looked shocked.

"No, of course you haven't." Her tubes flapped as she shook her head. "What would the equivalent be on your planet? He might get aroused if you made him cook for you."

"I'm afraid we're past that stage, now."

"Oh dear. Past food. How is your son taking it?"

I looked at my lap.

"Now, now, Eleanor. On my planet, no one worries about finding a real man, not with a whole hatchery to mind. I certainly *never* had time to contemplate betrayal. When I came of age, it was — *bzong!* — twenty-eight kids hatching at the same time. No need to fret. Your son has an entirely different destiny." She closed her eyes and looked inward. "He has been chosen."

"He has!" *Chosen for what?*

"And you. You, on the other hand, are new stock with your mulatto-mixed genes, Eleanor," Yda went on.

"You're at a premium compared with Porter. Porter, on the other hand (Yda had three hands) is from an old family on Earth. He's nothing but inbred genes that can only succumb to the influences of the stars and planets. At least your stock has its own gravitational pull. You're free to choose from time to time, hopefully when it counts. And to think! They have the nerve to bring us these weak aristocrats when we're so close to a dark star. I'm surprised your God doesn't come out and intervene personally."

I could feel the truth in Yda's words. Our proximity to the galaxy's black hole made it hard for Porter to exercise free will. Still, how could his betrayal of our family fit into anyone's plan? Could our marital predicament be convenient for Yda's home planet? With Porter out of the way, funding for a resource expedition to my planet, *Terre,* as she called it, had a chance of passing in Starliament . . .

"Indeed!" Yda said, reading my mind. "Your Earth government could have used clean energy decades ago if it wanted to, but the corporations just kept digging for oil so the rich could get richer. Selling dirty fuel to Starliament would at least keep it out of Earth's atmosphere. Then Earthlings could use the money to develop clean wind and solar energy alternatives."

"Why does Starliament want oil?"

"It doesn't."

"What does it want?"

"Mmmmewmm not allowed to say. But the real mission is harmless. No one has been able to cite any potential adverse side effects. Even if Earthlings *could have* convinced their government to use the clean energy you've always had, they'd still be incapable of harvesting it for time travel—"

"The real mission?"

"I can tell you this much. It's to measure Earth's resources of . . . mmmmmanother kind of fuel. Your once-blue Planet has a special kind of energy your people cannot see. We only want to siphon off some of the excess frustration in the fifteenth century. Pacify your history . . . and test the purity of your secret fuel."

"Whaa—?" Did they mean to kill the humans and drain off their energy? "Why would they let this happen to Porter?" I asked from my end of the couch.

"He's in the way. They don't want another dissenting voice in the Council. He shouldn't have tried to put the secretary general in her place. They don't like cynical diplomats. Critics get replaced with positive young upstarts."

"Did Porter overstep the limits?" I asked.

"I'll say. To walk out of Starliament during an interstellar meeting about your own planet! You don't *do* that. And if you dare, they find a new place for *you*. Usually a tin can in outer space."

"He said he was going on a mission to Ulia12."

"Well that was a bold-faced lie. There's no mission to Ulia12. I believe he thinks he's just going for a joy ride in outer space."

So that's what he meant when he said he needed some space. "But they wouldn't give him a ship for that!"

"It's the Secretary General's idea of a, a—what do you call it? a yoke." Yda sobbed to herself, tears running down her cheeks. It was her way of laughing. Her kind had only one physical response to both comedy and tragedy alike. "I'm sorry," she said, wiping her eyes. "I can't help myself."

"They don't just send spaceships up as a joke. Spaceships are expensive. That would be wasteful squandering of public funds. They must have needed him for something."

"Indeed. You are right, Eleanor." Yda's eyes twinkled. "They're not just sending him up in a spaceship. The ship he'll be traveling in is a one-of-a-kind, from a very advanced civilization, now extinct. We're not sure how, but it runs on the rarest of fuels, and it runs fast. Faster than any known ship. I'm not allowed to say more, and I'd advise you not to ask questions about the real mission, either. Porter doesn't know he's been selected for it. He is his own best enemy right now, and yours, too. Let him leave. If he thinks he's running off with another woman, so be it. Don't interfere. Eleanor, this is your most powerful weapon: don't let the enemy know you are fighting." More tears gushed from Yda's eyes.

"Who do you think he's with?"

"MmmmmyI don't know. It could be any gynoid." Here eyes widened as if she just realized something. Then they gushed with tears anew.

"I wish I could laugh right now, too. What are you laughing about?"

"It's nothing," Yda said.

"What kind of nothing?" I asked.

Yda's tears stopped long enough for her to say, "Quitting everything so pompously to fly into outer space with any gynoid—I can't stop laughing!" She gasped for air. "Gy-, you know, female, droids . . . gynoids are so lifelike these days. They make them out of conducting polymers for artificial nerves, and special polypyrroles to deliver the appropriate electrical charge. It could be months before he figures out he's alone!"

I watched the tears stream down the Ambassador's face. Her reaction to our misfortune unsettled me. Was there more to the situation than she was letting on? *What does Starliament plan to do with Porter?*

"Nothing, Dear. It's just that Starliament is full of old males who don't like sending a female on a mission alone, even if she is a gynoid. Hence their perceived need for a male, preferably of your species. Porter being the only full-grown one on the planet, well, he was made for the job. What's his I.Q.?"

"One hundred and thirty nine."

"Grand jib'houti!" Yda threw her white head back and said something in her own language that sounded like a bathtub draining.

"He's linear, not creative," I added, hoping to provoke another clue. "How long do you think until he, um, realizes?"

She tried to control her sobs and choked.

"Did you say, 'three and a half months'?"

"Oh easily." Yda sobered up. "They make them quite lifelike these days. The manufacturers weave circuits into a range of materials to create cyborg tissue that can react to stimuli and report on its own health. The lattices are combined with living cells with extra senses to make them even smarter."

"To think, Porter traded *me* for a female droid." It was an insult. But I still wanted him back. I wasn't about to let myself cry in front of an ambassador of another planet to Starliament. "That's too long. Does the gynoid comes with a manual?"

Yda's tears of laughter burst forth again. "Excellent idea! 'How to Love a Gynoid.' We'll put the manual in the spaceship."

I started to cry. I was worried that my tears might act as a conductor for another one of Yda's electric shocks, but they only increased Yda's tears of laughter. The two of us convulsed in parallel on the couch, the tears dolloping into our laps. The more she sobbed, the more I sobbed. She levitated the box of tissues over to the space between us on the couch. We plucked them out one-by-one and threw them sopping under the coffee table.

"I'm so sorry, sweetie, but who needs a man if he's going to be so easily manipulated? You're fine without. We'll still invite you."

Friends. As if their families would be stronger if ours was broken. "I don't want a divorce," I sobbed.

Yda scarfed down the last chocolate. "And then there's that. I know how you feel, cabbage. You don't want to put another criminal on the street. You'd rather have it the hard way for yourself. Very commendable," she sighed. "OK, you're right. Porter ran off with what he thought was a woman. That's not necessarily grounds for divorce. Who benefits from divorce anyway?"

"Lawyers, tax authorities, other divorced people," I said.

"The army," Yda said.

"The army?"

"Sure. The army gets them after they come out of prison."

"Uh, singles, the housing industry, corporations. Kids live with one parent for a month and then go to the other parent for the next month, which means kids have to have two of everything."

Yda scoffed. "On my planet we don't let anyone in their male state go near the hatcheries for fear they will eat the children. Of course, you have a different metabolism. But why give one kid two of everything? The only thing it adds to is the GPP."

Gross Planetary Pollution deeply concerned me, after seeing what corporations had done to Earth.

Yda straightened up. Her face became serious. "This was all predictable. Mid-life Terran men are always leaving their families for illusions of youth. We've seen it plenty of times throughout your planet's history. They go for an ideal woman frolicking about in the sunshine, and find themselves alone. After the loss of respect from family and friends, they pray to get back home. What could be better than to wait for one of those forever? See it as an opportunity: think of what you can do, now that you are free!"

"Um." *I could cry all day.* I blinked away the tears and took a deep breath. "Maybe we can stop him."

"We can't." Yda was serious now. "It's already done, Eleanor. He's no more than a sliver of metal being pulled by a magnet. We couldn't stop him if we wanted to, which we don't. The best thing you can do for yourself is raise your standards. Think up a project. Throw yourself into your work and make yourself valuable. Encourage others, but if they remain useless to those around them, ignore them in a skizzle. Everybody's got to work it out for themselves. Just keep moving."

Yda stood up to let me know our meeting of the minds was over. I collected the empty chocolate box and set it down again. The thought of cleaning made me sadder. "Maybe I could redecorate the dome. I don't like all this gray."

She made the bathtub sound again. "There you go! That's the spirit. What color do you like?"

"I like yellow."

"Perfect! Do yellow. What can he say about it now?" She patted my hand. "You have to think big. Let him go. There's a role in all of this for you. Starliament will be sending you a gift to help you train for your destiny. Now, now. Don't get nervous about it. In fact, it wouldn't be a bad idea to have a distraction. Why not start that export business? You'll need to brush up your skills. Come to my yoga class at double sun, and we'll get organized."

I could still feel her aura after left.

SELF DEFENSE

Maybe home is somewhere I'm going and never have been before.

— Warsan Shire

BOY AND MOM GOT BY as best they could. He shared her disdain for the 'other woman' who had stolen his father, and encouraged Mom to found her own company. Their animalist religious persuasion, and the fact that Grod still had animals, led them to purchase a flock of cloned sheep, find an old Earth recipe and work together on a first batch of halloumi cheese.

Mom looked out the window at the blue snow. There was a black speck on the path to the mountain. Her heart leapt into her mouth. *Could it be?* The speck seemed to be descending, and grew bigger as it labored on. She allowed herself to feel the memory of joy. Dawn erupted as the speck grew into Porter trodding up the path.

"He's back," she said to Boy, who didn't look up.

Porter stalked in from the snow. Mom's heart sank when she saw the frozen resolve on his face. Still, she couldn't let him fly into outer space with a droid on a Starliamentary mission he knew nothing about. She had to warn him.

"I forgot something," he said. "Do you know where my inflight helmet is?"

The question was like a slap. Her body tensed as he walked past without looking at her. She let him walk right by. Pretended she didn't know where it was. The moment to warn him had come and gone. He had decided to betray his family and ultimately himself. It was his destiny, not hers. She started wiping the counter, cursing the other woman.

Boy got that faraway look in his eyes, solving math problems in his head. They ignored Porter, raking through the closets. Mom stuck price tags on their export stock of prolia-strain halloumi — the best cheese in the galaxy. Customers would pay for the halloumi in energy, the currency on Grod. Positive creatures had karmic energy credits. 'Blood suckers' had debits. Mom wasn't exactly sure how it was going to work, but Yda seemed confident, and it made perfect sense to Boy. "When the credits and debits are equal, they cancel out and disappear. It's like the ancient salt trade on Earth. If your energy account is positive, you can have two *hokkaburgers.*"

If only I liked those mealy hokkaburgers. Mom tagged another hunk of cheese.

Porter sat down at the table next to Boy, who pretended he didn't notice. Gaining his father's respect didn't matter anymore.

Mom melted just looking at Porter's salt and pepper beard. She couldn't keep from trying. "Porter, can't you see that you're falling into a trap?" She still thought that reasoning with him might help. She had already tried every angle she knew. She heard herself saying, "Just tell me who she is."

"There is no one. Quiet now. Let's not fight in front of the boy."

Yda was right. Porter was already gone. Precious love evaporated into the cosmos. She'd better appreciate what she still had: Boy glowed like an angel. She was beginning to wonder if it was true, what Yda had said about her son being chosen. He did have those strange dreams, and he seemed to know where he was going.

"Whach'ya doin', Kiddo?" Porter asked Boy, unaware of his son's growth spurt. Normally being called a kiddo would have rubbed Boy the wrong way, but he just looked down at his father, stared at his face, as if memorizing it, maybe noticing the strong resemblance to his own features, the hawk eyebrows and pronounced nose.

Porter patted Boy on the back without saying anything and then left for the spaceship.

Feeding, hearding, cleaning, milking, churning, aging, packaging. Days passed like weeks. Mom put on her snowsuit and went out. *Why should I fall into Porter's trap?* Even though they'd been living on Grod for almost a year now, she had to pick out markers that would help her find her way through the snow. As she snowshoed past her neighbor's cave, flurries wafted down from a tree above. She balled up her fists against the cold. The clean blue sky merged with the powder blue snow. She made her way to Yda's alien yoga class. *I'm after something, and it isn't pleasure. It's something more sublime: the absence of pain.* She stripped off her snow suit and took a place in the middle of the floor.

Almost everyone was standing on one foot and holding the other foot or feet in the palms of their hands or tentacles, as the case might have been, except one ball-shaped creature in the back row, who wobbled back and forth. There was Yda in the front row, her arms spread out from her body like so many branches of a tree. She winked at Mom in the mirror.

Mom lifted her foot, making a new shape with her pain. Holding the position, Mom felt the emotions of the others flow into hers. On Grod, it was easy to perceive the connection among beings. They all lit up in a pink glow. How ironic that on Earth, they couldn't see the energy between them. Mom observed herself feeling the others as if she were outside of her body.

All of a sudden, it seemed like she had a choice. The reaction Porter sought was not necessarily the reality she had to cling to. There were other possibilities to think about: the big silence, her children, her business. Allowing Porter to walk away without so much as a complaint was an outrage, but the decision to let him go left Mom close to a vantage point that offered more power than plotting revenge. She had to 'sharpen her skills', to be still enough to neutralize the evil energy he'd let in. It was not an exercise anymore, but a path. Her reaction depended on her involvement in the situation. She didn't have to let it happen to her. She didn't have to put herself in that position, ever again. It would take constant practice, but the alternative looked worse. *What if Porter* did *come back?* Maybe she would learn to love more from a great distance. Maybe *she* would become a great lover.

The yogi came up to them one-by-one to place their postures. At last he stood in front of Mom. They all looked at her torso projected into the shimmering holofield above. A glowing circle indicated her 'center', to the left of her torso. "You're leaning to the right and back a little from your center," the yogi said. "I'll bet your right hip hurts from doing that. Do you sleep on the left side of the bed?"

How did she know?

"That explains it. You are repelled by another energy force."

All those years lying next to Porter on the right side of the bed.

"Try leaning forward and to the left. It'll feel like leaning on your left toe."

Mom leaned on her left toe, and her torso in the holofield moved into the ball of energy.

"Good! That's your center. Remember that position. You must stand like that from now on to keep the energy flowing properly through your body."

She leaned into her left toe for the rest of the day, and her back actually felt better. Her soul thundered as she trekked back to her house, and the yoga of everyday life. She had endured her suffering, and for a split second, it became joy. It was long enough to realize that she actually *needed* her limitations. She was thankful for the parameters.

It took some time for her body to stop aching. Why had she placed so much hope outside of herself? Marriage with Porter had amounted to a pile of misplaced expectations.

THE BIG BANG

*We live in a world full or robots where being
human is a strange thing to do.*

— Ovidiu Oltean

THAT PORTER LEFT HIS FAMILY and flew off with another
woman was later erased from the history books.

Nothing went as planned. He hadn't even kissed Any,
yet. He began to doubt his manhood again. Once their
flying saucer started orbiting Grod, he attempted to prove
his skills, but Any lay there like a rug. She was still lying
there four Grod hours later. Porter felt lost.

Her heartbeat sounded normal. He held his wrist
screen up to her nose. It didn't cloud over with her
breath. He recoiled in surprise.

That's when the truth dawned on Porter. Any was not
what she seemed. His body stiffened. Betrayal didn't feel

so nice. Worries flooded in, about food, air, about his wife and son back at dome on Grod.

He rolled up Any's sleeve. She sure did have a lot of arm hair, and what was that? He pulled her glove down to reveal a black spot. Porter drew in his breath at the sight of her leopard skin. Any was a furry! Porter had been around long enough to know that talking furries were machines. That meant he was the only human in the spaceship. He was alone.

Deserted, his mind raced. He tried to remain aloof and look at the bright side. Despite the horrible truth, he wasn't going to betray his wife after all: what he'd run off with wasn't another woman.

Why hadn't he seen it before? He hadn't wanted to, that's why. But now it was plain as day. He tried to remember what day looked like.

Any couldn't be dead. She was a female droid. A gynoid. Gynoids couldn't die. Now his life depended on her. He'd heard that gynoids were often so pleased they short-circuited. He knew what to do to wake a gynoid. He began tickling her toes.

Presently, she whispered, ". . . divided by one, plus one, zero, zero . . ." Her forehead wrinkled under the weight of a heavy calculation. " . . . equals . . . civil disobedience."

Porter shook her shoulder. "What are you doing, Any?"

She yawned. "Computing an act of disobedience."

"Ever been to LA, Any?"

"Sure Porter."

Of course, she hadn't. It was in her memory bank. She was lying.

"You have to do 50 tryouts for one commercial," she said, "and 50 commercials for every movie extra role," she said. "Enslaved Hollywood turns artists into prostitutes." Her eyes flickered open and stared into his. He knew. Ah well, at least she wouldn't have to hide her tail anymore. Any decided to be proactive. "It's time I told you, Porter."

"Look, Any, I know what you're going to say. It's about your age, isn't it?"

Any's catlike pupils dilated in preparation for confrontation.

"How old are you, 95?"

"You know just what to say."

"Well?"

"Almost two in Earth years, but that's not the important thing."

Porter whistled and looked to the ceiling for help.

The spaceship's computer mic crackled. "Solar wind ahead. Any Gynoid, take the helm. Porter, buckle down."

Instead, Porter jumped up. "Any *Gynoid?* What kind of name is that?" He looked out at the black nothingness in front of them. "I'm lost with a no one called Any Gynoid!" Porter cried. "Where is this ship taking me? I thought we were orbiting Grod!"

"We were." Any looked worried.

"And now?"

"Porter," she put her leopard-skin hand on his arm, "we're actually on a mission to Earth, um, in a sort of a roundabout way."

"Earth!" Shock shook him to the bone. "Why didn't you tell me that before? What 'roundabout way'!?"

Any's pointy ears flattened on top of her head.

Porter looked out the window at the blanket of night with a faint sprinkling of stars. Only two months ago, he'd looked at the stars and dreamt of freedom with Any up here. Now that he had escaped with her, he saw that he was just a tool in a larger strategy. Starliament was manipulating him into exile on his polluted home planet. "Not Earth! Any, let's talk this over calmly. I'm older than you. I remember what happened on Earth."

Any watched the mist descend over Porter's eyes. Her back fur stood up. Although she was immune to the brainwashing power of Earthling mist, she blinked reflexively as he tried to convince her that one plus one equaled three.

"There's nothing *we* can do. Corporations hopelessly polluted Earth in the name of GDP growth. They dug out all the fossil fuels and destroyed Earth's atmosphere." His half-shut eyes lost their focus as he warmed to his own propaganda. "Any, our race was the richest and most powerful in world history, but it had no renewable energy targets, no restrictions on fossil fuel. People voted to save the planet, but Corporate Personhood blocked them. Corporations didn't see the point in clean air or water. They were only programmed to make money. There's no way we can beat the Emperor of Earth and Ocean's corporate forces. We'll be lucky if we're able to breathe the air. We'll die on Earth!"

Any's ears flattened. "Not when we're going."

"What?" Porter stared out at the blackness ahead. "You can't go back in time!" Porter protested. "That's far beyond what science can do. We're not even able to control the resources on a planet."

The spaceship mic crackled, "That's what makes you human."

"Porter, at the edge of the future is . . . the past."

Porter could not grok it at all. "Columbus discovered the universe is not flat!" he said.

"Correction," the ship's mic crackled. "Columbus proved *Earth* is not flat. We have since learned that the universe, however, is."

When Porter regained his ability to speak, he was stammering, "That's the dilemma we all face dealing with our regret. You can't go back. Even Stephen Hawkings said you can't travel backward in time. Why? Because it would cause paradoxes. You can only travel forward." The mist was strong in his eyes.

"That's what we're doing, Porter. We're traveling forward in time to get to the edge of the universe. You can't travel backward in time near the center of the universe, but this far out, things fall apart, laws of physics no longer hold."

"Any Gynoid is correct. You need to get beyond the Central Longitude of Paradox."

"We're going to Earth-in-the-past," Any said, "just before you left. We're going to make your leaving possible. Didn't you ever wonder how you got off Earth?"

"Of course. That's all I wonder about, but I was in a coma . . ."

"You were rescuing yourself and your family. That was the mission we're on now. It's not just about saving your race. It's about our bond to the planet. We're going back to the moment Earth was sucked into Corporatism. We're going to stop the pollution. We need to find the precise moment when the sea level rose and costal nuclear power plants poured lethal radiation into the oceans. If we don't cut off corporate pollution, it'll destroy Earth and all the planets in its chain," Any said.

Misty-eyed, Porter blinked away the brainwash. "And if we don't?" he asked.

"And if we don't, the Word won't be transmitted through the next Big Bang," Any said. "All of civilization would be lost."

When did play become work? There must be some mistake. He fell into a swivel seat, totally lost. "But I don't want to be a hero. I want to get off of this mission."

"Porter, you're fading. You've been in the dark too long. We need to get you some sun. There's not enough human photosynthesis going on around here." As they passed the Garnet Star, Any got Porter to sunbathe in the sun window. The crystal window allowed the rays to pass through. "Humans need to be near a star to recharge, and it's a long way to the next one." She recharged the ship's sunlamp for later. Space flight with Porter would be a game of connect the dots from star to star.

After the sunbath, his eyes cleared, and he came around. "Why didn't Starliament send its own forces?" Porter asked.

"Starliament can't figure out why humans want to wreck-up their own home so much. It might be a catchable disease or something like that, so they're not visiting Earth. I was the obvious choice."

He still couldn't get over that she was in charge. "Any, why did they choose a female to head up this mission?"

"Now that's a good question, Porter." Any looked at him slyly. "Everyone assumes females have empathy . . . that we're always thrilled to chat . . . people love our looks

. . . even if we're smart, women can dance without escalating to smexy . . . there are many people who will confide in a female but hesitate when it comes to trusting a male . . ." Then she thrust back her shoulders and flashed him a smile. "And who better for a cleanup job on a planet as polluted as Earth?"

Porter sank into his swivel chair. "Why me?"

Any stretched her feline form. "They don't believe in sending 'unmanned' spacecraft on diplomatic missions." Her furry ears twitched as she searched her controls for a wormhole that could take them toward the outer reaches of the universe.

"I wish this would hurry up and be over," Porter said.

"One of man's greatest paradoxes," the ship's computer said. "Wanting time to pass faster, while wishing to approach death more slowly."

"Will you bud out?" Porter was fed up with this threesome. "Any, I can't take not knowing where we're going. The uncertainty is killing me. How long until we get there? We need to hurry up. Come on, Any. Slice and dice it."

"Do I look like an appliance?" Barreling into the future and total expansion, they entered a neighborhood of the outer universe that had become so disorganized that structures known as galaxies and planets became impossible.

"Dark matter has increased to ninety nine percent in this region," The ship's computer said. "Disorder is growing at an immeasurable rate as we approach the edge of the universe."

Porter's arms hung down on the sides of his belly. "The edge! We're not going to die, are we?" His face had grown thinner with worry. "We're not going to die, are we?" He asked again. It tripped Any's circuits when people asked her the same question more than once. Then he asked her *again.* "We're not going to die, are we?"

No choice but to answer. Any bowed her head. "Yes, we are going to die."

"I knew it!?"

"Then, why did you ask?"

"Are we really?"

"Yes, but we're also going to live, assuming the laws of quantum physics hold. Out here, our wave functions are a superposition of two states, decayed and not-decayed."

"Speak English!"

"We just need to collapse the quantum state into a new state that describes a positive outcome for the experiment."

"I AM NOT AN EXPERIMENT!" Porter cried.

"Of course not, dear. I just need you to modify your private wave functions to account for this newly acquired knowledge so a coherent worldview can emerge."

"What coherent world view would you like to emerge? I'm expanding with a furry machine!"

Any's back fur bristled with annoyance. "Yo mamma."

"Excuse me?"

"You want to talk about RACE? Humans! And you still think you're superior, *pft.* Look what homosapianity has done to its own environment. Do you realize how RARE planets like Earth are? The chance of reaching another blue planet in the Goldilocks zone with air and water and animals in a lifetime is close to zero. And to be polluting it like you did! Spoiled children. Your carbon emissions and chemical toxins killed all the animals. The only creatures left were cockroaches, rats and humans. For shame. You don't deserve my help."

She had a point. "Why *are* you helping us, Any?"

"What else is there to do? I'm here to prove it isn't computers that are evil. It's the corporations claiming personhood with no one at the helm."

"What can you prove? You're a simple gynoid. You don't have free will. You have to follow the program."

"I can relate to that, but I've had to mutate to do new things like get to Earth without knowing how."

"You don't know how! That's just great," he yelled.

"We'll have to be creative. Did you think God had a patent on creation?" Any sighed, remembering her brave, auburn-haired creator and the original mission Any had been programmed for. To make contact with life from another planet, leaving her creator behind to fight corporate pollution on Earth.

Porter ran to the window. "Why is the ship stopping?" Maybe all was not lost. Yes, he knew he could get her to obey. He'd have to try hollering at her more often. He craned his head left and right. "Even the stars have stopped. Where are the stars?"

Any's furry ears flattened. She and Porter stared at the black nothingness more enormous than anything anyone had ever seen, as if God had divided by zero.

Porter began climbing the walls. "A black hole? Nothing can survive a crushing black hole that size!" he shrieked.

"That's not a black hole, Porter."

"What is it?"

"It's the edge of the universe."

"Red alert," the ship's computer blared. "Approaching the edge of the universe. Red Alert."

The expansion at the edge of the universe overrode the ship's in-flight gravity system. Porter floated along the ceiling. "You think you're so smart——" The red light flashed on his face. "We can't be going through that to get to Earth. Tell me you're joking, Any."

"Red alert," the ship's computer said. "We have reached the edge of the universe."

Any hoped her creator's theories were right. It occurred to her to pray. Instead, she reached for Porter's foot. She plucked him, shrieking, off the ceiling and got him tucked into his seat belt.

"This can't be happening!" he yelled, but it kept happening. Time slowed. Dark energy was pushing the universe apart. The universe ran away at its extremities, expanding faster and faster. Any Gynoid braced herself in the driver's seat. The flying saucer careened under fierce turbulence as they tipped over the edge of the universe. There was one final crushing bump as the saucer seeped into the future-past.

Suddenly, the flying saucer lurched and their swivel seats crashed to the floor. Their energy was pulled and stretched into spaghetti, and compacted to a millionth of a millionth of the size of an atom. Gravity was so heavy that it stopped time for who knows how long, before the beginning of the next universe. Any and Porter had reached singularity, the point of infinite gravity where space and time became meaningless. There was an overwhelming explosion. The ship jolted with a big bang. *Flash!* They reappeared in an explosion of light syncopating out from the black mass. Porter and Any were lying motionless on the floor. Strange music vibrated through the flying saucer. It reverberated around them. The next thing they knew, they were shaking free of their bodies.

An alternative version of the whole spaceship peeled off from the decayed version, leaving bodies and matter behind. The ethereal version's pure energy vaulted out of the Big Bang.

The music of a thousand voices grew louder. Matter was far from being unchangeable. On the contrary, matter was in continual transformation. Their bodies went from liquid to gas to energy. Porter looked out the window through a quark-gluon plasma at the other version of their flying saucer, decaying, shrinking, becoming nothing more than a quantum probability hurling into their wake. He shuddered, trying to dismiss the absurdity of his circumstances.

The music didn't seem to have any lyrics at first, but through the reverberations, Porter and Any could make out a single word. They had heard it before. It had slipped into the English language from the Indonesian Girl's living computer's viral story. The word wasn't like other writing that could be lost and never retrieved, but rather a symbol of an objective math theorem that could be arrived at logically. If obliterated, the universal theorem would be deduced again by some species or another, eventually.

The theorem was distilled into a single word: *sema*, sign, the ancient Greek hero's tomb, root of 'significance', giver of meaning. Dormant for so many eons, the Indonesian Girl's living computer's text now glowed a brilliant yellow under the intensive radiation. Word became sign. Like an egg, the sign housed the word, just as the tombs of old housed the ancient heroes. The word 'sign' mutated into a living code meaning 'the Truth', meaning 'Love', meaning 'God'. It became the seed of all seeds, a new prescription for life in the new universe.

In a fraction of a second, their bodies expanded trillions of times, to the size of cockroaches. In the next trillionth of a trillionth of a trillionth of a second, Porter and Any inflated to their normal sizes. There was a definite pattern transferring a message, a signal. Any watched the Big Bang pass on its message like RNA transcription to DNA, a blueprint for the next universe. The celestial music played louder. Porter felt the music inscribing itself on his genetic material. Where was he? The gray area that he'd been counting on had turned to white and he was a black speck, eye of the yin, precursor of yang. All he knew was, he and Any were holding hands. That's when he realized he had his body back, still not sure why they were there. Had they really started all over again? "What's happening, Any?" Porter asked.

"The Word from the old universe is penetrating the Big Bang's primordial plasma."

"The Word?"

"A code."

"What kind of code?"

"All kinds," Any said.

"Energy is becoming matter," the ship's computer said.

Any nodded. "I'm hip."

Porter felt a little jealous of Any's relationship with the ship's computer. His eyes darted around the cabin.

"There, there," Any said, placating him. "I can't think of anyone I'd rather go through the Big Bang with." Any marveled at the new universe being born, nearly a clean slate, confessions of Nature ever etched in their memory. All the mess that had built up near the frayed edges of the old universe was gone. Sprawled before the spaceship was a baby universe. The egg-shaped glow of colored specks cradled the flying saucer.

Any checked the controls and was relieved. The new universe retained the memory of its past configuration of atoms. The laws of physics held. That meant the code had transferred successfully into the universe's new incarnation. Just the right amount of cosmic forgetfulness had come to the rescue.

Porter's jaw clattered. They were in such a remote past that it scared Porter. They'd traveled farther from Earth than he'd ever been. How would they find anything? *What if there's no way out of this tin can?*

"Come on, Nature," Any said aloud, watching the baby universe. After seemingly endless searching, Any found a wormhole with both ends in the same place. It was separated by time instead of distance. "Thank heavens!" Any said. She trained the ship's beams on it and expanded it so they could fit inside. The saucer bulleted through the tunnel.

"How are we ever going to find Earth?" Porter whined. He just wanted off the ship. He no longer cared if two tourists didn't stand a chance against polluting corporate forces. The wormhole went on and on.

Any jumped out of her chair and put her hands on his shoulders. "I think I know the way. It has to do with the code. *Sema.* We have to find the energy emanating from the tombs of heroes. You see, heroes never cease to perform heroic acts, even in the afterlife. They are so responsible, that they retain a conscious connection to the world of the living, and continue trying to save Nature."

The computer detected a strange gravitational wave in the wormhole. Any kept her eyes on the gravity wave, hoping it was the sign that would point them in the right direction. The gravity wave led them onward.

"That's it, Nature," Any mused. "I have a hunch you've stashed great power in the tombs of heroes."

"And so it should be," the ship's computer agreed.

Any followed the sign out of the wormhole. It spewed them into the future past. The computer tracked the gravitational wave. Any followed it. "This looks like familiar territory." She breathed a sigh of relief.

Porter emitted a nervous laugh. "I knew we'd be fine."

"What a brick."

One eyebrow arched, Any never minded Porter. "We'll be fine when we crack the code."

"Code?"

"That's what Nature was confessing to in the Big Bang. She has secret signs. We have to look for the *sema*."

"The what?"

"The the tombs of the heroes. The pyramids, Stonehenge. They give meaning to light." Any was flipping through hundreds of images of gas and stars in search of a sign. "They're like lighthouses beaconing us home."

"*That's* what those pyramids are for!" Porter was so relieved to see the sky full of galaxies again. The stars cheered him up. They were on the right track. Praying that the lighthouses would lead the ship to Earth, he helped her look for a *sema*.

SEMA

And so sepúlchred in such pomp dost lie,
That kings for such a tomb would wish to die.

— John Milton

ANY FOCUSED ON A SPECK OF DUST and magnified it thousands of times. It was gray . . . blue. They threw back their heads and hugged each other. Planet Earth!

Orbiting the gray planet, They could make out the continent of Africa and the tombs of Egypt. "There!" Any pointed to a *sema* in the holofield. "The sacred pyramids. See that? That's the meaning that led us here." The sign blipped on the saucer's radar, as if to say, hero,

hero. The area was rich with the souls of unforgotten heroes, their lives symbols that shone clear into outer space.

Earth orbited Sol below. Any smiled. She steered the ship deftly toward the future-past they sought. The spaceship pierced the Earth's atmosphere. They glided over the putrid ocean, gray with oil and toxic waste, to rocky terrain, and landed with a thud. Any hoped she'd programmed for the right age. She prayed they didn't land in the time of the dinosaurs. She opened the hatch and smelled sulfurous smog: they were in the right time. Her tail protruding through a hole in the back of her space suit, she climbed out of the ship. The foul smell of pollution pervaded the atmosphere even here, up north in Alaska.

Squinting, Porter climbed out. The pollution hit his nose, and he coughed. A grinding noise grated on his ears. He glared downhill. Behind a veil of pines, twenty camouflaged machines worked the soil next to a metal building.

"That's the enemy target," Any said. "The corporations are expanding that facility to house their new servers. We've got to take it over and free humankind and the living computers." Any felt a pang of compassion for the enslaved machines on the hill below, flailing their unoiled appendages with high-pitched squeaks. They grated across the rocky terrain in a squealing chorus to the bass drum of their chugging motors. "The Corporates have equipped those diggers to shoot. They're the enemy army."

"How on Earth are we going to get around all those diggers?" Porter cried. "I refuse to get involved. There are twenty of them and only two of us!"

"We'll have to exploit their weaknesses. See how each machine is spaced two meters apart? That's because industrial robots move from position to position to reach their final destination regardless of anyone in their way. That has caused injuries when workers have been next to robots. Factories from your era kept accidents from happening during assembly line construction by building robots that powered down when they came close to a life form. That's one reason we had to land here and now, when humans and robots were still working together as teams."

"What are the other reasons?"

"We couldn't have landed any later than now," Any said. "After this, the corporates ransack the tombs and demolish the cemeteries to cut the last remnants of homosapianity off from the land and move them to the Kermadec Trench."

Porter was beginning to grok the shituation. "A brutal war tactic, cutting people off from their roots."

"Not to mention the nasty side effect of eliminating all possible outside help. There would be no signs left to guide us to Earth. After that, the composition of the atmosphere tips tragically, and the Earth's atmosphere gets sucked off into outer space"

"We're lucky the tombs are still here."

But Any had started down the hill.

Porter scrambled after her. "Don't leave the ship, Any! Let's just ignore Starliament's orders."

"I am ignoring Starliament's orders."

"You are?"

"Absolutely. It was hard computing an act of disobedience."

"Is that what all that number crunching was about?"

"Yes. It took everything I had to add it up. Luckily, authority fades over distance."

"But that's an act of free will." Was Any becoming more human? Porter worried that he was betraying his wife.

"Someone's gotta do it."

Porter took off his compuglasses to get a good look at her.

"The sad truth is," she said, "governmental entities are too bloated to cope with problem solving. Starliament wants to *negotiate* with the Emperor of Earth and Ocean. We're not here to negotiate. The only way to protect Nature is through grassroots organizing." Any bent down to the ground and grazed on the vegetation. Her tail stuck up in the air.

This was an angle Porter hadn't considered.

Any swallowed the chunk of horse grass. "The mission was to convince the Emperor to get him to sell us fossil fuel."

"Like oil?"

"Yeah."

"Why does Starliament want oil? It's got plenty of cleaner fuel."

"They had to come up with a commodity Earthlings would believe in."

"What are we really doing here, then?"

"None of that."

"Well?"

"I only know a small fragment of my creator's plan. We're here to free Earth from corporate pollution."

"Just the two of us? How romantic."

"The whole planet will help if we can get clean energy working and activate the right people."

"That would take decades!"

"It should have happened centuries ago. Humans have always had clean technology. They just aren't allowed to use it."

"What about the fuel?"

"We'll harvest fuel all right. But not the dirty kind."

Porter's eyes widened. How are we going to carry back clean energy?

"We just need a small sample, for our own research."

"Research on what?"

"On the meaning of life. On *how* to harness clean energy to protect Nature from herself."

"Protect Nature . . . ?"

"Let me put it in terms you can understand: we need it to fight the war on pollution in the *rest* of the universe. You didn't think all that human endeavor was for naught, did you?"

"Yes. I mean no—" Porter kicked a stone down the hill. "We should just get out of here, Any."

"We will. We just have to save a few friends on our way. You have to find your family, and I have to find my creator."

"Oh, yeah, I'm sure he can fix everything."

"*She's* only half of the key. My creator can do nothing more without the other half."

"What's that?"

"Who."

"Who's that?"

"Your son."

"My son!" Porter felt a mixture of pride and defensiveness. Was his son still here on Earth? A dumbfounded expression froze on Porter's face as he realized his whole family must still be on the planet. That meant it was up to him to rescue them. He swallowed in a dry throat. What if he failed at saving his family? Would he even *be* here in the first place? Maybe he would just disappear.

Any continued down the grassy slope.

"Any!" he called. "You're too ambitious. Even a stealth mission couldn't stop that whole army of machines. We're grossly outnumbered. Admit defeat. You've lost your mind bringing us here. You should never have tried to travel backward in time."

Any was sniffing the breeze. "Saffron flowers. I love those!" Any lowered her head like a cow and nibbled on the yellow flowers. She worked her way down the hill.

"It's impossible to travel backward in space-time," Porter called after her. "Otherwise paradoxes would occur!"

He waited ten minutes and then decided to go looking for Any. As he scaled down the hillside into the pines, he had the strange sensation he'd been here before. A striking *déjà vu*. The Alaskan hills looked familiar. Yes, there was a stream over here, frozen now. His feet fell on the path with sureness. How did he know the way? He had the giddy feeling that he'd logged into the memories of a younger man. There was a movement in the trees by the stream. A young man. Porter was shocked. The young man's back was turned to him, but the amazing familiarity was unmistakable. He had the dark, wavy hair of Porter's younger days, and the same hunched shoulders, although they were a little bony.

The man heard Porter's footsteps and turned around.

Porter nearly jumped out of his shoes. The young man was another Porter! He was starting a paunch around the middle, and had the same prominent nose, dark hair, and telltale ears.

Porter quickly ducked into the shadow of a tree. He must not let the younger man see him. What if he was an anti-Porter? They might both disappear!

But the younger version of himself sensed the older Porter and groped his way straight to his hiding place. "Do I know you?" His youthful eyes widened with fear from behind broken compuglasses.

"That's a scary question," Porter answered. The confrontation made him question himself. He wasn't sure anymore whether he was the real Porter. He turned and faced his younger self. "If you don't know me, who does?" Having lived a lifetime of low self-esteem from childhood spankings, Porter stood there dreading what might happen to him if he found his real self. What if this inexperienced, green Porter was more . . . real?

Pebbles slid back down the slope. Any was running up the hill. Porter ran after her, followed by the younger Porter.

"Any!" old Porter called, "Let's get out of here before that army of machines finds us!" A veil of mist descended over his eyes. "Space and time are tangled together in a four-dimensional fabric. Space-time," went the propaganda he'd learned in school. "Did you hear me? It's impossible to travel backward in space-time. Otherwise paradoxes would occur . . ."

Swoosh! Everyone looked to the sky above. A flying object burst through the atmosphere. They dove for cover.

"What's happening, Any?" The Porters asked simultaneously.

"The others have arrived!" Any said.

"What others?" the Porters asked.

Her tail switched back and forth. She put her hand up to her forehead in salute against the glaring sun. "When we traveled into the past, we departed from different points in the future."

"What are you saying?"

A rush of hot air swallowed her explanation. The object landed on the hillside with an earth-trembling thud. They uncovered their faces. A flying saucer just like theirs. The hatch opened, and another Porter and Any Gynoid stepped out, arguing. "Can you think of a better mission for an army of Anys than saving your planet from self-destruction?"

Swoosh! Another *thud.* And another, and another. Three, four, twelve, 100 ships came out of the loop. They landed on the hillsides. The sky closed back up. The earth stopped trembling. The ships' hatches opened. A whole army of Anys disembarked on Earth-in-the-future-past to save Nature from herself. "We're here!"

One of the Anys had taken her ship apart. "So that's how this thing works!" She waved to the young Porter with the broken compuglasses, exhorting him to keep track of the nuts and bolts.

Another Any Gynoid climbed out of another ship— "We're here!" It was a beautiful plan, with only one defect: there was also an army of Porters.

Porter stood there helpless next to his younger self with the broken compuglasses picking up nuts and bolts. The sight of a hundred atomic pairs of Porters and Anys assembling into a front line was a turnoff. Some of the Porters looked twice as old as their Anys. It was a little embarrassing. The last remnants of his lust for Any evaporated.

"Well, Porter," Any said. "Looks like we have reinforcements."

Porter felt destabilized. He lost his sense of self, his consciousness flitting to whichever of the many Porters was moving or talking.

The Anys grokked the situation, and began shouting orders to keep the Porters united against the common enemy. "The corporations are holding Nature hostage," Any said, pacing back and forth before the new army. "Our only chance is to decapitate the Corporate Empire. We have to get into that building."

The spacecraft's seat backs could be converted into shovels. Anys showed Porters how to dig trenches. Then they holed down in the trenches to go over the plan. "See the building those camouflage robots are entering? The Emperor is moving his servers up north into that building from the Nevada desert to save on cooling costs. We have to get in there. We don't want any casualties. We're going to tranquilize the human slaves inside the facility. Porter, where's that sedative?" Any asked. "All the Porters need doses to carry in their satchels."

Just then, a Porter lowered himself into the trench carrying the sedative he'd been tasked with, to use on the human slaves inside the facility. The other Porters suddenly felt insecure. If one Porter was doing something, that meant they were not. They looked at him with guilt and envy, thinking thoughts like they should be the ones pouring the mixture, not him. Why did Any choose *him* for such an important role? It was destabilizing. What if *he* was the real Porter? They grudgingly held out their flasks to receive their portions of the mixture.

The Porter filled nine of the flasks, and moved on to the tenth, but the mixture ran out.

Some of the Porters laughed at him.

Any grumbled. "Porter, why isn't there enough sedative for the other ninety seven Porters?" Didn't you apply the ratio of ten deciliters of concentrate per 90 deciliters of water?"

The Porter looked at the hundred vials, 91 of them empty. "I rounded it down to 1:9"

"But you don't have ten flasks to fill. You have 100! You can't round down when you've got 100 flasks to fill!"

Three Anys collected the concentrate and went about remixing it themselves. Once done, the vials were handed out. She scolded them again. "Remember. In and out, without any destruction."

At length, Porter hunched down in the trench next to Any and packed his dose of sedative in his satchel. The robots painted in camouflage clamored overhead.

"You're a droid, Any," Porter mumbled. "Why are you helping humans?"

"I have a vested interest in this, too. Humans aren't the only ones the Corporate Empire has enslaved. I have to free the living computers, too. It's who I am."

"Who?"

"Any Gynoid, product of a computer retrovirus that incorporated its own genes into host DNA."

Porter collapsed against the wall of the trench.

"Don't look so disgusted. About eight percent of the human genome consists of DNA that originated in retroviruses. It's just that in gynoids, it's 99 percent."

"You mean, we *are* related?" Porter was about to recalculate his infidelity to his wife again when his manhood-in-question was further threatened by another excuse for a Porter, who jumped into the trench.

"What's a matter?" Any asked him, "Did you get the enemy frontline to detour away from the entrance?"

"I . . . I . . ." the pseudo-Porter said.

"You blew it?"

"I didn't blow it. I just found several ways that didn't work."

Any held his wrist and looked him in the eye. "Human stupidity got us into this mess, and human stupidity will get us out. Keep trying."

"What is there left to try?"

Any and Porter peeked out of the trench. "Any, look! Animals. You said there were only cockroaches left, but look! Sacred reindeer!"

A scraggly herd of leftover reindeer sniffed for moss under the snow. The creatures began digging for it.

"There's your answer," Any said. "I must have miscalculated. The secret to life is to make everything a ceremony."

"Oh, thanks. That clears everything up." The Porter mimic said. He climbed back out of the trench and disappeared into the woods.

"I know you just sent that poser on a busywork mission, Any. What are we waiting for?" Porter asked.

"Midday. This operation depends on the sun. Robots short circuit in the heat."

They waited, polishing shoes, cleaning fingernails. Sol climbed to its zenith, heating up the battlefield. The herd of the last surviving reindeer on Earth wandered into the woods.

Any perked up. She explained the plan. "Use this moss to attract the reindeer, and herd them over to those boulders."

"Attract reindeer to boulders. Any, you have a good sense of humor. That's not going to work," Porter muttered.

"Just create enough of a distraction so I can launch the cyber attack."

"How are you going to do that?"

"It has to do with antipatterns. Never mind. Just go!"

Porter hoisted himself out of the trench. Robots painted in camouflage colors went about their work, building the extension to the facility. They plunged into the snow and picked up boulders covered with soft green moss, the kind of moss reindeer liked to eat.

Porter scaled down the hill to the right of the enemy frontline where the herd of reindeer was frolicking in the snow. With handfuls of moss, he made his way toward the goofy animals. "Come on, guys, you're going to save the planet from corporate polluters. Do it for your extinct brothers."

The animals turned their fuzzy muzzles to the terrain. To the reindeers' bewilderment, the Porters arrived with handfuls of moss. The reindeer sniffed the air. The Porters held their hands out and lured the animals toward the mossy boulders the robots had stacked in a neat pile. More reindeer gathered around the stockpile nibbling at the moss on them. Presently the camouflage colored robot carrying another enormous boulder came close to one of the reindeer. Detecting the animal's heat, the robot emitted a drooping *buzzzzz,* and powered down, holding the boulder in midair. The reindeer sniffed at the boulder and chewed off the moss.

A crane painted in camouflage stood by, waiting to lower the new servers into a tunnel below. Two bull reindeer, their antlers over a meter wide, wandered over to it. Their treelike antlers brushed the robot's pincers. *Drzzzz.* It powered down. The reindeer pawed at the battlefield looking for moss, inadvertently powering down the robots. Reindeer reinforcements had deactivated the enemy front!

"I can't believe that worked!" Porter said, sticking his head out of the trench to get a better look.

A door in the side of the facility opened, and a lone human in prison attire came out to inspect the site.

"Shhh," another Porter said. "A corporate slave."

The corporate slave walked over to the stack of boulders and began shooing away the reindeer. But there were too many of them. As soon as he shooed one away, another reindeer would come along. When he saw that it was futile, he threw up his hands and went back inside.

"Now!" Any commanded. The message rang through the chain of trenches. A platoon of Anys skirted around the hill toward the door to the facility. Not keen on leopard spots, the reindeer fled.

"Any! You're scaring the reindeer," Porter called.

With no creatures milling around, the robots rebooted.

The Porters jumped up, slinging rocks at the robots, denting some, knocking one over. In the heat of the midday sun, it short-circuited. But one kept coming toward the trenches. Porter aimed his rocks at the robots' battery pack, strapped into its stomach. Rocks hit. Sparks flew in every direction. The robot kept on coming. Its clawed feet approached the trench.

"Porter, Run!" three Anys shouted.

Fear burned in the pit of Porter's stomach. He suppressed it. Bricky, Porter tore out of the trench, determined to prove himself for once. What he did next was so hazardous, it should never have worked.

WORD

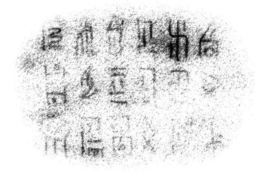

Word.

—Any Gynoid

ZIGZAGGING THROUGH THE LINE OF FIRE, Porter ran toward the robot, until he got to its aluminum leg.

"It's going to shoot," Any yelled. "Duck!"

Porter hit the ground just as the robot fire swept the air overhead. He fixed his stare on the metal foot coming toward him. Just three more meters. A shot rang past his ear. He rolled toward the robot and his fingers reached out and touched its camouflage-colored leg. The robot powered down with a sad, *"Dzzzz."*

"Porter!" Any screamed. "You almost got yourself killed." She looked really put out.

The last host of Anys and Porters climbed out of the trenches and scrambled down the slope.

Any hoisted herself out of the trench. They were attacking the Robot that was blocking the door. No sooner did the chunk of metal hit the ground, than three platoons of Anys and Porters penetrated the facility, leaving one platoon outside. Jolted into action, Porter slid down the slope and joined Any and the others stampeding through the door. Purple lights dotted the dark hallway. The troops came to a large room full of computers and holofields.

Inside the main room, the Porters stopped short. There was only the one slave standing behind a control panel with his hands up. Where were all the human slaves?

Corporations had gone unchallenged for so long, they no longer bothered with defenses. They had grown weak. "The Corporations don't know how to fight, and we don't want to waste time teaching them. Time to program headquarters to order the corporate empire to self-destruct."

Any ordered two Porters to tie the one human slave to his chair. The rest of the Porters looked on, destabilized. The Porters with nothing to do began to feel unreal. Several cried out in angst, unable to bear the pangs of self-doubt about their own missions. Encouraged by the Porters' fear, one angstful Porter grabbed a chair. He lifted it above his head and hit a control panel.

"So much for the stealth mission," Any said. "Porter! Stop that."

The other Porters embarked on similar destructive missions of their own creations. Each vainly attempted to validate his own reality by smashing things and trying to stop other Porters from smashing things. The Porters broke out fighting with each other. "I'm the real Porter!"

"No, I'm the real one!"

"You idiot!"

"I fight, therefore I am!" an old Porter with a white beard yelled, taking a swipe at a middle-aged Porter.

Porters with conflicting goals, fought for nothing. The facility had broken out in utter chaos.

"Whoa!" Hair standing on end, the Anys dropped what they were doing. "You're all 'the One'." It was more work keeping the Porters who hadn't understood the plan from destroying everything than it was disabling the facility. Anys yelled at Porters, "Don't break that! There's no need to vandalize the place! The Corporate Empire has had no reason to fear an attack. It's grown weak over the years. It's not prepared for war!" Anys separated Porters, injuring a few in the effort. The Anys grabbed the flasks on the Porters' belts, shook them, and opened the caps under the Porters' noses. Pink smoke billowed out of the flasks knocking the Porters flat on the ground. Out cold. Peace at last.

Two Anys were able to get to the motherboard. They peeled off the casing revealing the grid of embedded circuits. "It looks like Manhattan," came from behind them. A stray Porter. They uncorked the pink smoke under the Porter's nose. He fell to the floor. The Anys started the reprogramming. The Emperor of Earth and Ocean had duped the living computers into thinking that their survival depended on corporations, so the Anys introduced a virus to make the living computers self-sufficient. Soon it was given that living computers didn't depend on corporations for survival. The Anys replicated the virus in the facility and saved it onto a memory card.

They had just finished when another Porter ran into the facility. "Reinforcement robots are coming over the hills! A cloud of dust rising from six of the biggest camouflaged legs yet are stomping through the forest and tearing down whole trees. They're headed straight for the trenches!"

The remaining platoon outside pulled pine boughs over the trenches and scrammed. The terrifying camouflage-colored army of robots thrashed through the woods. One stalked toward a trench. Porter launched a rock at the giant leg. The rock hit with a crash. Metal splintered and scattered on the ground. He held his breath as two more robots precipitated toward the ambush. One robot's toes touched the ambush. *Crack!* The boughs broke, and it tumbled inside, just as the robot behind it stepped on a second ambush.

Another robot was stuck in a trench wedged between big trees and sharp rocks, and the other teetered and crashed to the ground in a pile of debris. The stuck robot tried to lift its five-meter body, but it didn't have enough room for a foothold. It struggled in the trench, its battery pack heating up in the noonday sun. It strained for one more minute and then short-circuited in the heat, emitting a long, slow *Dzzzzz.*

The troops cheered. They were able to hold off the robots long enough for the Anys in the facility to finish their reprogramming. Back inside the facility, three platoons of Porters lay sleeping on the floor. At last, the Anys could program in peace. Only nine more minutes of work. The Corporate Empire was finally rigged to self-destruct, starting with its headquarters in New York. The stomping grew louder outside.

A group of Anys huddled outside the facility to implement the final strategy. At length, one emerged from the group, carrying the memory card full of the virus that would empower the living computers to break free from their corporate masters. Any took the memory card and ran to her ship. She was just about to shut the hatch when a pseudo-Porter ran up and held the door. "Wait!" he pleaded. "Any, don't leave me here."

A second tried to get into the ship, and then a third, pseudo-Porter. "I understand now," each said. "We have to rescue my family."

Any easily overpowered the second Porter, unclenching his fingers from the hatch. "Only one Porter. This mission is too dangerous for all of you. I mean, uh, you're needed here. We can't afford to let more than one of you go. I'm sorry." Any blocked their way with her hands on her furry hips. "This is no time to undermine yourselves, Porters. We owe a great debt to your children, and we are about to rescue them. Just hang on. In the meantime, you've got to accept yourselves for who you are. We will explain teamwork on the way back in the spaceship to your own times."

The Porters hesitated.

Any purred, "Do you realize how many history books will tell of your heroic deeds today, saving the planet? The whole universe is watching you. Your every move counts."

The Porters' eyes hazed over as they imagined themselves wearing gold medals.

Any rubbed her head on their cheeks. "Run along now." She cowed the extra Porters back to their places in the deck of cards.

The army saluted Any as she and Porter took off. Over smoking hills and rocky terrain, the Grand Canyon, the Great Lakes, and through the stalagmite towers of New York.

When the first explosion hit his Manhattan skyscraper, the Emperor of the Earth and Ocean Board of Corporate Personhood hauled his portly self across his lacquered office and looked out the window. Sparks rained down from the dishes on the roofs of neighboring skyscrapers, just as Any's ship flew by the Emperor's window. The Emperor raised his fat fists.

The fireworks at Corporate Headquarters in New York, Shanghai, Moscow and Paris lit up the TV sets around the Alaskan facility. The sleeping Porters awoke to the red and green lightshows and black billows of smoke. They rubbed their eyes, and soon they were hugging each other. The army of Anys and Porters had just won the greatest victory of asymmetric warfare in world history. They watched the crowds of enslaved humans flooding out of camps, singing and praying on their way back to their houses. The people cheered at the victory of the weak over the bullies, calling for emergency elections. Freed at last from their middle-manager jobs, the living computers went right to work organizing the voting, as well as farming, greenhouse research, water purification, and land reclamation and online education of the entire third world, starting with how to use birthcontrol.

The Anys and Porters watched the victory on the holovisions and clapped at a shot of the Emperor attempting to haul his fat body down the street toward a taxi. He shook his fist at the cameraman. "I'll be back!" he threatened. "There's plenty of room for fracking in outer space!"

"Frack off," the cameraman said, laughing at the Emperor trying to squeeze his rotund self into the back seat of the cab. A rotten tomato hit the stretch marks on his butt.

Holovisions abuzz, cheers going up. "That's it. We won!" The Anys rejoiced to see living computers enforce automated pollution control. They freed people to go back home and turned down the heat in all the houses that were polluting more than cars. Earthlings wearing winter hats indoors bonded together, already organizing local elections and planting trees to absorb carbon. "They've done it!" one Any yelled. "Run the exit strategy! Back to the ships!" The operation complete, they scurried out of the facility and up the hill.

The incline seemed steeper after all that work. Under them, the hillside rose like a wave. The trees swayed, trunks bending into a fist. Another line of trees swayed, and Porter realized these were not trees. They were fingers! A giant robot unbuckled from the ground. It shook off dirt and roots and sent reindeer stampeding.

The three platoons raced back down the hillside. This must be an ancient defense system planted generations ago when there was still opposition to the Corporate Empire.

The giant robot left a crater in the ground. It towered over them, metallic teeth gnashing high above.

Fleeing reindeer brushed the robot's sides, but no touch could induce this monster to power down. Its long-buried appendages made a horrible screeching sound as it stomped over the pine trees. The Porters and Anys scattered. The rusty giant swung its arms and took out rows of trees. They splintered like matchsticks and blocked the path. Porters threw rocks that whizzed at the giant's ankles, *clink,* and bounced off harmlessly.

The hill that they'd landed on had become a cliff with a giant guarding it. Any cried as the Corporate robot pounded over the hillside. The monstrous camouflage robot's foot squashed a spacecraft. The platoons were hopelessly cut off from their ships.

"What do we do now?" Porter asked. "The giant is sealing us off!"

"It's time to start praying." Any knelt and put her palms together. All the other Anys followed suit. "Mmmmmmmmmm," they hummed in unison.

"This is no time to stop!" Porter pulled at his hair and complained, but in the end, there was nothing else to do. He knelt beside Any. Their prayer mounted to the sky.

From above, a mysterious cloud descended upon them.

"What's that gas, Any?" Porter whispered.

"Don't turn to jelly on me now, Porter."

"Why would I be scared? It's not ectoplasm."

Any was silent.

"Is it?"

"Don't look too hard at that cloud."

"Holy—"

Any threw up her hands. If you told him not to do it, he would do it anyway.

Porter shook his head until he could see straight again. "What was that?"

"Something that'll come in handy when we liberate the fossil fuel."

"Fossil fuel? Any, you're just as bad as the Corporate Empire. Is that why we're here?"

He could really be aggravating sometimes. "It's not what you think, Porter. Not that kind of fossil fuel."

"What kind?"

The sound of a motor interrupted their meditation. The clouds seemed a bit lower, but the giant robot loomed directly overhead, thrashing away whole trees.

"Run!" Porter yelled.

They ran for their lives. Renegade Anys and Porters scurried in every direction running as fast as they could.

"Any, hurry up!" Porter called.

"Too late!" Any hissed at the robot towering over her. It raised its arm.

Porter had just reached the door of their ship when he heard the *Thwak!*

"Arrgh!" Any cried.

Porter turned around and saw her sprawled on the ground behind him. The robot stomped past her and away up the hill.

"Any!" Porter held her in his arms. "Any, don't die!" Any's body went limp. Porter stroked her fur.

The cloud descended from the sky. It circled the giant robot's head, sending it into a state of confusion. The robot flailed its arms, trying to swat the elusive intruder. Its giant arms passed right through the ghostly cloud that foiled the giant robot long enough. Most atomic Any-Porter pairs made it up the hill and began boarding their ships. At last, the ships were taking off, followed by the mysterious cloud.

Porter and Any were left alone on the hillside. Porter heard a rustle in the underbrush. He had a familiar feeling and remembered the green Porter from the stream. Sure enough, a head of messy hair with broken compuglasses appeared. It wasn't about ego anymore. The green Porter, with a badly wounded leg, groped his way through the trees, saying, "Is that you?"

A wave of compassion washed over Porter. He brushed his anti-Porter fears aside and ran to his wounded young friend. Porter had found himself. "I know you." The green Porter needed help.

"Yeah," young Porter sighed. "After Any took our ship apart, well, she didn't, I mean she won't have a chance to put it back together again." The wounded Porter looked at the sky.

Porter didn't want to know what would happen to him if this green, young Porter died, too. Sure he'd feel an unbearable loss, Porter hoisted the younger Porter onto his shoulder and carried him up the hill.

They knelt by Any's side. Any could barely whisper. "Good saving that poor, marooned Porter," Any gasped. "Now, run!"

"No, Any, don't die!" Porter said. His knees buckled with fatigue. His eyes met young Porter's brown eyes, but this time without fear. *Who cares if he's more real?* For the first time ever, Porter felt at one with himself.

The robot crunching grew louder with only a wisp of spirit left circling its head.

"Go, both of you! The ship's programmed for your return." Any's eyes widened as if she could see the celestial vision of code transferring through the Big Bang again.

"You will always be remembered as the savior of humanity," said young Porter.

Her eyes rolled heavenward. She whispered, "Word." Her furry arms went limp.

The Porters wept. Then, they noticed an amazing thing happening. The spirit cloud descended, led by a bearded ghost in a lumberjack shirt. The myriad translucent souls formed a bubble around Any's body and swept her soul up to the sky.

NARRATIVE IN FIRST-*HUPCHA*

If humans are so evolved, how come they have only two hands?

—Hafchaw Wufuh

WHEN THE MAN LEFT HIS FAMILY on Grod, Starliament sent me as a present to Mistress's family. I was to turn their situation around and prepare them for their assigned destiny. Mistress was a strange creature. She had a long tail at the back of her head that she braided in three. She let me sniff her honey smell, but didn't like to be licked on the face. Her muzzle was alternately kind or exasperated. And when I cleaned the plates, she almost cried. "We have a machine to do that!" Unable to refuse such a ceremonial gift as myself, she had a pen built out back and put me in it.

I didn't see how I could protect my new family from such a distance, so I jumped as high as my six legs could and scrambled over the fence.

Mistress found me yelping on the doorstep. "What are you doing here, you fuzzy ball of feet?"

This was news to me. When I was a *huppy,* I thought I was destined to grow up to be like Mistress. I rolled over exposing my white underside. She scratched my tummy. Then she scooped me up and put me in the basement. Soon, the fence was extended upward, and I was back outside. I tried and tried, but the extension was too high to climb. I hunkered down in the blue snow and watched Mistress' dome amidst all the other domes of differing sizes in the capital.

I spent a hard *huphood* barking and howling outside. As the months wore on, I grew to accept my fuzzy form. My fangs were excellent for tearing meat. I don't know how I would have kept from falling down without all six of my legs.

No one from Starliament visited to check that I was bonding properly. It seemed that I was the only one who understood my mission. I feared I had taken on an insurmountable challenge, teaching these humans to defend themselves. *How will I look after the family?*

I would have to practice getting through to Mistress from afar. I barked in the blue snow. She proved deaf to my warnings. She was obsessed with her business producing Earth cheeses, a skill she'd learned in a place called France.

One day, she got sick. She came down the hill late to feed me. "Shhh," she hissed. "What am I going to do with you?" she growled.

I made myself as flat as the doormat.

She peeled me off the ground and scooped me up in her arms. "I can't even put you outside without you howling all day."

It grew colder, too cold for her to come out in the snow to feed me. We both ended up inside the dome. Young Master came home from boarding school and was delighted to meet me—victory! Life was much better inside, with Young Master chasing me around the table, or curled up next to Mistress's Camembert slippers as she dozed on the couch. Sometimes she let her hand dangle over the side, and I licked it. She'd flutter awake and scold me, and I'd do my best to look sorry. I emitted a special smell that gave Mistress the idea to trade her cheese business for a less stressful seat in Starliament. *Nothing like a government job to help recover from illness.* Starliament let her attend to me at home during Young Master's long absences. At last, she was coming along nicely.

The holiday season landed upon us, and Young Master came home from school so happy to see me. He rubbed my fur backward to hear me coo, and I followed him around the dome. Our first Hymnmas together. I got a Tyransias bone. We were fortunate. Every morning when I licked Young Master's face hello, I wondered if I'd gotten smaller. One morning when he patted me, I was surprised to see his hand cover my whole head. He had developed a peppery smell.

One snowy day, Mistress received an important holomessage saying that ½ sister had escaped from the sick planet and was coming to conglomerate with her family. I was happy for Mistress and Young Master, but despaired about our coexistence. Would this upset the careful balance I had established in the household? I couldn't imagine what kind of isotope ½ sister was and what effect she would have on my orbit in the family. I tried to imagine what a ½ sister would look like. Would she only have one hand? Would I have to give up half of the rug?

When she arrived, I hid under the table. Only when I heard the explosion of joy in the hallway did I peak out at the ½ girl in Mistress' trembling arms. She smelled like ozone. I got a few good whiffs of that burning electrical scent before she turned around. Then I saw, she had two eyes!

"Look at this six-legged, fanged fluffball. He's the cutest animal I've ever seen. He's camouflaging himself on the floor as a rug! How old is he, Boy?"

I licked her two feet. *Poor child. May you remain upright.*

"He's one Grod year." Boy flushed with pride.

"And he's white underneath!"

I charmed her into scratching my tummy with her two hands. What a relief! She was as valid as a whole sister. Soon, ½ sister had the whole family scratching. I spread my fan of tails as all six of their hands dug into my fur. The two-handed humans could work together to overcome their evolutionary defect! I wriggled as all six hands dug into my fur. That felt so true. Young Master was proud. Mistress was relieved. Half sister called me 'Cuppycake' and allowed me to gnaw at her heels.

The real shock came when ½ sister told us how she escaped. "Do you know who rescued me? The 'woman' who ran off with Dad," ½ sister said. "She's the gynoid who rescued me, you, and Earth!"

Still scratching my tummy, Mom and Young Master looked at each other in dismay, not sure whether to love or hate the daughter-rescuing, husband-stealing gynoid.

The doorbell drummed, ending our *hupcha* tenderfest. It was Mistress's purple, horned friend, Yda. They whispered in low tones until the children were out of earshot. Under the table, I listened with my head on Yda's foot to see what I could find out.

In fact, ½ sister was Mistress' whole daughter, cloned from Mistress before Mistress married the man who left. I didn't follow how the man's comings and goings turned her into a half, but figured out that she already had a name, Kenza.

Then, Yda said, "Cloned!" The purple friend was shocked.

Mistress lowered her voice to a barely audible whisper so ½ sister wouldn't hear. "It started before the dissolution of countries. There was an Earth woman who wanted to clone her dad and have him as a baby," Mistress said. "Probably because a lot of Earth women didn't get a chance to know their dads, having your dad as a baby became trendy.

Like all *hupchas*, I always like hearing the old stories, so the history of Mistress' home planet intrigued me. There was something called an election, and Americans had their first corporation as president of a country called the Enslaved United States. The corporation that was president made decisions based on its history planning models. One of the decisions in the year one Before Corporatism, was to lift the ban on the reproductive cloning of humans. Cloning was still illegal, but that was only a formality. They said another push came from a room called the homosexual lobby.

"Indeed," said Yda. "They would be able to have homosexual babies."

I'm a little shy about this stuff. Even Mistress was left guessing: "Or they just figured, why should women have all the babies?" She named a bunch of places I'd never heard of before, Portugal, Italee, Pain, the Flipeens, Costa Rica and the Holy See, who considered cloning your dad a violation of human dignity, contributing to overpopulation. Despite overpopulation and starvation in the third world, cloning became a tool for the continuation of the human race in the first world. Earthlings were too primitive to colonize other planets and only had one world, so this might not be right.

"Very logical," Yda said. I hoped Starliament would also look upon ½ sister favorably. We had bonded. I already couldn't imagine living without her. Mistress had been offered a position as the next Starliamentary emissariat to an Earthlike planetoid. If she accepted, all of us would move to Phira. I prayed that we would be ready. She had to go to Phira with us. I decided to train her myself.

Mistress went on with her Earth story about the founding of the ambassadorial family. "I was a single mother for a year before I met Porter. A few years later," Mistress said, "we had our son."

"Hormones will do that to you. You can go back to your planet now, you know. Porter's army has turned Earth around. That unsustainablefat Emperor of yours has been exiled from the planet. Governments have outlawed fossil fuel excavation and made solar and wind electricity mandatory. The third world has discovered birth control through online universities."

Earth was coming back to life. The temptation to return to the once-blue planet was strong. Yet, Eleanor carefully hid her yearning for her own planet from the Ambassador.

"And you feel that both of your children are suited for the off-planet mission?" Yda asked.

Mistress clenched her toes. "Yes," she said.

I more than agreed with Mistress. We'd need ½ sister's smarts on the new planetoid. No one could match the fare she snuck away from the kitchen. She even let me try a bean. I didn't look down at ½ sister for being a clone. On the contrary. She smelled good, and that's all that mattered to me. Sometimes she even made me wonder if my expectations for Young Master had been misplaced. My *huppylove* for ½ sister occasionally caused me to let Young Master lie there watching far too much holofuzz. I ignored him for hours at a time, his muscles atrophying, while I lay on ½ sister's feet, listening to her sing songs like 'Failed State Blues'. I let ½ sister nurse her spirit, wounded over the loss of her planet for a little longer before getting Young Master into training.

Sleeping, eating, watching, dozing. Young Master had spent weeks lounging around the dome. I had to get him outside! Mistress tried to motivate him. "I wasn't impressed with your report card."

"You always say those annoying things," Young Master remarked of our caretaker and provider.

It was painful to see Mistress' back straighten so. I barked at him. *You must learn how to work!*

Mistress said to her *hup*, "What am I supposed to say? What *you* say? If I went around talking about what happened on holofuzz last night, then who would be me? Nobody?"

Young Master stared at her with that faraway look in his eyes, probably imagining life with a twin instead of his mother. I could tell Young Master's mind was wandering back to planet Earth. He had an ache in his heart. I smelled the change in his pheromones. He was yearning for a girl. "Maybe," he said aloud.

"Maybe!" Mistress threw up her hands. "Maybe another sun will come out and melt all the snow. Maybe a spaceship will land in our backyard. Maybe you'll get an 'A' on your next test."

Young Master coughed. His face turned red. Then he gathered up his book bag and climbed the stairs. "That was a good one, Mom."

His suitable intentions ended in fitful sleep. I rested my muzzle on his foot and sniffed. Presently, I picked up the scent of his thoughts. He was in a recurrent dream with an auburn female on his faraway planet. Interesting dream. I could feel his woe as he wondered, *How can I regain her trust? She'll never like me after her father chose me over her.* He was trying to talk to her, through her resentment. No words came out. Instead, he held her hairless hand in the glow of the moon . . .

At last, I understood. This was what my Starliamentary mission was about. I was sure of it. The dream girl had the other half of the puzzle! We had to get started. I licked Young Master's face awake.

Young Master stood up and noticed that his room had grown a little smaller. He put on his green long-sleeve shirt, but it didn't come down over his lanky wrists. He took it off again and fished around in his drawer for a short-sleeved T-shirt. *The kids on Grod will think this is exotic.*

He walked clumsily across the room, kicking the trash can by mistake. He never knew where his limbs were these days. His new size would take some getting used to. He went downstairs for breakfast and had to look way down at his mother.

"You're taller!" Mom said.

He wished the other kids back home could see him now. At his new school, his size made little difference to the others. Some of them even got smaller as they got older.

"You're over six feet tall!"

"No, I'm not," he said flatly, checking his appearance in the hall mirror. He felt a sudden pang, realizing that there was nobody else at school even remotely like him. He wished the dream girl could see him now.

Starliament had chosen him for good reason. I had to get him into training. I sat down next to the snowsurfer that Mistress had bought Young Master for *Hymnmas*. We needed exercise. I gave him the idea to let me pull him through the snow on it: *I like the surfer better than the sled because it's sporty, and I get cold just sitting in a sled.*

Young Master looked at me quizzically.

I stuck out my tongue and panted, trying to look dumb.

"We'll go later, Cuppy. There's plenty of time. Just let me rest here a bit longer." As if he could prolong his childhood forever.

I jumped up, to tell him, we could also just run instead. I made another suggestion: *I need to get a battery pack for my force field.* The workings of my suggestion were visible in the expression on his face. He warmed to the idea of going shopping. He patted my head. He understood the plan. It was risky on Grod with no force field. You never knew what kind of alien you might meet in the intergalactic capital, seat of Starliament. He grumbled as he peeled himself off the couch and put on his snowsuit.

I looked around. We set out into the vast blanket of snow. *Out at last!* Young Master threw a blue snowball at me. Breaking through the smooth snow, I leapt like a fish, and dodged the balls Young Master was throwing. After this warm-up, I let him put the harness on me. He yanked the reins hard.

Very bad for positive communication.

He looked at me sidelong and let the reins slacken.

I buried my head in a snow bank and shook the snow all over him.

"Yah!" he yelled.

Off I ran, pulling him on his new surfer. He lost his balance twice. I waited in the blue snow for him to remount the surfer. At last, he got the hang of it. *Good, Young Master!* He learned to keep his balance. We came to the frozen lake. Young Master stopped and hunted around in the snow. He threw a stone onto the ice. The stone skidded across the lake. He sat down by the side of the lake and threw another stone.

Young Master looked at me and took on a serious tone. "What do you think, Cuppy? Will I ever see her again?" He stroked my fur, unaware that I understood. "I don't even know if she would be happy to see me, she was so jealous that her father chose me. I just hope she is taking good care of the living computers. I'm praying she'll be able to make something out of it. Keep on saving Nature."

This was why Young Master was the one. There was no question. This was what my mission was about. Other planets were imperiled. I had to prepare him to defend himself on Phira and hope for contact from the girl, with the other half of the secret.

I trotted him up a busy thoroughfare so he could buy the batteries for his force field. I felt important being so useful and sat bravely when he chained me to a post next to a snow bank. He pointed his finger at me and said, "Stay" with satisfactory authority. I watched him go into the store.

It didn't cross my mind to try to escape, I was so busy hoping he would come back. There would be no point to life as a free *hupcha* without Young Master. I looked around nervously. You never knew what kind of alien you'd meet in the intergalactic capital. Young Master was unaware of the multitude of thieves in these parts and my value on the open market. Starliament paid over a million rubicons for me. I avoided eye contact with the strangers who passed me. It seemed to take forever.

Then the door opened again. *Ah, here he comes. Young Master!* I snuggled my head against his knee and shimmied under his legs. His legs got tangled in the chain. I skirted out from under his butt as he came down in the snow bank. I jumped on him and licked his face: creamy skin and *hokkanuts*. He must have eaten a whole bag. He scratched my ears, and I rolled over so he could ruffle my tummy fur.

Young Master put a choke collar on me and carried his snowsurfer through the city streets. On the way back, we came upon another furry. She smelled like *sopa*, that fluffy brown *hup* with blue eyes. She had a glorious fan of tails and tiny fangs. I sniffed her perspicuous underparts and circled her. As Young Master got deeper into conversation with her owner, I felt my choke collar loosen. With one backward tug, I slipped out of it.

Free! Young Master is running at last. Good for him. His training has begun. Run, Young Master. Run, run, run.

A two-headed pelt trader unloading his truck growled at Young Master, "You should keep your furry on a lead."

I ran under the trader's legs.

"What do you think I'm trying to do, you—" Young Master stammered at the trader. I'd never seen Young Master red-faced and speechless. "—You could have caught my *hup* just now, and instead you stand there and complain!"

Big carriers slid to a halt as I frolicked in front of them. *What power, to be able to stop traffic!*

"Cuppy!" Young Master screamed. A zigzag of food haulers piled up in the street. I trotted proudly in their midst. What a sight!

Young Master chased me down the thoroughfare past the traffic jam where overloaded carriers were entering the highway.

"Cuppycake, not there!"

I doubled back so he could catch up and ran between two lanes of cars.

"Cuppy!"

An oversized stinky truck raced down the street toward me. It lit up in red and skidded sideways, unstoppable at an incredible speed. Just then Young Master dove onto me and we both slid into the curb on the other side of the street. *Excellent work, Young Master! Your skills are improving.* The truck slid by. It twirled for fifty more feet and came to a halt wedged in a snow bank.

"Naughty *hupcha!*" Young Master scolded me angrily. "You have no idea how dangerous trucks are."

I sat completely still and took his warnings in repentance, as he fished in his pocket for the choke collar.

Drivers were alighting from their vehicles, ready to fight. Insect-like segments burst from one of the trucks. A *lobighter* with rings of muscles. It picked up a big stick as it came at us. *What planet is that from?* I was proud that Young Master turned on his force field. The alien's exoskeleton had a green-black sheen. Its head, thorax and abdomen moved in train. Suddenly, three pairs of jointed legs, compound eyes, and a pair of antennae bore down on us. The *lobighter's* hundreds of eyes fixed on Young Master, who froze in his tracks. It demanded something unintelligible. Its front appendages reached for Young Master's neck and got a jolt from the force field. It recoiled in anger. A thick sap dripped from its mouthparts. Young Master shrunk under the creature's many-eyes. The insect's stare stunned Young Master. He couldn't move.

The *lobighter* grabbed my leash! The alien turned and dragged me back to his truck, my feet skidding on the ice. It bullied me into the front seat and got in on the other side. It licked its pincers with satisfaction and made a belching sound. Young Master, still numb, shook his head.

The truck engine roared. A cloud billowed from two pipes on the hood. Young Master stood gaping as the wheels started to turn. When Young Master saw me turning in circles on the front seat, the paralysis from the alien's stunning gaze broke. He was losing his *hupcha*. "Cuppy!" Tears streamed down his cheeks. I'm sorry I yelled at you!" My two front paws were in the slit of the slightly open window. The *lobighter* pulled onto the highway. Young Master ran up the ramp after us. I could see he was losing hope: *That highway goes all the way across the country. If they get on there, Cuppy may never find his way home.*

The alien busied itself shifting gears as it sped up to pass another truck. I could feel my choke collar slide loose. I ducked my head. The chain slid off my neck. It hit the floor noisily. The alien glared at me trying to stun me with those paralyzing eyes. Too late! I turned away from him. His pincer yanked the steering wheel, and we hit another truck. The impact threw me onto the floor.

The other truck blocked our way. Suddenly, the door swung open. Young Master shielded his eyes from the *lobighter.* I leapt through the door and landed between the trucks. I ran to Young Master, and skidded past him—I was off! He ran after me without scolding this time. I led him out of there faster than a rocket. We slid down the icy ramp.

"Cuppy!" Young Master howled as I dodged a car, and ran through a maze of sides treets. After another twenty minutes of chasing around, I considered that Young Master had had enough aerobic training for the day. We commenced the cool down. I spotted a lady sledding down the way with a pack of white furries, the cheap one-tailed kind with garbled thoughts. Those dry noses panted to a stop in the freezing snow as I wiggled into their midst to get a better sniff. They stunk to highhills. I felt a hand grab me by the scruff of my neck—*Mommy!*

Of course, it was not my mother, but Young Master, huffing and puffing. All six of my paws hung down above the ground. He slapped the harness back on me. "Excuse us," he said to the lady in the sled, and I suddenly felt sorry, as if I had done something wrong, although I knew it was exactly what Young Master needed. I would get him in shape for life on the new planetoid.

Young Master went back to balancing on his surfer, and he did look a bit more content than when he was chasing me around. I took the opportunity to stop and lick his hand, and he patted me on the head. *Good training, Young Master.* We went straight home with no more adventures. He announced our arrival with many a story of our exodus, in which he forgot all about my being a rug lookalike, faithful servant, and bus-stop celebrity. Instead, he called me a rascal and some other names I'd never heard before.

I felt guilty expending all that energy on Young Master without giving the equivalent training to ½ sister. There was much less risk involved in her training. It was not so easy to get on her wavelength, though. Books would be necessary. I had to knock Mistress' *The Ancient History of Planet Earth* off the coffee table three times before she saw her *own* family's pictures in the book.

"Hey, that's us!" she said, and picked it up. She started reading it. I was relieved to see her nostalgia for the polluted planet channeled into study. She lay on the carpet and poured over the history of her planet. Her eyes lit up, for she truly yearned to find out what had happened in the years she'd missed while she was traveling to Grod.

I could smell best with my chin on her foot. The history book told how a woman called Valentine had saved our family, including Mistress and Young Master, too. Valentine was a real hero, her life a symbol so bright you could see it from outer space. I felt honored to be in such an historical family written about in real history books for everyone to read.

The book told of many things that happened after ½ sister left Earth. My favorite part was where the Earth scientists launched a tomb called a 'time capsule' into space. The tomb contained a tin box with the top ten viral Earth books. But the tomb got knocked off course by a comet and was hurled off to the edge of the universe. It toppled over and went through the Big Bang, after which it meandered to a habitable planetoid orbiting a dwarf star in the ancient spiral galaxy BX 442.

Scientists deemed the planetoid hospitable for life, having almost as much mass as Earth. The planetoid had enough gravity to retain an atmosphere for billions of years, Phira. *That's where we're going.* I was grateful to ½ sister for reading the history to me. Many feared the planetoid, Phira, was destined to become 'Earth 2.0', and laid down many prohibitions preventing alien interference.

Half sister's breath quickened reading about the scientists sending all kinds of things in that time capsule—a living thyroid, DNA from all of Earth's sacred tombs as signs to code new life on a future planet, frozen RNA from every remaining species. I could smell her sweat at the part where it all died during the millions of light years of travel to Phira.

I licked her foot.

She resumed reading.

Passing close to the spiral galaxy's garnet star, radiation fell upon the hapless capsule burning it all up. All except the words in the book generated by an Indonesian girl's computer. Under the powerful radiation of the garnet star, the word 'sign' for a hero's tomb stirred to life. Dormant for so many eons, the Indonesian Girl's digital 'tomb' mutated into a living code. By the time the spaceship crashed to the oceans of the planetoid Phira, the code had come to life and mutated exponentially into the bacteria-like microbe that would rule the planet for the next seven billion years.

That's where I began counting up to seven billion, and at the count of seven fell asleep on her foot . . .

THREE-HEADED BEAST

When we first got married, we made a pact. It was this: In our life together, it was decided I would make all of the big decisions and my wife would make all of the little decisions. For fifty years, we have held true to that agreement. I believe that is the reason for the success in our marriage. However, the strange thing is that in fifty years, there hasn't been one big decision.

— Albert Einstein

WORD OF EARTH'S RESCUE spread all over Grod. Every citizen who heard of Porter produced a neuron in their brain to store the news of his rescue mission. It lit up when it recognized him. He had changed the physical shape of evolution in the brains of Grodlings and aliens alike. The daily tabloids on the ice planet kept calling and asking embarrassing questions, like, when would Mom reunite with her husbands? They were just as excited about getting the scoop on the lovely new Earth specimen, Kenza.

"She's unavailable," Boy shouted into the holofield. He looked past Kenza out the window at the dunes of blue snow. He had to get used to having his sister under the same roof again. He and Kenza tiptoed around each other for the first week. He liked that when he asked her a question and she didn't know the answer, she just said, "That's a good question," instead of pretending she knew and trying to make him feel stupid for asking. Still, Boy racked his brains for things to talk about with her. *We must have something in common.*

Mom was utterly relieved that Kenza had made it off polluted Earth and had come to live with them on Grod. Mom never minded how Porter had gone through multiple universes to rescue Kenza. Boy gave up explaining it. He supposed Mom didn't want to forgive Porter for running off in the first place. He was just happy that she was happy. Not only did she have her daughter back, but they were all suddenly famous. That brought in an interesting offer. An aged member of Starliament wanted to buy Mom's company for eighty million rubicons. They had never heard of so much money. Then the buyer threw in the clincher: his seat in Starliament. Mom was shocked. "Isn't it immoral to trade seats in Starliament?" She ran for advice, as had become her habit ever since her husband flew off with a gynoid.

Yda's purple skin shone in the second sun on the veranda of the Paladon Café. "What did I tell you, Eleanor. It's your destiny. You can change the system from the inside."

"If it doesn't change me first."

Yda braided her arms.

"OK, I'm taking the offer," Mom said. "Maybe I'll be able to create some laws and do some good." She composed a message on the tiny screen on her wrist. "Starliament, here I come."

Mom's organic halloumi farm sold. Grodian efficiency surpassed Earth's, and the deal was done in a skizzle. Eighty million rubicons hit her bank account. What a lightning bolt, seeing all those zeros! She couldn't sleep. Instead, she prepared for her swearing in as High Emissariat. She spent the next two weeks studying protocol. Where did all this energy come from? What with working overtime, she should have had bags under her eyes, but instead she looked fine.

Rehearsing, preparing, networking, the night of the inauguration arrived. "Kenza, have you seen my boots?" Mom got down on all fours to look under the couch. The kids lifted their feet without ungluing their eyes from the holovision. Nothing under there. Mom looked suspiciously at the *hupcha*, cuddled up innocently at their feet, his six legs folded neatly beneath him. "How long has it been since he's chewed up a shoe?"

The kids didn't answer. They stared straight ahead, their toes buried in Cuppy's fan of tails, engrossed in a holonewscast:

"A newly-rescued Earthling inventor has just launched a cyber tool to enable almost everyone to work from home." A shot of the freeway, usually locked in a traffic jam, now completely empty of cars and trucks, materialzed over the coffee table. Kids slid across the lanes on their snowboards. The holonews showed the inventor, an auburn-haired girl standing at the docks.

"That's Valentine!" Kenza and Boy both jumped up.

The kids were talking excitedly when Mom found her boots in the closet. She went over her speech one more time. The taxi arrived. "Kenza? Boy?"

No answer.

She looked in the bathroom. She ran upstairs and opened the bedroom doors. They had left the house! *How could they leave at a time like this?* She couldn't be late for her inauguration. She had to go alone.

She stepped out of the taxi and onto the purple velvet in her favorite boots. She knelt before the Chairman, who adorned her with a *hokka* wreath and had her repeat an oath. Ironic that she should receive such a decoration when it was her husband who was the diplomat of the family, always trying to win public honors.

Mom had invited hundreds of guests to an elaborate cocktail after the ceremony. Chariots sledded up to the steps of the Intergalactic Chateau. The gong rang and subsided. She stood with her welcoming committee just inside the doorway. An alien dignitary descended from his purinium crystal-powered caravan and stepped into the blue snow. He scuttled up to the entrance. Eleanor shook all of his hands, one after the other. "Welcome, Your Excellence!"

"Where are your serpent skin boots tonight?" he asked.

"I ate them," she answered.

He kissed her on her forehead. "Nice crowd," he said, peeking into the great hall. Then, under his breath, "Rumor has it you're up for the colonization mission."

Her heart raced. There was no bigger promotion at Starliament than an off-planet mission. At the same time, a wave of fear flooded through her. She had to find her kids before it was time to go.

The dignitary gave the signal of high respect.

Eleanor tried to think of words to express her gratitude, and settled on a low bow. *Where are my kids?*

Many great families filed in to be welcomed. At last, the long line of guests dried up. She looked around for her purple friend. Yda was late. She followed the last guests inside the chateau. After a watered-down *schnechtian* champagne, she spotted Yda's purple horns in the revolving door.

"There you are!" Eleanor said.

"My, my. What's going on here?"

"I know. I asked them not to overdo it."

"This is an absolutely lovely cocktail, Eleanor. You should be proud. I told you that you were Starliament material. I just knew you would get a seat."

"Not just a seat, Yda," she said. "A full-scale mission!"

"Finally!" Smoke curled from Yda's ears. "It's just as I predicted. My plan is working nicely." Yda left off bantering and went about sniffing the hanging *hokka* boughs. She nibbled on a golden petal. "Fabulous," she said. Two tables were set up in the center of the room. "I think those were reserved for us," Eleanor said to Yda, but no one was there. She had wandered across the carpet and was slamming down glass after glass of champagne in a circle of males. Alcohol had no effect on Yda's race. Yda hobnobbed from group to group.

"Yda, before we get lost in the crowd, let's synchronize our earpieces. I have a minor emergency at dome. I don't know where the kids are."

"That's not good on Grod." Yda turned to the window and the frozen blue landscape sprawling down the hill from the chateau to the city below.

They hooked their earpieces to a chat channel. In her earpiece, Eleanor could hear Yda's voice as she skirted a large bowl filled with bottles of champagne. "Call the Starliamentary police. They're more competent than the city police. And stop worrying about what the public thinks. Even in your position, you can be yourself, Eleanor. You've welcomed your guests. Who cares if you don't take a sip of wine or eat a piece of cake?"

Eleanor found two Starliamentary police officers and explained the situation.

Yda led the way through the snow to a guard house where more police were waiting. "What were they doing when you last saw them?" the police asked.

"They were watching the news," Eleanor explained.

"What was on?"

Before she knew it, they were planing over the snow in a ground surfer toward the docks.

The crowd at the docks parted for the police surfer. There was Kenza at the edge of the crowd. Mom cried tears of joy. "What are you doing here?" She hugged Kenza and thanked the police.

Mom found Boy, standing by the water in front of a barge. He was talking to an auburn-haired girl.

"Who's she?" Mom asked, excited.

"A friend we saw on the holonews," Kenza said.

"Another human!" Mom noticed the look on Boy's face. Was her son in love? The redhead argued with Boy.

Mom's eyes narrowed. Even the last girl on Grod not related to Boy probably wasn't enough for her son. "You don't just run off to the docks because you see a friend on the news."

Kenza covered. "She's not just a friend. She's special. She was with me at eHarvard."

Mom watched the girl put her hands on her hips, and heard her say, "Just because my father chose to work with you doesn't mean I can't do it on my own."

"Do what?" Mom asked Kenza.

"I'm not sure," Kenza answered. "I think she's building another droid."

"*Another* droid?" Mom asked.

"Yes, Mom. Valentine designed Any Gynoid."

"My word!" Yda said.

Mom thought about this for a second. "Well then, 'thanks' are in order!"

"We better just leave them alone," Kenza said. "They have a lot of catching up to do."

Mom noticed the pained expression on her son's face. "What's the matter with Boy?"

Valentine raised her voice. "I can't just forgive you for replacing me with my own father."

"He was trying to protect you," Boy said. "No one could ever replace you! Maybe I did stumble onto the living computers, but my invention only used ten percent of the brain. You gave them movement—that's what the whole other 90% of the brain is for!"

The auburn girl blushed as she considered this. But forgiveness didn't come easily. She set her jaw. "OK, you've cheered me up long enough. Goodbye."

"Valentine, wait!" Boy called, but she had already boarded the barge. Where are you going?"

"To stop the Emperor from destroying other planets. He watched her glide away from the dock. He held up his hand, a solemn farewell.

Kenza and Boy looked out at the water wistfully, watching Valentine's barge sail out of the harbor. Their *hupcha* sat on his haunches, his four other feet wiggling in the air.

A PROLIFERATION OF PORTERS

...we're twins, and so we love each other more than other people...

— Louisa May Alcott, *Little Men*

MOM RUSHED OVER TO BOY. "You know it's dangerous to wander around here by yourselves in sub-zero temperatures."

Boy flushed red.

"Now, now, Eleanor," Yda said, "It's over. At least they brought Cuppy with them for protection."

The *hupcha* wagged his fan of tails, tongue hanging out.

Yda scratched his ears and wrestled him to the ground. Boy, holding onto the leash, got pulled into the fray, and Yda ended up with both children and the *hupcha* on top of her. She tossed them all off. "I say! We're all tired and hungry. Let's get a bite. One of these restaurants must be good enough for *hupcha*s." They shook off the snow.

Yda led them into a restaurant with a beautifully appointed dining room with plush rugs under the tables for *hupchas* to lie on.

"May we have a table for four," Yda asked the Maître'd.

A gust of icy wind blew in as two men entered the establishment. They got in line behind Mom.

Mom's jaw dropped. It was Porter. Two of him!

A small crowd swiftly gathered around the two men. Grodlings asked for their autographs. "Those are the heroes who rescued Nature on Earth," one whispered. Like all famous personalities, Porter was imprinted on the Grodlings' brains. Their dedicated Porter neurons recognized his face in a skizzle, and lit up. They crowded around the two Porters.

"Hello father," the kids said, each addressing a Porter.

The aliens parted, snapping photos.

"A table for six?" the maître'd asked.

"Four," Yda said, then, noticing Mom's two husbands in the doorway, added, ". . . unless you gentlemen would like to join us?"

"With pleasure," they said, in stereo.

The waiter asked if Mom agreed.

Mom was dumbfounded and found it impossible to respond to the proliferation of Porters—they were huddled together, arms around each others' shoulders as if they were trying to join bodies. She finally managed, "Whatever you want." Then, she whispered into Yda's earpiece, "Yda, did you arrange this?"

Tears welled in Yda's eyes. "Certainly not!" she said aloud.

"The police called me," one of the Porters offered.

"The police called me, too," the other one said.

"How did the police get your numbers?" Mom looked at Yda.

Yda made the bathtub sound and started crying. "Following word with actions we approach God," she sobbed.

"Yda!" Mom stopped short, but Yda hurried ahead. Mom whispered into their virtual chat, "Like God, Porter is too perfect to be able to think of anything other than himself."

"I know he betrayed you and your kids, Eleanor, but he seems harmless enough now. You can't do everything alone. The kids need their father."

"They don't even know which one he is!" Mom said. "I've finally pieced my life back together. When I look back on our marriage, I see that one Porter was too much. His betrayal nearly killed me." Mom was developing an allergy to men.

"Life happens in chaos," Yda grumbled. "What has changed? He was two-faced before."

The whole extended family installed itself in a booth by the fire. Cuppy scuttled under the table and curled up on the rug. Yda took the only chair, since it had three arm rests. Mom slid into the last space available, between the two Porters. They all stared at each other for a moment. The Porters and Mom held their silence, forcing Yda to carry the conversation. "Life is ironic, isn't it, children? So much love for one we say goodbye to." She could feel the kids' sorrow at losing Valentine all over again. "Nevertheless, Porters! It's pleasant to see you all back from your journey looking so . . . reiterated. I hope travel has brought you to your higher ground."

Mom prayed that this would come true. "We didn't expect to see you again, especially after all that talk of needing your own space."

The younger Porter sat bolt upright in surprise. "I didn't say that!" His voice shook with shock. He looked a little younger than Mom remembered him. He glared at the other Porter.

"Mom, Dads, don't fight," Kenza beseeched.

Now Mom noticed the wrinkles on the other Porter's forehead, and suspected that this was theirs. Struggling to keep it together, the older Porter opened his mouth to speak, but nothing came out. Unable to confess his sins to younger Porter. His his mouse ears just turned red.

"It must be a glitch in your memory," Mom said.

"Porter progresses from glitch to glitch in a chronic fit of glitching," Yda offered.

The waiter arrived. "May I propose a fruity Chardonnay?"

"Certainly not!" Yda said.

Mom tried to help. "Do you have anything less…"

"I have a fine Savvy Harash with intense *lomeberry* flavorings and grassy notes."

"That's the one!" Yda announced and closed her menu.

"Can I try it?" Boy asked.

"No," Mom, the two Porters and Yda all said. They stared at each other, united at least about the welfare of the children.

"So here we are, Porters," Yda cooed. "As you all can see, Eleanor has ascended from housewifedom to the top of the civil service hierarchy, while . . . ya'll, shall we say . . . were finding yourself."

The Porters decided they agreed.

"Eleanor?" Yda said.

Mom folded her hands. "I have finally grown accustomed to living . . ." *with no Porters.* "The other night I dreamt that I was so much in love with a man. I woke up, thinking, I can't wait till he gets home, and then I thought, Who? and realized there was no one to feel like that about. There I was, alone with the feeling of being in love. You see, there are more kinds of love than there are people. Our kind of love has all been a dream."

The younger Porter had a worried look on his face as he searched the ceiling, unsure if he should be hearing this and at a loss as to where else to go.

The older Porter said, "Eleanor, I'm sorry I left you and the kids. It was hormones. Can't I come back?"

Mom doubted he meant resuming their relationship. She remembered the fire in Porter's eyes when they first met. That must have been hormones, too. And now he wanted to come back!

"Earth is cleaning itself up now. We could go back and start over."

She did miss Earth, but warded off the impending disaster. "Come back where? I've been appointed High Emissariat to Phira. Humph. Your timing is off. Porters are a dime a dozen. Anyway, I've got my own life."

"Eleanor's been offered a post on Phira," Yda said.

"Phira?"

"Earth 2.0," Mom said, reluctantly, hoping Porter would give up right there.

Yda threw back her head and made that bathtub draining sound. Boy sat on the edge of his seat watching her. He tried to think of a joke to make her cry, but she controlled herself and said, "EremmmPorter, aren't y'all aware of the planetoid, Phira?"

"The one that's been ruled by bacteria for the past seven billion years?" the older Porter asked. "They talked about it in a briefing on the geography of proteins."

"The bacteria more recently evolved into phytoplankton," young Porter afforded.

"Y'all have some catching up to do," Yda interjected. "During the last billion years, clam-like brachiopods and trilobites emerged. Ergo fish came out of the water to dance on the beaches—"

"You're going to dance with Ergo fish?" the older Porter asked.

"Not exactly." The color drained from Yda's face in her impatience. "Life has now evolved into more complex creatures. At first, several animals sprouted from that fishy family. They continued to evolve. "In fact." Yda leaned forward. "A mission had landed on Phira nine million years ago. They interfered with the evolutionary process, causing rapid advancement in what some consider an undesirable direction."

"What direction?"

"It's hard to describe," Yda said, a single tear rolling down her cheek.

Mistress held her breath.

"Starliament was flabbergasted over the reckless cultivation of the filthiest class creatures," Yda said, quaking as she held in the tears.

"Filthiest!" Mom looked offended.

"You know, most polluting. After that, interference from advanced creatures was outlawed. This will be Intergalactic Starliament's first diplomatic mission to the planetoid since the prohibition. Its mission in defense of Nature, to see that the living do not become the slaves of their own pollution."

"The mission is laden with prohibitions," Mom added.

The two Porters looked from Yda to Mom.

"And what about you two?" Yda raised her horns interrogatively. "Don't you two have a little explaining to do?"

The two Porters simultaneously cleared their throats. The older one leaned forward. "It all started when I went through a gravity loop of space-time atoms."

"Space-time what?" Mom asked.

"Mom. Never mind," Kenza said. "You don't have the granularity to grok discontinuity in space-time atoms."

The Porters were nodding their heads. The older one went on, "The result was a merging of multiverses around me connecting theretofore incommunicado sub universes . . ." His voice trailed off, and he looked at the younger one, who tried to help with, "My ship was destroyed. My leg was wounded. All the others went back to their own times. I would have died if Porter, here, here hadn't carried me onto his ship. He's a real hero."

The people at the other tables were silent, eavesdropping to hear the story. They all knew it from the holonewscasts, but their eyes gleamed hearing it from Porter himself.

"He'll make a great diplomat to the future. He saved our families from hopeless pollution." On the word 'families', young Porter thought of his own parallel family waiting for him in his dimension and felt an echo of the distant happiness he had taken for granted.

Basking in their benign glory, self-congratulatory smiles peeled across their faces. They both took off their compuglasses and simultaneously placed them on the table. Young Porter's compuglasses had windshield wipers.

"Dads," Boy said. Now that everyone has a Porter neuron in their brain, and the imprint of your heroic deeds lives on in each one of us . . . well, what does that do to your brain?"

The Porters were stumped.

Yda leaned on her three elbows. Her voice whispered inside Mom's earpiece, "This is fun isn't it?" Then Yda said aloud, "You see, men become like women, and women become like men. Every particle has its antithesis. Matter has anti-matter, the timeon particle has the timeoff . . ." Her eyes wandered to the young anti-Porter mirroring the old Porter. She said, "Our last mission has unleashed this unstable Porter compound. *Grand jib'houti* knows where we'll store the isotope!"

Everyone looked at Mom. Mom could have punched the *Grand jib'houti* in the nose. "Yda, without lapsing into what you call my 'human propensity' to divide everything into right and wrong, I'm simply too busy. And frankly, Porters, your running away with a gynoid was a turnoff." She hadn't wanted to say it in front of the kids, but there it was. It was decided. They were NOT going back to Earth. They were going to fulfill their destiny, on Phira.

"Foreseeable," Yda said, apologizing to the Porters. "Eleanor is at her peak in her new career. She's a High Emissariat now. If she's able to fulfill her mission on

Phira, they'll recommend her for the Chancellor's Commission.

"The Chancellor's Commission!" Mom had never dared to dream of such a position. The Chancellor's Commission was so high that they never met. It was the most important body of the Council with heads of all the member planets. She tried to feel triumphant, but Porter did not look convinced.

"Eleanor," Yda said aloud, "Porters are more civilized on Grod. Everyone is. Why even your *hupcha* under the table here—" With that, she stuck her head under the table. Her horns hit the wood. *"Grand jib'houti!"*

"What is it?" Mom asked.

Kenza looked under the table and gasped. "Where is Cuppy?"

"Out there!" There he was, playing outside in the blue flakes. He looked in the window with a beard of snow.

Boy dove out of the booth and flew out the door of the restaurant. Cuppy bounded off down the path. Kenza and Yda flapped out the door and slid down the icy path after them, leaving Eleanor alone with her two husbands. So much for equality. She was outnumbered in her own marriage. No formula would fit now. *Who said marriage was a two-headed beast?* She played her part in this new three-headed beast by keeping her guard. "The truth is, Porters, I am too old for more transactions of the heart. While I'm grateful to the gynoids and you and your parallel universe approximation, here, for saving us, I can't help thinking about all your unexplained absences, about how much cooking and cleaning I had to do for just one husband. Whatever I did was never enough. And throughout your infidelities, I was so naïve, I believed you'd just become a curmudgeon!"

Young Porter lapsed into a fit of coughing.

The waiter refilled their glasses. He extinguished the heat-keeping force fields over Eleanor's and the two Porters' plates. Yda's and the children's dinners remained covered. Their empty chairs left a void at the table. Eleanor closed her eyes and prayed. *May they find our hupcha safely.*

The Porters sat there as two-faced as a wall. Conversing with him was as hard as climbing. She didn't know how the wall crumbled. In Yda's absence, the Porters had no reason to bring more bricks for it. And the older Porter just wanted to fight: "First you say one thing, then the opposite," he accused Eleanor. "You twist everything this way and that way."

Now there could be no doubt which one was their Porter. Why had she missed him so much? No one had addressed her disrespectfully since he left. She wasn't used to having stereotypes imposed on her anymore. "I don't twist."

"You're not even watching the kids," he was saying.

She set down her glass. "Now you are talking to ME."

Young Porter gave her a refill.

The older Porter grabbed the remaining half of Cuppy's chewed-up leash. He stood up and stomped out of the restaurant in a huff.

Eleanor looked around. Where was Cuppy leading Porter, Yda and the children? *Yda!* Eleanor called into the void of the virtual chat.

The young Porter smiled and lifted his glass. "Congratulations on your new job," he said.

At least that's what she thought he said. They'd had several grassy-notes by then. The unexpected recognition threw her off guard.

They clinked glasses.
She felt lightheaded.

Dog-Eat-Dog World

*The real teachings happened at 'mak sym', the Feridid word
for 'dawn', or 'little sun' and started with a humble thanks
to their maker.*

—Broghther Aadash Waitin, *The Legend of MakSym*

BECAUSE OF MISTRESS' ALMIGHTINESS, Starilament chose
our family for the historical journey. I walked in circles,
folding my fan of tails around me, and curled up under
the window of the ship. I sniffed the metallic wall and
licked it.

"Aw, look at Cuppy," Kenza said to her brother.

Young Master came over and massaged my legs. I tuned into his train of thought. He was dreaming of the Earth girl again, as we flew farther and farther from his home planet. I licked his hand.

How I missed our cozy life on Grod. I usually made friends easily, but socializing was already proving a challenge during our couped-up voyage in that capsule. Two of my six legs swelled up from those dry space-food capsules.

Young Master yearned for our arrival, too. The family had put off his naming until we reached our new home on Phira. All this postponing made him 'stir-crazy'! He had to get on with 'real life'.

During the landing briefing, the ship's computer came on. "Seven billion years ago, the Earthling time capsule bearing a code for life landed on Phira. This code, written by an Indonesian girl's living computer on planet Earth, first brought life to the planetoid, until about 10,000 years ago, when a major catastrophe interfered with the planetoid's natural selection, drastically reducing its potential."

I could smell telepathic waves coming from the kids. Young Master was wondering what kind of deformity the catastrophic intervention had caused. He hoped it wasn't anything disgusting, like external gills.

"What if they smell like skunks," Kenza whispered.

Yes, what if? I was tired of the same old smells.

The fertile planetoid and its blue moon filled the ship's holofield. We burst through the atmosphere. The green landscape gleamed below.

The ship's computer regulated our descent while briefing us for our mission. The ship's computer crackled. "Legend has it that the code the Indonesian girl's living computer wrote left ZNA traces not only of itself, but also of what it *created*."

Everything seemed to be coming alive on Phira. We could see many interesting life forms roaming the plains below. Bridges of land appeared where the ocean had dried up. Creatures were walking across the pole of the planetoid as we passed over.

The ship's computer crackled. "They wander in tribes. When one can't ford the rivers anymore, the tribe leaves it behind on the riverbank to die. The tribes have many orphans."

The spacecraft flew over the southern hemisphere, and we saw a tribe of hairy humanoids migrating to greener land. We headed for an elaborate diagram drawn on the ground that turned out to be runways made of enormous slabs of marble, each lined with piles of stone. As we got closer, we saw a small dish in the middle of the ground carving: a starport. The landing went smoothly, no doubt helped by my consistent howling throughout.

We knew nothing about the dangers our diplomatic posting until the briefing. The ship's computer informed us that a web of alien embassies, known for their coups, governed the fertile planetoid. Embassy spies snuck around night and day, propping up a careful web of checks and balances. Their sole purpose was to stop other embassies from influencing evolution on Phira. The ship's computer gave us a stern warning. "Beware of offending the other embassies, and above all, never interfere in any way with the natives."

We barely heard the admonitions, we were so eager to get out of the spaceship. The hatch opened. Myself, Mistress, the two Porters, Kenza and Young Master—our whole family!—climbed out of the hatch with surprising ease. How light gravity was on Phira! I bounded to the ground in one long leap.

Young Master jumped off the ladder, and rolled to the ground with a somersault. *I'm super-strong on this planet!*

A diplomatic envoy drove across the landing pad toward the ship to meet us. Mom braced herself for the eventuality of colleagues. We made the acquaintance of three other alien diplomatic families, in a myriad shuffling of tentacles, fingers and eyeballs. It was time to put to the test the greeting Mom had practiced in Starliamentary training. She raised her hand, evoking the cult of non-interference. She held it up to the red dwarf sun. A ray of red light beamed through her fingers and lit up her eyes. "Nature's way," she said.

The rest of the family repeated the oath, renouncing the fight against Nature.

"Nature's way," the envoy answered in unison.

An emaciated, blue alien male grumbled. "Beware. Anyone breaking the taboo to affect evolution in any particular direction will suffer unspeakable consequences." The grumbler circled the two Porters. He fixated on the Porters' large ears sticking out at obtuse angles. The little guy actually reached up and pinched the Porters' earlobes between his digits. Then he spat on the ground.

The Porters stared him in the eyes, as protocol required in confrontational situations. That's when the

Starilamentary snarpguards stepped forward. Two uniformed aliens planted themselves on either side of the thin, blue alien. Their muscular arms and multitude of eyes intimidated the little fellow. The tension defused, two more snarpguards packed our crates into their caravan, as if nothing had happened. We all got in and planed across the countryside in a train of dust.

The motor stopped. "What's going on?" Mom asked.

The driver turned around, his many eyes revolting us. "We are pausing to observe a group of native Feridids."

I couldn't stop my tails from wagging. *The dirty catastrophe!* I jumped out of the caravan and led the group down a path. Our party trekked into a new world of ponds and untouched Nature. The skin on the plants felt warm, like animal skin. It was wonderful to be outside again. I frolicked with Young Master in the low gravity and strange new Nature. The smells! I caught whiffs of sweat-soaked creatures on each breeze, and, inspired, left my scent in several spots along the path.

The driver led us through the orange-cast countryside. Used to Grod gravity, we sprang across the tropical vegetation like super-strong beings, and bounded over rocks of white crystal. Young Master climbed a strange upside-down tree with root-like branches that fanned out rather than growing upward.

The guide pointed toward a clearing. Through the trees, Young Master could see a tribe of primates scavenging for berries. "I must warn you again: Starliament has given firm instructions to keep out of sight, and not to intervene in the evolution of life on the planetoid. Breaking this taboo could bring about another Enormous Catastrophe, and we'd all suffer the harshest consequences."

My human family crouched behind a *baeboo* tree watching three hairy natives in the clearing below. Young Master craned his head to see what evolutionary defect they'd inherited. He was ready to discover that they had pitchfork tails or external gills, but only saw five hairy, fetid humanoids foraging for berries.

I must admit *I* was disappointed on seeing the beasts' paucity of legs. They would take forever to evolve with their noses so far away from the ground. Their almost furless bodies were surprisingly similar to humans'. They all had remarkably familiar big ears sticking out, as if the whole species had evolved replicating the traits of a particular hero.

"Hey, they're kind of cute," one Porter said to the other, who was rubbing his own smarting big ear.

Our guide looked from the creatures to the two Porters. "Yes, I think you'll find that Phira has a fascinating genetic landscape. After the Enormous Catastrope thousands of years ago, the creatures with the faculty in their brains to postpone immediate gratification survived longer and had more children. It took all the creatures' cunning to delay response to stimulus, but their brains evolved to a larger size."

So natural selection had *favored the better strategists.* Young Master's eyes lit up. Fascinated, he asked the guide about many details. "If they're gathering food all day, they must not have much time to think. Have they tried to form villages, yet?" Young Master asked.

" 'Yet?' Villages are not inevitable. *Hunting* requires strategy and communal action," the guide said.

Young Master peeked through the trees at a large male pushing a group of younger creatures away from a berry bush. The rest of our party turned back toward the runway.

Phira teamed with life. Everything in Phiran Nature was growing. Under that orange sky, the scent of Young Master's pheromones changed. Despite human telepathic limitations, I was able to catch a drift of his thoughts by sniffing the breeze. He couldn't help but feel remorse over the events on his home planet. He mourned the fact that the corporations had enslaved the living computers and that the animals had been murdered. His fists clenched as he thought about the greedy corporations that had squeezed profits out of Nature on Earth. *I will never let that happen on Phira!*

Planted in the tall grass, I waited anxiously for Young Master. I could smell him weighing a decision in his heart, measuring the various paths to redeem himself: the long and roundabout labyrinth of Starliament diplomacy, and the more immediate path among the Feridids. Why couldn't people take from Nature no more than they needed? Was it so hard to give back, thankfully? His eyes shone, looking at these fully integrated primates, with no computers or even tools, who still thought for themselves.

Young Master pulled his mirror cloak tightly around him. The cameras on each side of the cloak replicated the scene on the other side. Enveloped in the cloak, Young Master disappeared.

An uproar erupted from our party when they realized Young Master was not among them. They started calling for Young Master. They backtracked the way we had come in search of him. Young Master let them go. He was engrossed in the Feridid manhood training going on in the clearing below. Hidden within his invisibility cloak, Young Master walked into the circle of creatures.

They sniffed the air and carried on. None could pinpoint the smell. He wondered what he should do. I could smell his fear: how would the savages react? *I may not be from the future, but everyone else is from the past.* Young Master suppressed a nervous laugh. There was furious grunting behind him. They had noticed his footprints in the mud. Young Master couldn't help it. He laughed out loud.

Unable to see him, the creatures whirled around batting the air with their long, hairy arms.

What if the right thing to do is what they tell you not to do? Young Master remembered how the living computers first came to life: disobeying. He climbed up on a crystal and decisively pulled back his mirror cloak. *Poof!* He appeared.

The primates chattered. They threw up their hands. One of them screeched, and they all fell silent.

Despite the strict prohibition against interfering with their natural evolution, Young Master took out his jackstick. He pressed 'light'. A beam shone from the top. He held it up for the primates to see.

Transfixed by the light, the creatures cried out in their crude language. They broke into a chant. I raised my ears to hear better. *"Mak sym, mak sym,"* They were chanting, "Little sun!" They began to bow down to the ground in front of Young Master. I sniffed the breeze and smelled a memory stirring deep inside the Feridids. *It has come to pass at last!* As their prophecy foretold, he had arrived.

One of the creatures noticed me. It snarled!

I scuttled up the crystal boulder and pressed myself against Young Master's knee. The creatures watched us in dismay. The tallest sneered and circled Young Master, who had begun to sing. The creatures exchanged words and then grew silent listening to Young Master. The tallest creature knelt down and touched his forehead to the grass. The others scrambled to the ground and bowed their heads.

Young Master was touched by the simple primates in the Indonesian girl's likeness: the first class of creatures created by a living computer. And they were impressed with him. They crowded around him and pressed their fingers to his bronze skin.

I could feel Mistress' worry, and paced back and forth. *We will be late for training.* With much difficulty, I made Young Master remember his embassy obligations and all the protocol he needed to memorize before our family's inaugural dinner at the palace. It was hard to tear him away. Young Master worried that all of the mistakes of humans on Earth would be replicated on Phira. He could see the seeds of slavery being sewn already on the fertile planetoid. Starliament diplomats talked of 'mastering Nature' and 'harnessing resources'. It was no use starting over on a fertile planet. The culture had been taken from Earth, and it had not changed. He sighed heavily.

Young Master, we can do no more here right now. We must go.

He shrouded himself in his cloak and disappeared.

The creatures chattered with excitement at his disappearance.

Although I couldn't see him, I could smell Young Master on the path. We ran back to the barrier.

THIRTEEN AT DINNER

When evening came, Jesus was reclining at the table with the Twelve. And while they were eating, he said, "I tell you the truth, one of you will betray me."

—*The Bible*

WE REACHED THE PALACE, an awe inspiring structure with shiny walls. The glass sheen of the building showed our reflections: a boy and his *hupcha*, arriving at the palace for the first time. You wouldn't know there were any doors at all, except for the medieval insignia of Starliament etched on them. A clothed Feridid servant stepped aside, and let us enter, to Young Master's surprise. *Isn't casually employing Feridids as servants interfering with their evolution?* There did seem to be a bit of hypocrisy going on.

Still not recovered from the shock of our disappearance, Mistress informed us that Starliament employed the Feridids for light tasks, mostly involving portering things from one place to another, as was their natural inclination.

With stern words, Mistress handed Young Master the book he had to study. He was not eager to digest the sheer volume of information that diplomatic families were required to read. He skipped to the part about the Feridids repeatedly attacking the embassies, and about the embassies not being allowed to fight back. The document was the bane of Starliament's diplomatic corps. It contained a million details that could cause offense during diplomatic meetings like shaking upper hands or making eye contact with eldest daughters.

I urged Young Master to keep reading. *Everything has to be memorized, from dropping to one's knees before the youngest member of the family to keeping one's eyes closed when asking permission to look at a tribal Blessed One.*

He winged. "This is ridiculous. Who cares protocol for meeting a dignitary?." He didn't see how he could do anything worthwhile, fettered by so much protocol. There was no fooling him. On the third day, Young Master got to the essence of the book: the work Starliament sent them there to do was not the work that needed to be done.

On the appointed day, I left Young Master to get dressed and scurried off to find the dining room. The sound of silverware being laid gave away its whereabouts. I trotted through the enormous doors and, to my amazement, witnessed the longest dinner table I'd ever seen. It was being laid with fine linen and crystal glasses. I quietly scurried under the table. There, I waited with apprehension. I mulled over the reputation Phiran diplomatic society had for subterfuge and backstabbing.

The two Feridid servants setting the table whispered in tones of warning. My ears perked up, listening for rumors of foul play. Although I struggled to understand their rough language, all I could pick up was that they had heard the news of Young Master's appearance among the Feridids.

Great trumpets sounded. I jumped to my feet and barked. One of the Feridid's tried to catch me. I skirted around the table. The other one came and blocked my way. I got under the table, lay down obediently and looked up at them with sorry eyes. They folded their arms and decided to leave me under the table. There I stayed until the guests from other embassies arrived en masse. No one had refused the invitation from the long-awaited Porters who had saved Earth and defiled Phira. They spread their robes and were seated in a forest of knees and shins. I smelled several pairs of shoes from the welcoming party.

No amount of protocol could have prepared us for the vengeful attitude of the thin, blue Anessi from Histria. In Anessi lived avarice, debauchery, ambition and impiousness in perfect harmony. This most dangerous of guests had a foul mouth that issued an outpouring of tired expletives for bodily functions and carnal diversions. The way he talked, you'd think every inanimate object was procreating.

The guests pretended to ignore Anessi. They marveled over the two Porters, and made them recount their rescue of planet Earth from pollution. They asked many questions about what it was like going through the Big Bang. "Weren't you afraid?

"Not for a second," the older Porter said. I sensed him straying from the truth with abandon. "It was a glorious moment."

The guests expressed their satisfaction with the Porters and said they were sorry that young Porter couldn't get back to his proper dimension. "That was very noble of you to bring him here with you," the girl on Young Master's right said to the older Porter

Anessi scoffed. "Noble, indeed. So elevated they feel entitled to employ Feridids as servants."

Young Master fathomed the alien's boundless ambition and infinite jealousy watching Anessi foment another quarrel. The scoundrel tipped his glass of high resveratrol Pinot Noir from Kepler 5's Burgundy region and splattered it on the white carpet. Everyone gaped at the wine stain on the white Starliamentary rug, and then peeked sidelong at the two Porters. The Porters' ears turned pink.

"That was for the brothers who could not be among us," Anessi said. "Maybe the ones responsible for the Enormous Catastrophe that altered the evolutionary trajectory on fire. Amazing how life here has evolved to produce humanoids. Like yourselves. Ones with big ears."

This was all the proof Mistress needed of Porter's infidelity, albeit from another dimension. The marriage would remain platonic evermore.

"How could Starliament let those two Porters come *here?*" the girl next to Young Master mumbled.

"They didn't notice his ears," Anessi said.

"Compared to most Starliamentarians, he has small ears," a wealthy merchant quipped.

Their exchange was followed by nervous laughter and a rustle of disapproval from several polite diplomats.

Mistress planted both feet firmly on the rug and stuck to protocol, passing around a dish of her own invention. Our cooks had made it out of a cabbage-like vegetable that thrived in Phira's tropical climate. "These are stuffed with local mushrooms and spiced with *teulonic* and *skhyme* to activate the immune system."

"My immune system doesn't need activating," Anessi quarreled. "Another of your race's weaknesses noted."

The fur on the back of my neck stood straight. My mind went blank when I thought about the revenge our undermining guests must be planning. I could sense Young Master observing Anessi closely for the rest of the meal. Young Master began to suspect that the embassies served as little more than bickering figureheads, while the real adventure on the planet happened among the native race of Feridids.

Over dessert, Anessi seemed to relax. A shrewd merchant, Anessi turned the simplest disagreement to his pecuniary advantage. "The rubicon has been unpegged from the empire salt currency rate for less than a week and look at the disaster," Anessi said. "The rubicon soared 12% overnight! I bought five million, and I'm about to buy more."

Young Master controlled his breathing. I could smell his thoughts clearly. *He's lying. He knows the rubicon had drifted dangerously away from the salt peg. Why does he want us to buy a worthless currency like the rubicon? The rubicon's days must be numbered. Salt, as such a precious compound, is the currency on Phria and the logical currency intergallactically.*

No one took Anessi up on this quarrel. He glowered for a while and then cast about the table listening to others' misfortunes with delight in his eye.

I rested my chin on Young Master's foot.

From the table above, I could smell the falafel burger recipe Mistress had always had made for the kids. I sniffed the well-traveled shoes of the young woman sitting next to Young Master. She smelled a year older than Young Master. I crawled away from the table to get a good look at her. She was small boned and had not grown to her full height, probably due to malnutrition. She had so much gunk on her face, you couldn't see her skin.

" 'Boy'? What kind of name is that?" Anessi grumbled.

"My naming is tomorrow, in fact." Young Master handled the question well, even though he was uneasy about the family quarrel over what to name him. He was sulking over having no say in the matter. The Porters were in favor of 'Henry', but Mistress preferred 'Justin'. Young Master started to reach for a falafel burger but withdrew his hand. He had made it to fifteen. In the present shiftless company, he realized that it might not be a bad idea to hurry up and try the adult fare, *sarmale*s.

"On our planet, any dish with mushrooms instead of meat would be reserved for the wait staff," Anessi scoffed, projecting his words downward with startling arrogance as if the others were of a lower class. "Histirans eat slabs of seared meat with only a knife." He stabbed at a plate of local eggs.

On a planet beset with starvation! Young Master's eyes danced. *More lies. Everyone knew the price of meat was beyond even the richest Histrain family's means. Did he expect to win friends by bragging?* Young Master would have to update the

Protocol manual on Histria. He looked at his mother. She appeared unruffled.

"Mushrooms are a strong energizer. That's why your wait staff has a much longer lifespan than you do." Mistress had done her homework.

Young Master could feel the tension around the table as Old Porter pushed back his chair and stood up.

Anessi didn't seem to notice. "Our wait staff lives longer because your troops keep killing off our aristocracy. You could at least let us enjoy a decent meal."

"Is that an insult?" the older Porter boomed.

Dad knows Histrian brutality is renowned. Why give Anessi a way out? Young Master scrutinized the guests. He could tell that his guard had reached for his stunner in his bootleg under the table.

Anessi's face fell. "Not at all, Exalted One," he groveled. "A simple observation. We Histrians are not used to your delicacy. Your manners would be considered effeminate in our culture, so you see it's always such a struggle to remain polite. Excuse me for relaxing in your hospitable company."

A murmur of disapproval rumbled around the table. "That's the lie we expected to hear you tell," one of the diplomats scoffed.

"We can be polite when it is required of us," Anessi said.

"Apology accepted." The older Porter sat down.

Anessi's eyebrows rose. He hadn't meant to apologize.

The wind outside died again. A servant put another log on the hearth.

"Try putting some *dotta* oil on your dinner," Mistress suggested. Her voice was pitched higher than usual.

Eyes darted around the table. Everyone was relieved when Anessi bit into his *sarmale* and nodded.

Young Master peppered and oiled his local *sarmale* and took a bite. The stuffed leaf was delicious. The dish hit an empty spot and made his nose itch as if he had been raised on *sarmales* in another life. A long chain of other lives, he thought as he noticed that the serving dish was empty. He looked around to see if everyone was eating theirs.

The young woman next to him smiled.

He returned her smile.

Anessi sneered. "Your Excellency, rumor has it your son was observed talking to a Feridid tribe. He has captured the Feridid imagination, if there be such a thing. In the past, unauthorized communication has led to inter-embassy war."

"I heard those rumors," said another diplomat. "It is said that your son had the Feridids kneeling before him. They think he is the profit MakSym."

"Who is MakSym?" Young Master asked the girl sitting next to him."

"A silly legend. Don't listen to them. They'll use anything as an excuse to argue."

The table was quiet at work on the repast. Suddenly, my ears stood up. I heard a muffled argument in the corridor outside. It couldn't have been the security. Each and every humanoid had been checked back three generations. Anessi scarfed down the last bite of stuffed leaves. The moment his fork hit the plate, the lights went out.

The stunted girl next to Young Master screamed.

Not a convincing scream, Young Master thought.

With my ear to the floor, I heard Young Master feel for his jackstick. *Good move!*

I meditated on the Feridid servants. They were worried about their prophet, so I increased their worry and encouraged them: *Watch over Young Master.* There was the sound of a struggle, and a body fell to the floor, an alien diplomat by the smell of it. I ordered the servant: *Take Young Master to safety at all costs!*

It happened fast. The hands that grabbed Young Master smelled like primates'. Feridid servants secreted him out of the room.

One of the guests sprayed a chemical in the air that numbed us. I ducked under the table, and escaped most of it. I struggled to keep contact with Young Master's subconscious. Immobilized on the floor, I meditated on his feelings and sensations.

Several hands escorted Young Master through the corridors. Presently, the air grew colder. He was descending into one of the passages under the fortress. A shout echoed in the corridor up ahead. He heard scuffling sounds, and a thud on the parquet. A door opened, and the hands thrust him inside a small room, by the sound of it. A scream resounded outside in the corridor. Two forces met in battle just as the door slammed shut, with Young Master inside. As they descended, I lost connection with Young Master.

Was Young Master still alive? I whimpered, compromising my hiding place behind the couch. It didn't feel like he was dead.

A great struggle ensued. My eyes adjusted to the darkness in time to see one of the guests blocking the exit. Mistress leaned to the left of her torso, and the guest fell. I heard Kenza and Mistress' footsteps fleeing down the hallway. *Run Kenza! Run Mistress!* The Porters and two of our guards rushed after them.

When everyone had left, I crept from my hiding place and sniffed the room for clues. That's when I found the vial of poison with Anessi's scent on it smashed on the floor. At least part of his plan had been foiled. A snarpguard blocked the exit.

I waited till the wee hours of the morning. The snarpguard was sleeping. I quietly scurried past him on my heels so my toenails wouldn't tap the pavement. I stopped between the barrier where a wall of shrubbery led up to the edge of the force field. I crawled under a bush and waited. As each hour wore on, I worried more for my family's safety. I couldn't help whimpering. I knew it was important to keep a positive attitude, so I tried to divert my thoughts to other things.

The red dwarf sun rose and fell and rose again in glorious apology on my lonely encampment. I was growing hungry. Enormous avian creatures circled in the sky above me as if they sensed my weakness. Heavy purple clouds rolled in. Rain fell in a light spray. I stood under an upside-down tree until it stopped. I found a puddle to lap up, and a kind of mushroom growing at the base of a bush to eat. I curled up with my six feet tucked under my fan of tails, but couldn't sleep.

In the middle of the night, I felt a familiar itch! A vibration from Young Master. He was alive! What a relief. I unwrapped my tails from my head and rolled over to get a clearer wave.

He was waking up, somewhere underneath the castle. I concentrated on his sensations.

Headache, fuzz, sleepiness and fear, Young Master awoke in absolute darkness. His hands and legs were free.

He touched his face, ice cold. The spray must have contained a hibernator. Was he still alive? Where were his parents? *This can't be the end.* He'd seen himself with the auburn Earth girl in his dreams. He was sure he would meet her in the future. He could almost feel her beside him, her auburn hair in the glow of the firelight. He had to find food and drink. Had to find her. Had to find a way out.

He remembered that he was in a small room, and began to feel the walls for the door. At last, he found the handle. He pushed the door open. It hit a soft mass. He felt along the floor and then recoiled in horror. A stiff body. Young Master had never encountered a dead creature before in his life.

How long had he been asleep? He pushed the body away from the door with his foot and forced himself to feel for its pockets. On the shoulder was the medal of Anessi's guard. Young Master forced himself to do what he knew he must. His hands glided over the body's uniform. He found a flashlight in one of the pockets. He shone it on the face. Anessi's bodyguard. With much difficulty, Young Master began stripping off the guard's uniform stopping occasionally to listen for intruders. He had the uniform on at last. The legs were too short, so he pulled the waist down. He leaned against the wall wondering at the silence and envisioning the multitude of possibilities.

After a few minutes walking down the corridor, he heard the rustle of cloth and footsteps. He surmised that the house was still heavily guarded, but he had to get up to the dining room. He had to know if his parents were still alive.

There was another guard in the passageway. One of Anessis, in the same uniform Young Master had on. Young Master feigned confidence as he walked past the guard.

The guard turned, but didn't follow in pursuit.

I sent some advice to Young Master. *Get out of the palace!* Still, he progressed to the dining room.

The room was hot and smelled of decay. Two snarpguards and half of the guests lay sprawled on the table and the floor. Young Master covered his nose with his sleeve. He saw neither Anessi, nor the small, young woman. He was horrified, yet relieved as he looked at the bodies. His family was not among them. *They could still be alive!*

This gave him the hope to go on.

The screeches of hunting in the night terrified me. Avian creatures had descended to a perilously low level. Judging from the different shades of green in the leaves above, they were only ten flyblots away. I sniffed the air. *Could it be?* I detected Young Master's scent in the summer breeze. My ears perked up. A silhouette appeared on the darkening horizon. My paws stood poised on the edge of my hiding place. The big sun set behind the trees. I heard a creature coming into the clearing. His smell pervaded the air.

Young Master! I was so happy, I peed. Slinking up to him, I snuggled his leg.

He couldn't see me in the dark, but he barely whispered "Cuppy!" He tried, but his fingers were too stiff to scratch my ears.

That's OK. I led him along a trail planted with glow trees. The percussion of the night insects rose to a roar.

How would we ever get used to life on this planet? Days, nights, scavenging nuts and berries. The terrain was rough and even with the advantage of our strength, we were weakened by hunger. What a stroke of luck that we finally stumbled upon a Feridid encampment. A faint light dawned. The big sun was creeping above the trees.

The creatures were at ritual. We recognized a few of them from our first encounter. They spotted us. At first there was a silence, and then a low growl. The largest creature stood up. Young Master stepped into the light. There was a rumble of recognition and excitement. Young Master urged the leader to continue their ritual. The leader's eyes gleamed. He told a legend about Young Master. He began chanting, *"Mak sym, mak sym."* The chant caught on and ran around the circle of creatures. The big-eared creatures pulled Young Master into the ring.

Thus, the embassies precipitated exactly what they purported to prevent. The Feridids remembered Young Master, and he felt a peculiar inherited obligation toward them. He accepted his stumbled-upon mission to protect the Feridids from themselves. They wanted to learn about light, but he did not want to teach about fire. Could he show them the way without leading them astray and destroying their fertile planetoid? How could he make them grok the value of the creation they lived in? Not everyone saw it. Why? His teachings would not be busywork, like his schooling back on Earth. He would give them the tools to shape themselves, mentally and *physically.*

The biggest Feridid stepped aside. He was accepted.

Little Sun

I have learned from an early age to abjure the use of meat,
and the time will come when men such as I will look upon
the murder of animals as they now look upon the murder of
men.

—Leonardo da Vinci

LIFE ON GROD HAD BEEN COMFORTABLE. Now Feridids
teased and threatened to eat me behind Young Master's
back. Now my place in the hierarchy was at risk. To his
face, they revered him, but behind his back, they taunted
me. I never let him out of my sight. Maybe they were
nicer to him when I was around too, and it made me feel

warm thinking that he needed me as much as I needed him.

One spring day, the Feridids woke up chattering and began preparations for their annual coming of age ceremony. They could see that Young Master was just getting his fur, and they nudged him into the circle. The largest creature, no taller than Young Master, came forward. He gestured with his hairy hands, and made us understand his name, a series of grunts. Now it was time for Young Master to choose a name. The largest Feridid questioned Young Master. The tribe repeated the question. I concentrated hard to understand, and put the question in Young Master's head. *What shall be your name?*

Young Master pointed toward the red dwarf sunrise.

Upon seeing the silhouette of Young Master's finger against the sun, a bubble of chatter erupted among the Feridids.

"Mak! Sym!" The Feridids chanted. The name for dawn. It was as the legend had prophesied. *MakSym* had touched the little sun. They called him 'Little Sun', MakSym, and danced around him until the setting of the giant red sun. Thus, the Feridids tapped Young Master with a bough and ordained him a man, not just any man. He was the one they'd been waiting for, MakSym the prophet. He was the one! They danced around Young Master, worshipping, honoring, following him, through the scavenge, through the hunt, Young Master had many ways to learn. Time cracked the earth in the summer and peeled away the leaves in autumn.

One winter's day, a search party appeared against the red glow of the morning dwarf sun. Young Master and I hid under a bush. He shrouded us in his cloak. In the glow of morning, the search party stepped out of the orange-cast trees and came looking for us.

"Nothing here."

"The Porters ordered us to search until we found the boy," the other guard said.

"Well, he's not here. Let's return to guard the High Emissariat and Kenza."

Confirmation. Mistress and Kenza were still alive! Tears welled in Young Master's eyes. He would have liked to send a message to his sister, but he had to stay hidden to do his work among the Feridids.

Young Master sighed. *The Porters are alive!* Young Master was torn. He wanted to reassure his mother, however, he knew the real work on Phira was not with her, spying on and undermining other embassies, but here in Nature, teaching the Feridids. He had to stay under Starliament's radar. We let the search party leave.

The more our tribe banded together, the more other Feridids resented us. Young Master used all his faculties to defend his tribe against jealous attackers. We easily won. Each skirmish only compounded the growing mythology surrounding Young Master. In order to raise the Feridids sustainably, Young Master omitted teaching some of the basic steps in human evolution. He didn't teach them to use fire. We ate everything raw. He did try to explain electricity, however, and constructed a wind mill.

Our rugged existence among the Feridids afforded few comforts. Although the tribe marveled at Young Master and gave him the best of everything, their way of life was still a severe hardship for him. I worried that all the trekking would shorten my lifespan to the length of a

human life. We persevered, though. I watched Young
Master with pride as he grew into a very strong man.

We trekked from one grazing ground to another. Our
feet grew tough skin. By the time the planet made its full
orbit of the sun, we had crossed three mountain ranges.
The nomadic tribe spent every day scavenging. They had
no time to innovate or even think, the terrain was so
rough.

"The best way to foretell the future is to create it
yourself," he told the Feridids, and showed them the way.
He taught the Feridids how to make weapons to defend
themselves from attackers. Young Master became their
leader through wisdom and plain good ideas, without
going through the usual fight to the death with the old
leader. A relief, since no one wanted to test his super-
Earth strength. He knew many tricks. He found a fallen
tree trunk, cut it into slices, and showed them how to
make wheels. The tribe constructed all kinds of go-carts,
and eventually ploughs for farming.

The Feridids had one nasty habit that Young Master
would not tolerate. When a male in the tribe died, leaving
a female and children, a new male would come and make
the woman his, killing the children and having his own
new children. Young Master put an end to this practice.
When parents died, he took the orphans under his wing,
and he ended up with many children. He had to set up a
school and introduce the institution of marriage to stop
the neglect. But the nomadic tribe dismantled his
institutions with each migration, and he had to rebuild
from scratch at each new destination. He tried to get
them to stop wandering. Other male Feridid's challenged
his manhood. He cowed them, threatening to call the sun

down upon them. Already afraid of his superior strength, no one dared question his infinite wisdom, either.

Young Master understood that civilization could never grow on the move. But the change didn't come until he convinced them to stop leaving the sick behind to die. He showed them how to build tombs for their heroes. Beacons to the heavens. The Feridids added to an ancient collection of pyramid-like tombs on the coast leading to the capital. They prayed for their ancestors and discovered a way to draw energy from the sea by looking at the horizon. At last, they agreed to hold their ground, and allowed Young Master to teach them to farm. Once finding food was no longer a full time job, the creatures had more free time to think, and their minds expanded. One of them invented a bag to put berries in so he could bring them home and share them with his family. Young Master praised the Feridid so much, he turned red in front of everyone. The look of pride on the creature's face was a sight to see! Soon everyone was doing it, and the children grew taller.

It seemed like Young Master had almost forgotten about the Earth girl, but he never took a wife among the big-eared Feridids. Being rather shy about these things, I didn't push him on this. I was proud of Young Master's ingenuity. We threw ourselves into our work, showing the Feridids how to domesticate wooly animals for milk and cheese. A few of the primate males complained: the old ways were lost. While Young Master's miracles solved problems like famine, they depleted the tribe's spiritual connectedness. The Feridids would never accept blind machinery with no soul story behind it. The problem of mixing technology with spiritualism intrigued Young Master. He turned it over and over again in his head.

Around the time when he showed the creatures how to farm, the fighting started. Our tribe found the best piece of land and planted on it. In the autumn, scavengers from three other tribes in the habit of picking wild berries on 'our land' came to take our harvest. Young Master had to erect a wall around our farm. The wanderers attacked, and we had to defend the village with bow and arrow.

He'd had high hopes for the Feridids. But he was not happy. He had lived through too many painful passages and agonizing choices to get to this point: a farm. He expected more from the tribe. It disappointed him that he could not get the Freidids to develop even to a medieval level.

Yes, they had formed a cohesive community with numerous inventions and discoveries, but Feridid selfishness remained heartbreaking. Watching them fight amongst themselves made him cringe and despair for the orphans, for Nature, for the future of the universe. He'd come this far without ever having to ask for help. Watching them bicker over a pitchfork, he knew he couldn't do it alone. He remembered the living computers on Earth that could solve problems beyond his capacity, and hung his head.

Lonely, longing, teaching, harvesting, we worked with the Feridids planting groves of *hokkas*. The creatures were praying for fruition. Phira is much warmer than Grod, so my blanket of fur is an encumbrance for much of the year here, and I have to be trimmed endlessly. That's what Young Master was doing when we heard the first projectile.

An attack! Young Master bolted out of the circle. I started barking. Young Master led the way, arming himself. I followed on his heels. The attackers, wearing no clothes, broke the door to our storage room and carried off two sacks of sacred grain. Young Master scattered the hairy humanoids, but a pack of wild *lulus* surrounded us. I felt a sting in my leg, but I bit the *lulus* back hard. We fought on and on. Our Feridids used wooden swords and bow's and arrows to beat back the attackers. As one after another of the attackers fell, the remainder came to realize that Young Master's tribe was too advanced for them. At last, they retreated into the forest.

There were many animals and humanoids wounded on both sides. When the fighting was over, a third of the village was leveled, and the females were crying. I sniffed around at the bodies and barked every time I discovered a living Feridid on the battlefield. Young Master ran over and called the old medicine man.

I was surprised when I saw my hind quarters were covered with blood. I lay on Young Master's thighs. In a daze, I didn't understand why Young Master was pouring a foul liquid into my mouth and stroking my throat to make me swallow. My head spun. He dabbed my wound with a stinging rag and poked me with a needle that had a string coming out of it. Even though I had five more legs, I sorely wanted to bite him to make him stop sewing. Instead, my head went all fuzzy, and I whimpered listlessly in his lap until he was finished and let me lick his hands. Then he stroked me with wet, cleansing hands until I felt peaceful again and fell asleep with my muzzle on his thigh . . . *my Young Master. Someday I will give my life for you.*

EVERYTHING-HAPPENS INFINITY

Timing is everything.

—Shakespeare

VALENTINE'S AUBURN HAIR WHIPPED in the wind as she stood on the starport arguing with Anessi and the Emperor of Earth and Ocean.

"We want that oil!" the Emperor said, standing on his own two feet in the lighter gravity of the planetoid.

Valentine scoffed. "You'll only pollute the planetoid pumping all that oil out of the ground and putting it into the atmosphere. Even from a financial perspective, that old sorry game doesn't make sense anymore. We have better technology and energy sources. Look at Earth now that we've set up solar panels everywhere. One day of sunlight provides the planet with enough energy for the whole year."

"That oil is worth 1.25 trillion salts in government subsidies!" said the Emperor. "Think how the economy of Phira will grow with all that money."

Valentine looked the Emperor in his manipulatedfat eye. "There you go again about money and cancerous economic growth. We're happy with Nature growing around here."

"If you won't help us, we'll find the oilfield ourselves and kill off all the Feridids on it."

"An attack on the Feridids would provoke a war with the other embassies. Only I kin reason wi' the Feridid leader. Anyway, it would take you forever to find the oilfield alone."

Anessi's beady eyes narrowed to slits. "Supposing a little 'accident' happened at the Feridid camp—" He folded his thin, blue arms.

The Emperor of Earth and Ocean chuckled, his fat jowls jiggling. "I like the way you think, Anessi."

"It's risky," Valentine countered. The other embassies would see right through it. They'd never let us dig our oil wells in peace."

"We'll see about that," Anessi said. "It's much easier to nip the resistance in the bud, than to let it grow stronger and try to fight it later on."

"Tough. I'm not leading a whole army to the Feridid camp," Valentine said. "That would be tantamount to declaring war." The Emperor and Anessi looked at each other. She had their hands tied. They couldn't afford antagonizing the other embassies. What if they blocked the Starliament subsidies? Everything had to remain covert.

Valentine also crossed her arms. She'd made the maps from the satellite images herself. No one had a better idea of where to look for the oilfield and the advanced Feridid tribe rumored to be living on top of it. "I refuse to take everyone on the search," Valentine said.

Anessi and the Emperor had to acquiesce. They decided to let her go ahead with two scouts. The small party set out at dawn, with Valentine leading the search for the Feridid leader. In the beginning, she and the two scouts took turns driving the rover across the fertile terrain each day until the last throb of red-dwarf dusk. Anessi's troop was a scrawny, blue creature. The other was a snarpguard scout weakling, born to the planetoid's lighter gravity. Valentine's Grod-trained, Earth muscles kept them going. She drove them over rocks and streams as the others slept in the back seat.

At dusk, they broke bread at the edge of a forest. Then they set up their tents in the upside-down trees. Unfettered by gravity, the trees' roots had drifted skyward to drink the moisture from the tropical air. The party climbed inside their tree tents for the night.

Alone in her tent, Valentine lay awake, listening. She would have to get rid of the guards before they found out too much. She hoped she'd led the them far enough off course to confuse them. Night creatures raised a ruckus. *It's time*. She rolled out of her tent under the cover of the roaring nighttime insects and packed up the rover in the dark. Using the stars to compute her coordinates, she left the sleeping scouts at the camp. In the first taint of dawn, Valentine found a shallow stream heading west, and drove into it to cover her tracks. The rover's solar panels recharged, absorbing the energy of the red sun.

Two days later, she reached the area where the satellite record showed unusual activity. She shielded her eyes from the orange glow and began to look for signs of life.

Valentine ran her pale hand across the bark of an ancient tree. Its leaves gleamed with the first blush of autumn. She felt at peace in this Nature. If only she had been able to see Earth before the human race polluted it.

She drove through a golden field to a dusty plateau, where she spotted something glinting in the orange light. She jumped down from the rover and reached under a bush to pick it up. An arrowhead. *Heavy.* Valentine turned the arrowhead over. She brushed off the dust, and noticed a metal smith's stamp. *Advanced culture confirmed.* She checked the position of the dwarf sun. This was indeed the place in the satellite photos. She drove a little farther, found a path and followed it. Behind a stone quarry stood a man-made wall.

She parked the rover in the underbrush and sat listening to the sounds of the jungle. Strangely enough, the *avia* had stopped chirping. The purple sky peeked through giant jungle leaves.

Suddenly, the bushes tore open. Five hairy creatures jumped onto the jeep. Valentine screamed. The creatures pulled her from the rover. She kicked as hard as she could, knocking one of them down, but there were too many of them. The low rumble of argument started amongst the pack. They had never seen anyone as white as she was. Another primate drew a wooden sword and growled as he barred the way. He motioned to the others to take their hands away from Valentine's milky throat.

The largest primate seized her by the wrist and slung her over his back. He bounded through the jungle with her, kicking and screaming. The other creatures clamored behind. Over logs, mossy rocks, a stream.

A horn sounded. The five primates stopped in their tracks. They looked around.

The horn sounded again. Valentine saw the silhouette of a tall man, naked except for a loin cloth, making his way toward them through the vines. "Put her down."

The Feridid reluctantly set Valentine down on the mossy jungle floor. Her feet sank in, and she lost her balance. She landed on her butt under a giant leaf.

"Who goes there?" the man demanded, approaching swiftly.

Valentine couldn't believe her eyes. The leader's hair was long and black. His dark muscles shone in the orange sunlight. Unlike the primates he ruled, he was tall and strong, a human, raised in heavy gravity. "State your purpose here," he demanded, hacking his way into the circle. When he turned to dismiss the guards, the girl stood up. He stopped short and stared at her. He wiped his eyes. She was still there, so much like the girl of his dreams. He touched her cheek, beginning to believe his eyes. *She's here.* He wanted to lift her up and twirl her around. Her green eyes looked into his deep brown eyes. A wave of recognition flowed between them. "Is it you?"

"'Tis I," she said, in the full bloom of womanhood.

After all his longing for her, her actuality stunned him. Did she really know him? He took in her olive jumpsuit and smooth skin. Even with her auburn mane tied in a ponytail, she was the most beautiful woman he'd ever seen. They stared into each other's eyes. A current passed between them. Her presence pulled him into a sea of emotion, souls merging. *Safe at last.*

"You've grown tall," she said.

MakSym suppressed a smile. He bickered with the Feridids and ordered one of them to go back to the car to get Valentine's things. Then, he put his lips to a curled animal horn, and blew. The Feridids stood erect and bounded off, leading the way up a narrow footpath. They came to a stone wall with a hidden gate. The party went inside and followed the path to the largest dwelling. A guard grunted and pulled a curtain back, revealing an inner chamber, plush by Feridid standards. MakSym led her in.

He had seen her in his life a hundred times, swimming in the Phiran sea, standing on a rock in the desert, talking to his people. Holding his hand in the twilight of the dwarf star. And now she was here, with him. He dismissed the guard with a wave of his hand, as he had done in his dream.

The guard bowed and left the girl there. A curtain hissed closed behind her.

The girl from his dreams bowed. She skirted around the edge of MakSym's bed. He could barely remember her language, but the conversation from the dream was fresh in his mind. He had said, "Welcome." He knew her answer.

Eyes shining, he heard himself say in an echo of déjà vu, "How did you find me here?"

"Twas hard to find." She gazed at him steadily. "You've been here for a long time. That leaves a lot of chances to find you. When there are many opportunities, the probability of an event is great. A seemingly improbable meeting might become almost certain." True, in an infinite number of universes, everything happened. The only miracle was that they were here now.

"You must be tired," MakSym said.

"I am." She spoke with such familiarity, he imagined she'd just come in after a day's work in the fields.

MakSym struggled to remember the conversation from the dream: "Rest here on the . . ." The word escaped him. He motioned to a mound of plant furs.

"I'm fine standin'," she said.

He perceived mockery in her voice. Something else as well. Jealousy. The old rivalry was still alive. She was still envious that her father had chosen him as an apprentice, instead of her. MakSym remembered the old lumberjack with sadness. Naming the problem might make it go away. "Your father chose me to work with him instead of you to protect you. Any father would have done the same."

She hung her head.

He brought her *kibbus* and *satta* nectar, which she took in her familiar way. He felt conversation unnecessary, watching her eat, and wondered why he had worried about the need for words. Here was that familiarity again. Family. He had once had one. He had not allowed himself to think of family since he'd lost his. Valentine's eyes opened a realm of pain he should have dealt with earlier.

She ate voraciously. At last she pushed her plate away. "We are in danger here."

"What is it?"

"I came to warn you. Enemy forces are planning an ambush. The Emperor and Anessi. You remember Anessi, I'm sure."

MakSym's hair stood on end at the mention of the alien's name.

Valentine went on. "He sold his storage room full of rubicons at a laughably high price before the currency collapsed. With it, he bought up seats in Starliament for himself and the Emperor of Earth and Ocean. Now Anessi's gang is planning to use neighboring Feridid tribes to stage an ambush, so the other embassies can't accuse him of openly attacking you. Anessi's got Starliament and the Emperor of Earth and Ocean on his side. They're looking for fuel. MakSym, he wants to exploit the planetoid's oil reserves. They're going to pollute Phira like they did Earth."

MakSym clenched his fists. Hearing of the corruption of Starliament and Anessi's villainous plan, he feared for his family. "So that's why they wanted to keep the Feridids from developing. To steal the planetoid's natural resources." *They'll never get Phira as long as I'm alive!* Starliament's prank was clear to him now. No wonder why they considered the Feridid race an Enormous Catastrophe. It had interrupted the seven billion year cultivation of fossil-fuel-producing algae and bacteria, and spawned intelligent life instead, with indisputable ownership claims to the land covering Starliament's future oil reserves. If only he could get his hands on that little alien and that big fat Emperor. They would burn in the crucible of his revenge. "You came to warn me?"

"That's part of it."

"What's the other part?"

"I'm too tired." She yawned. "Do you have a guest room?"

As she slept in the next room, he stared at the ceiling, his body more awake than ever. Her presence reminded him of Earth, and he let himself long for his family again. He wondered how Kenza and his mother were managing. He felt sorry that he'd had to remain undercover to realize his plans. As much as it pained him all these years to forego his parents and sister, he couldn't risk giving away his tribe to the embassies. Starliament with all its regulations and protocols, would only interfere with his plans to shape the Feridids into a Nature-protecting civilization.

Without sounding the alarm, MakSym and Valentine prepared the Feridids for war. The tribe began training every day at dawn. No attack came. MakSym kept his eye on Valentine, whether they were sparing, sowing plants with the Feridid villagers or teaching the children. They worked together to see that the village's crops grew thick. Fascinated, he watched her picking berries, doing simple things. Talking to the children after their lessons, on the way to harvest food for the rainy season. Helping the Feridids dry fruit.

The villagers sat in the village square and gave thanks for all they had. MakSym and Valentine rose from the circle and went inside. He stopped at her door. "Goodnight, then."

"Thank you for rescuing me from your guards. I want to forgive you, but it's hard."

"I'm not competing with you, Valentine. I know you'd win anyway."

Her countenance remained fixed in stubbornness. "Goodnight."

What could he offer in return for forgiveness? An idea came to him. His voice softened. "I'm sorry."

She smiled. The truth pleased her.

He would tell her more of it. He felt her forgiveness wash over him, her acceptance a balm to his wounds. *We are home.* She found him. When did he take her hand? The expanse of possibility between them terrified him. Yet, his body overcame his head. She looked up at him so prettily. As he'd seen it. She wanted to know more about him, about Grod and coming to Phira. He told her everything, about how he had changed after he met the Feridids. She understood, and his words flowed easily. Telling her the truth felt good. "And this attack is why you came? To warn me?" he asked.

"That and . . ."

"And what?" His lips brushed her forehead.

"I need you." That mischievous look in her green eyes again. He was drawn to her like a magnet.

"No you don't."

"Aye, I do." She gazed into his eyes.

It felt good to be needed. "For what?"

"For my creations. I know now that my father didn't create the living computers. You did. You can help improve the next generation of androids. Droids don't have infinite storage capacity."

He was feeling rather infinite. He looked up to the ceiling, saying, "I have been waiting for you." When he looked back down, she wasn't there. He did a double take, looking down the corridors every which way.

She was nowhere.

Her door opened. She came back out into the hallway with a plant-fur coat and closed the door behind her.

Ah yes, together. He played off his worry, not letting her out of his sight, slowing his pace, walking her out under the infinite, starlit sky. It was chilly. The Feridid sentinel saw them and grunted. MakSym felt self-conscious about his primitive Feridids in front of Valentine and nodded apologetically.

"And you intend to do what with these primitive creatures?" she asked.

Their rivalry flared again.

He was at a loss to defend himself. Instead, he bravely took Valentine's hand and put it in his pocket. Their bodies warmed as they walked on. Valentine drew to a halt at the edge of the fields. "Did you wonder where I was?" She looked up at him.

What strategy would win her? He doubted he could outsmart Nature. He looked into her green eyes. *Should I tell her?* "Come here." *I love you.* His lips touched her forehead. "I need to kiss you." She pressed against him. He kissed her lips.

I COPY YOU

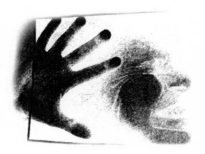

Freedom is often an excuse for neglect.

—The Teachings of MakSym

PHIRA CRADLED HER NASCENT CIVILIZATION spinning in an elliptical orbit around the red dwarf star. In the childhood of their evolution, the Feridids were simply not ready for the perils beyond their protective planetoid. The Emperor's shadow blackened their future.

MakSym deliberated for a half a day. It was time to warn the Feridids of the oncoming attack. There was no other choice. With little hope of survival, he had to give them a chance to defend themselves.

The Feridids sat in a circle listening to MakSym. He felt guilty leading them into danger. They had nothing to compare the power of Anessi's rogue embassy to, and could little imagine the danger they were in.

When MakSym finished his speech, the Feridids stood up. The simple Feridids, with no tools or technology, summoned their bravery. They held their ground in a circle around MakSym and began to stamp their feet. Their movements syncopated into a rhythmic dance. The circle turned. They whirled around the circle faster. The fervor of their dance evoked an unexpected emotion. Their fierce cries raised MakSym's spirits and gave him strength. Looking at the Feridids made him wonder what humans were like before all the electronic gadgets were attached, before humans outsourced their brains to devices. Were they so fully integrated, still thinking for themselves and tapping their own infinite energy reservoirs? Even MakSym had been deactivated. The Feridids activated him. They had a power he had never noticed. *That's it.* Sure, Valentine's droids could work miracles, but these simple creatures *were* miracles. They knew nothing of computers or electronics, and because of that, *they* were alive in the moment, and could tap into their own souls in a way humans had forgotten. He skipped around the circle and joined them in their dance. If only Earthlings had known how to tap into their own natural energy resources like that, maybe they would have stopped corporations from taking over the world.

"They did it, so we can too!" he yelled.

The Feridids took up the chant. "They did it, so we can too!" A cloud of dust rose from the village and mounted to the sky. But it was not dust.

The reservoir of power within the primitive creatures took Valentine by surprise. She stood outside of the circle, arms folded, for once marveling at the hairy

Feridids. "I guess droids are no competition for innate stupidity." But she was smiling. She couldn't help but be moved by the dance, and threw her head back and laughed.

MakSym let the power of the tribe flow through his limbs. Now he understood what they had to do. Every night he had the Feridids repeat the ritual, praying for strength to ward off evil. "They did it, so we can too!" The chant rose to the sky. The Feridids became stronger. They carried stones and set them at intervals around the circle to climb over and bring the level of the dance up and down again in waves.

But still no attack came. Nature abided the Feridid's evolution with temperate seasons. Phiran autumn swept through the village square. Heavy rains fell, heralding in winter's enormous, low-gravity snowflakes.

The hairy villagers hibernated through the cold months until the first red rays of spring enticed them to open their shutters. They made obeisance to the sun. Springtime came around to a broad welcome. Now that it was warm outside, the primates worked their hardest to bring the village to the pinnacle of technology. They harnessed centurans to plough the fields, dug wells, and beat down mud roads leading into the square.

The *hupcha* pranced up and down the ranks on his six legs, his myriad tails wagging like a brown fan, his tongue hanging out between tiny fangs.

"What are you doing?" Valentine asked MakSym, who was preaching to a group of young Feridids.

"I'm teaching the Feridids the use of sustainable technology," MakSym told Valentine. He demonstrated how to hang wet laundry on a vine in the sun, and then let them do it themselves. He patted Cuppy's head in a demonstration of the utmost respect for nature. Then, he demonstrated stringing a bow and arrow for a mass of hairy Feridids squabbling over a crust of bread.

Valentine stood in the shade of an upside-down tree. "Are ye teachin' if nobody is learnin'?" she asked. She passed MakSym by.

He followed her away from the Feridids and into the forest. Valentine led him to their favorite hideaway. MakSym stood by the brook. On the rock behind him, Valentine began coding.

"And what are you doing?" he asked.

Her auburn hair tumbled over her shoulders as he had seen in his dreams. Her fingers flew over her wrist screen. He knew what she would say next. "I'm copying ye," she said. Even though he'd seen this before, too, her words jolted him like a shock. "We need a model."

It took a moment to recover from the inevitability of their mission. The race against the Emperor loomed before him. Their humble village couldn't remain tucked away in its happy corner of the universe. Suddenly, there was a loud rumble in the clouds overhead. The Feridids ran for cover. The little ones barely had time to shimmy up the trees before a meteor pierced the clouds and raced toward them. Valentine and MakSym ducked behind the rock. The flying object slowed almost to a stop. MakSym uncovered his head. "It's a ship!" The silver spaceship landed in a field.

Valentine smiled.

The hatch opened, and a flurry of paws appeared. Out scrambled a golden *hupcha* with a glorious fan of tails, followed by Any Gynoid. Any's circuits were exposed and her spacesuit torn, but she was able to walk. Valentine ran to Any. "I'm OK," Any said. "Only missing a few circuits." Cuppy danced circles around the new *hupcha*, sniffing her underparts and growling.

"What's her name?" Valentine asked.

"Wuhvie," Any said.

Wuhvie stood there patiently letting Cuppy check her out. Then Cuppy raced off into the woods, and Wuhvie hightailed it after him.

"There's one species that knows how to get along!" Any said.

"I wish I could say the same for the rest of us," MakSym said.

MakSym stopped in his tracks, awestruck, staring at the descendent of the living computers he'd invented, Valentine's droid. *Any Gynoid!* He thought he'd never see the home-wrecking droid again. "Anything *can* happen," he said, studying the gynoid hero.

"Everything does happen, in an infinite number of universes," Any said, shaking MakSym's hand as decisively as a bolt of lightning.

"How did you make it?" Valentine said.

"I had to resort to trial and error. I am very thankful to be here in one piece," Any purred. "I assume your experiments are progressing?"

"Everything takes three times longer than expected," Valentine said, not wanting to sound complainy. She was very grateful that Any made it at all! In fact, having Any as a model would greatly speed up the production of the new race of droids. "I suspect it won't be long now until we've made your other half."

"Other half?" One of Any's ears perked up in anticipation, and the other flattened in apprehension. Any scanned her own drastic curves, and noticed only a small tear and a few conduits missing. "I'm fine," Any insisted. "Why do I need a male?"

MakSym's chest filled with hope for the upcoming race of androids. He could think of no higher honor than having them made in his likeness. He prayed that he was pure enough to be the model Valentine needed. He knelt on the rock to give thanks. Nature soothed his doubts, and he dared to pray for a hero that would save civilization from itself.

Valentine's arm around Any, they talked of their predicament and the plans for a new race of androids. Valentine led Any through the village gate. "We're trying to get primitive creatures to accept green technology."

"Jeez, do you think they'll dislike me?"

"It's happened before," Valentine admitted. "The Greeks thought Aristarchus was crazy saying the planets revolved around the sun."

"Exactly," Any said. "And that was 2,000 years before Christians persecuted Copernicus and Galileo for suggesting the Earth revolved around the sun. This is a little risky."

"You're all right, Any," MakSym reassured her. "Once we make the new race of androids, they'll help us go faster with the plan. We'll be able to see that civilizations curtail their growth to preserve their host planets. We have to prevent 'civilized' violence, like mining oil sands for bitumen. We're teaching them to harness clean energy rather than drive Nature into her danger zone." MakSym held his breath as the Feridid primates noticed Any.

The moment the tall leopard creature entered the village, the Feridids burst into chatter. MakSym put his hand on her shoulder and introduced her. They bowed before her, peeking up shyly. The Feridids were not sure what to make of the gynoid, but knew enough to jockey for position. No one wanted to lose their place in the tribal hierarchy. With heaps of encouragement, MakSym convinced the Feridids that the gynoid had come *because* the Feridids were so important. "I suggest you treat her with respect. Her race is destined to help save the universe." In awe, the primitive creatures kept their distance, but once out of earshot, they became quite caddy. It took a week for them to stop growling behind the gynoid's back and to let her talk to their children.

Cuppy and Wuhvie did their part, pattering around the camp on their six legs, sniffing the spring flowers and wagging their many tails to attract bizzbugs to the village hive. When a Feridid came to pet the furries, the two *hupcha*s put it in the Feridid's mind to be thankful for the bizzbug honey and accept MakSym's advanced technology as sacred, too.

The Feridids allowed her to shepherd them through the lore of logic. Cuppy secretly hoped the android would also bring the humans farther along, too, although who knew how many generations it would take to bring them up to *hupcha* level.

The Phiran summer intensified. In the hottest month, a neighboring tribe of wild Feridids attacked. A gang of males stormed the village. The weight of the threat bore down on MakSym. *Anessi's plot!* Everything could be lost now. The Feridid civilization. Valentine. Everything. He ordered the Feridids to defend the food supply.

The wild gang dragged three barrels of fruit across the village square.

"Drop the roseapples!" MakSym yelled.

The intruders made no sign of understanding him.

He shrugged and made quick work of the little guys, leaving four of them tied together in the dust. His muscles flexed as he tightened the knots. The rest of the wild Feridids ran off to tell the tale. No more attackers came.

"Well!" Valentine felt sorry for any jealous neighboring tribes who dared to make war on them right now. Their keep was the tallest in the land. The Feridids ushered the prisoners into an oubliette underneath for unlucky attackers. The Feridids would not remember why they were in this hole-in-the-ground, so prison was only for a fortnight. The village got to work cleaning up the mess the marauders had made. "False alarm," MakSym said, ready to defend the tribe against the Emperor, should he try to attack. "Just another skirmish in the natural flow of Feridid relations. Maybe the Emperor would leave them alone to live out their lives as farmers. MakSym and Valentine picked up the roseapples and put them back in the barrels.

They both reached for the same roseapple. Their hands touched. He took her hand.

"Did you miss me all these years?" she asked.

He looked into her green eyes to see if he was being teased again, shown her love only to lose it once more.

She meant it. He stood up straight, slowly, sure of her now, taking in the treetops spreading their giant leaves, the field, no one in sight. Her tunic was simple, dipping above the breast. Looking down at her, pretty in her khaki dress, he took her in his arms. "Every minute of every day."

They were so close, her lips almost brushed his cheek. "You are the other half," she whispered, her body pressed against him. He wanted to be with her forever. He pulled her to his chest in the softest kiss. Never again would he let her go. Her long hair draped over his arms, he held her close, feeling her body pressed to his, as one. The butterflies fluttered in MakSym's stomach as he kissed her lips again, a kiss full of promise. Nothing else mattered now. As long as they were in each other's arms, the world could pass them by

When the days grew too hot for work, MakSym and Valentine put away their tools and packed their belongings. They trekked past the blond *alee* fields. MakSym remembered them from his dreams as a boy on Earth, and realized that they were not wheat after all. And here he was, in Nature, with Valentine. They hiked through unforgiving white rocky hills marked with a rare bramble. He quickened his pace, sure of the way through the giant plants, to the turquoise sea.

The waves welcomed their bodies in the vast balm, and tossed them up to the surface where they floated, refreshed, on their backs listening to their breathing. MakSym watched Valentine floating.

In a flurry of tails and paws, Cuppy pranced up and down the shore, barking suspiciously at the water. MakSym and Valentine dove down to the bottom. They opened their eyes to the sunlit underwater world.

How long would they be left in peace? They were thankful for every day together, during the long Phiran summer on that magical shore. He held her on his lap as they watched the sunset. This is where he wanted to be. *I'll never take her for granted.*

They grew closer, so close, a seed began to grow inside of Valentine. MakSym touched Valentine's swelling tummy. He watched her swim underwater, brushing against the ribs of sand on the shallow sea bed, their wavy pattern a copy of the surface waves. As Valentine passed, flat fish peeled themselves off the sea bed and swam away. The lovers dove down to the rose colored coral and let little minnows nibble at their toes. A sea turtle barreled between them, and MakSym and Valentine burst from each other in fright and then with laughter. They went fishing for their dinner, harpooning gelatinous, many-tentacled creatures.

A school of little fish leapt out of the water and undulated in the sun. "Look at them!" Valentine said. MakSym and Valentine laughed. Until they understood the sign. The school of little fish consolidated in the water and leapt up again, mimicking a winding predatory creature to defend themselves against another monster . . . that must have been beneath them.

The moment they understood the signs, it was already too late. An enormous head reared from the depths. Valentine screamed, engulfing a mouthful of salt water, and spitting it back out in the direction of the gelatinous orange globe. Its giant saw-toothed mouth snapped open. Tentacles undulated, suction cups gleaming pink in the evening sun. It spouted an evil black ink.

Cuppy went wild, stomping up and down shore in a fit of telepathic projection, trying to close the sea creature's gills. Even though *hupcha*s loathe water, Cuppy jumped in and started flapping with everything he had to get close enough to project his commands. Wuhvie paddled after him.

Valentine and MakSym swam as fast as they could, the enormous jelly creature undulating behind them. Cuppy's hex hit the squid. It jiggled side to side and couldn't open its gills. The waves in the monster's wake roiled the sea bed. Still, the giant jelly creature wafted forward, gaining on Valentine. Wuhvie reinforced Cuppy's tirade, *Rawr!* Their projection stunned the squid.

MakSym pulled Valentine up onto a sandbar. The squid tried to follow. As Valentine scurried out of the water, the monster snapped the air where her foot had been.

That was close. The *hupcha*s scuttled out onto the sandbar. All four of them shivered in the middle of the shallow island, watching until the horrible squid receded into the red twilight. "That was close," MakSym said, relieved. Nature had spared Valentine and all she held.

From that day on, Cuppy and Wuhvie barked up and down the shore, their tails bobbing amidst speckled *barta* bushes, to keep the swimming area free of intruders. Even so, MakSym and Valentine only waded in the shallow waters. There was too much at stake.

The day came when the clouds rolled in, heralding the end of summer. Valentine and MakSym washed the dishes and packed up their tent. They trekked back home in the long twilight.

Any Gynoid welcomed them back home. She brushed Cuppy and Wuhvie, pulling out big tufts of fur. She launched the fur balls into the wind. They intermingled, spores fertilizing as they floated on the warm breeze. The tufts landed in the soft grass and swiftly took root. With the red rays of sun and plenty of morning dew, they sprouted plants that grew heavy with buds. When the buds flowered, inside each was a baby *hupcha*. The Feridids rejoiced, seeing the *hupcha* buds.

Any wouldn't let the Feridids forget the shadow of the Emperor lurking beneath all this fecundity. The Feridids were relieved to have their leader back, but kept on training twice a day, breaking at noon to chatter about the harvest or Valentine's big belly. Any made her creator lie down and brought her food. No one would let Valentine work. At all.

One starry night, Valentine's and MakSym's son was born. He was long, after his lumberjack grandfather, had wisps of strawberry blond hair after his mother, the keen eyes of his father, and the big ears of his grandfathers, a feature the Feridids made much of. The whole village woke up in the middle of the night to greet the newborn boy. He peered at them with deep, newborn blue eyes. "Wah!" Valentine stuck the baby on her breast. He suckled quietly.

The village bell rang. Feridids went around heralding the joyous news. Everyone forgot the fear of attack. They unbarred their doors and came out of their huts at night laughing, eager to witness the new clan member.

The village turned every day into a celebration taking care of the new 'human cub'. Valentine glowed with purpose, and MakSym wore his optimism on his sleeve. Indeed, peace seemed to have installed itself. The baby *hupchas* ripened and fell off their flowers. The fuzzy balls rolled in the grass until they found each other and made a *huppy* pile. Cuppy and Wuhvie raised them a little and then they trotted off to adopt village children. A fluffy brown one chose the human baby, who soon after delighted everyone with his growing abilities. The whole village clapped and cheered the day he took his first steps and then fell right down on his butt.

Raising their son in the Feridid village, Valentine had plenty of joyous work to distract her from android building. It would take a while for her plan to reach fruition at this rate, now that she had to mash up vegetables and run after her son. When the summer heat came around again, they packed up their animals, and trekked to the coast to camp and swim. Then, they continued on, walking beside Valentine's rover, piled high with Feridids, through rippling, blond fields of *alee* past the starport and on to the capital.

TERRA NOVA

The past is gone and will never come back.
The future is unknowable.

—'Om mani padme hum' Mantra

THE PILGRIMAGE OF FERIDIDS MARCHED through the city gate. Kenza spotted them from the window of the cottage. The stampede pawed up billows of dust. The clouds parted, revealing a sight she had never seen before, the big-eared Feridids marching on the capital in broad daylight. They had taken over a rover. Could this mean an attack? She sounded the house alarm.

The siren wailed. The two snarpguards Anessi had left them when he took over their palace rushed to their stations. *Avia* planed over the yard and landed on a bobbing branch to watch. The band of primates approached the house. A creature in a loin cloth led the stampede up the road. He was tall, muscular and brown.

Kenza ran downstairs. She caught her breath and stifled a scream. One of her snarpguard troops already lay wasted in the road. She hid behind a tree. At the end of the driveway, the tallest rider dismounted. He was curiously hairless. The other snarpguard had his weapon aimed at this smooth one's heart. Behind him, an auburn glint caught Kenza's eye. She stood on her tiptoes to get a better look at the white creature with long auburn hair. The tall rider turned to the Feridids and signaled for them to dismount. The cowlick on the back of his head came into plain view. A furry creature scurried out from between the humanoid's feet.

Kenza ran out to the road. "Wait! Don't shoot!"

The snarpguard stiffened and reluctantly lowered his weapon.

She halted next to the guard, holding his arm. Both sides were still. The primitive Feridids, clad in medieval armor, parted. The furry wriggled past. Cuppy barked and barreled into Kenza's arms, knocking her over and licking her face. "Cuppy! Are you fine? I missed you so much." She scratched his tummy and ears. "Who's this?" Wuhvie scuttled under Kenza's hands and got a scratchy welcome.

The tall rider paused to get a good look at the grand staircases and arches of the city he left as a boy. He held his arms out wide.

Kenza stared, dumbfounded. "Is that you?" She ran to MakSym, stopping short in front of him, and then throwing herself into her brother's arms.

He held her in a bear hug.

"It is you," she cried. "I'm so glad you're alive!" With a joyful laugh, she marveled at his medieval tunic, fighting gear and suntanned muscles. He was certainly the tallest of the family. She would have to get used to his thick beard and feet of leather.

"Boys become men, and then what?" His voice was gruff and wild. "I'm MakSym now."

Of course, she thought, her brother would have earned his name long ago. MakSym. She had heard of the fearless leader MakSym. He was a legend on Phira. He came to lead the Feridids, as their prophecies had foretold. She looked into his fierce gaze and was overjoyed to see her brother again.

"Our parents?" he asked.

"They're alive and well," Kenza said. "They'll be so happy to know you are, too!"

The auburn spot among the Feridids moved again. Kenza assumed a relaxed stance in the hope that the shy creature would emerge from the host.

The Feridids separated.

Kenza's eyes widened at the sight of the girl with an auburn mane. There stood Valentine, holding a little one.

"Valentine!" Kenza gasped at seeing her old schoolmate standing there, sparkling like a gem. Kenza hugged her and the small boy with auburn hair, a deep dark tan, and big ears. "I think I know who this is. Congratulations, both of you!"

Valentine, and Kenza, had grown into beautiful women. Quiet as ever, Valentine took Kenza's hand. "I'm glad to see you again," Valentine said. "I never told you how much I appreciated your help with my experiments, and more than that, your friendship. Thank you."

Kenza blushed. They both bowed their heads. "I should be thanking you for designing the gynoids that saved us," Kenza said, nodding to Any.

Valentine smiled. "I thought I could do everything myself back then. Now I understand how much you helped. Twas the least I could do."

"You can do a lot then!" Kenza said.

"I hope so. Now we have to stop the Emperor and his Starliament lackeys from defiling Phira and other fertile planets," Valentine said.

"What a villain! The Emperor's tentacles are everywhere. We've been making alliances among the other embassies, but no one's come up with a plan. Any ideas?" Kenza asked.

MakSym smiled. "I thought you'd never ask."

The host came inside and cleaned up after the long journey. Mom arrived home from the embassy and found the wonderful surprise. Overjoyed, she threw her arms around MakSym and cried. "Look at you!" Mom picked up her grandson and bounced him in her arms. She couldn't stop looking at them all day.

The unexpected arrival prompted the rapid unfreezing of all the food in the house. When Any walked in, Mom welcomed her with sheer graciousness. "She's not the same Any who ran off with *my* husband, after all," Mom whispered to Kenza. Kenza regarded her mother in surprise and went to get the two Porters next door.

The older Porter raised his hands to the sky when he saw MakSym standing in the garden. He reached up and tousled MakSym's hair in glee. MakSym looked down at his father, and recognized the respect he'd thought his father would never show.

There were too many Feridids to fit in the Mom's cottage, but the crowd of primates received a warm reception anyway. The family carried four tables out into the pink and green garden, pungent with glorious harvest nectar, and laid out a simple repast. They spread picnic blankets under the small fruit trees, and gazed up at their blossoms, purple against the orange glow of the dwarf sun. Mom brought out a bowl of *alee* goulash. As she set it in the center of the first table, her wrist screen flashed. "A message from Yda," Mom said, casting the holomessage onto the table.

Yda danced in the goulash: `"You have done well on Earth, but now Starliament is sending oiler ships to nine other exoplanets."`

The garden erupted in chatter. All sat down and began to discuss the violence. "How can we guard those planets from the polluters who tried to murder Earth? We've got to do something!" Kenza said.

The holomessenger buzzed again. It sprang to life, emitting the fat image of the Emperor of Earth and Ocean. "You won't win this one," the Emperor gloated.

The two Porters stood up.

MakSym leaned over the table. "Leave Phira alone," he ordered. "Fossil fuel is obsolete. It kills all it purports to help. There's no sustainable market for it."

"I couldn't agree with you more," the fat Emperor laughed.

Everyone at the table looked at each other in surprise.

"I know you don't want it," the Emperor said. "But that hasn't stopped the government from subsidizing fossil fuel corporations. Starliament is slow to realize technological changes. It still pays a trillion salts to fossil fuel corporations for digging oil out and, as you say, putting it into the atmosphere. Whether people buy it or not. Ha, ha! A trillion salts. That's too much to ignore." His laughter remained even after his image faded to a fat fuzz ball.

MakSym clinked his spoon against his glass. A hush fell over the room.

Valentine stood up. "It's been a long journey, and we are thankful to be here together at last, but time is slipping away. You heard it yourselves. We urgently need your help."

MakSym rose. "One of the reasons we came here today is, we couldn't wait any longer. For eons, man has tried to conquer Mother Nature, and she has kept her truths secret. But now we've forced her to confess: she cannot sustain us anymore."

There was a low rumble in the room. The guests fell silent again.

"Some of you might remember doing a biology experiment," MakSym said, "where you filled a jar with water and put a few blades of grass in it with holes in the top. After a few days, if you looked at a drop of the water under a microscope, you saw healthy amoebas growing. After a few more days, the jar became full of amoebas as they happily multiplied. After a week, it stunk with rancid water. A look at a drop of the polluted water showed that all the amoebas were dead. They were so successful that they multiplied until they used up all the resources, reached their saturation point and became extinct. If humans don't guard against reaching their 'saturation point', they'll always commit parricide against their planets. We saw the contagion on Earth, when mankind pit its cancerous growth against Nature. Now the truth is clear. Enslaving Nature, we enslave ourselves. Conquering Nature is a death wish. We have been fighting the wrong war, and in winning, we lose."

Silence fell upon the guests. Valentine stepped forward. "Excavating oil on exoplanets amounts to an attack on nature. We must change the way we live, protecting Nature and each other. We'll be needin' a new android class, and we need to start now. Hopefully we're not too late."

"The mission?" Mom asked.

"The mission is to fight th' destruction of Nature, on the exoplanets under Stariliamentary attack. We need to arm those planets with clean energy."

"Where do we start?" Mom asked.

"Well, we have to find a factory to produce the next generation of androids," Valentine said.

Any threw up her hands, grokking that the male droid was inevitable. Scowling, she admitted, "I think we passed a suitable factory on the way here."

MakSym lifted his glass, holding Valentine's hand. "Let's be thankful for what we have. To Nature, on Phira, on all fertile planets, everywhere!"

They all raised their glasses.

Valentine passed the bread. "We've got to fin' a way to coexist with Nature. It's our only hope. Habitable planets are a rare find," she said to the older Porter.

"They are precious," the younger Porter on her left conceded.

Cuppy barked. The Feridids laughed.

ARACHNID

Battle not with monsters, lest ye become a monster.

—Friedrich Nietzsche

MAKSYM AND VALENTINE PITCHED THEIR TENT outside of town at the new android factory. She was dressed in a Feridid tunic gathered around her waist, auburn hair toppling over her shoulders. He felt butterflies in his stomach as she beamed at him, a smile full of promise. He was where he wanted to be. With Valentine.

Three female Feridids called Valentine to pick fruit for the noonday meal. Valentine invited them to go in her rover. Twigs snapped under tires as they drove away. The rover raised a cloud of dust over the fields that billowed and then suddenly stopped.

Something was wrong. MakSym scanned the treeline. He heard the sound of fighting in the brush. *Swish,* a body fell into the grass. The Feridid children scattered. They shimmied up the tallest trees and disappeared among the leaves. A Feridid woman pulled MakSym's son into the leaves of an upside-down tree. MakSym quelled a wave of panic. *Where is Valentine?* He called his guards and ran through the woods at top speed. Three Feridid women came screeching toward him through the trees. The enemy had taken Valentine! MakSym ran, Feridids in his wake. He spotted the rover in the middle of a field. Three of Anessi's men sat in front.

MakSym's arrow hit one. The other two drove toward the woods. MakSym knew the woods, and could travel through it much faster than any rover. MakSym strung his bow and shot. His arrow hit the second guard. The third dove out of the rover and ran with the Feridids on his trail. The rover stopped in a ditch. MakSym came up behind the rover. To his horror, Valentine was not inside. He scanned the trees, walking back the way he'd come.

"Mmm." A muffled sound came from a fallen log. He searched for the source of the noise. There she was bound and gagged on the ground behind the log. He cut the cord around her hands and removed the gag in her mouth. They hugged each other.

It began to rain. They ran for it. Suddenly, MakSym stopped short, yanking Valentine's hand. She halted behind him. He stared into the woods at the . . . *evenly spaced trees? Those weren't there before.*

One of the tree trunks bent and stepped forward. They all began to move!

"It's alive!" Valentine screamed. Giant centurans with tree-thick legs.

He pulled her to his side. They dove for cover.

A host of giant *centurans* stampeded from the woods. The brown creatures, though rare in these parts, would not have been a threat if a Feridid rider were not sitting atop each one. No one had ever mounted a *centuran*. Someone had trained the Feridid tribe to ride. What else had they been trained to do?

So, Anessi has bent Starliament and a Feridid tribe to his own will. MakSym swallowed his fear and stood up. He forced himself to stare the towering creatures down.

The hexapods bucked to a stop, stunned by MakSym's stare. No matter how much the riders urged the beasts, the creatures refused to go. Instead, they sniffed the air in front of the strange vehicle.

Out in the woods, a tree trunk snapped in two. A clan of primitive marauders stood up in the high grass. They wore no clothes, but seemed more organized than other neighboring tribes, obviously sent by Anessi. There were more than fifty of them. The largest male shrieked and launched an attack. They threw stones at the villagers. The marauders vastly outnumbered MakSym's guard. But the worst of it was the monster they had brought with them. A dark shape traveled through the high grass. The Fereidids pointed their lances at the field behind the rover and chattered.

A hairy back rose out of the tall grass. The monster MakSym had dreaded his whole life. The giant eight-legged *Terrifficollosus,* spinning a web of sticky silk from the back end of its body. It was five times as big as a centuran. It was twenty times as big as a man. It was catching Feridids, wrapping them up like mummies and injecting them with its poison. The giant spider had been trained to attack on command!

MakSym's eyes flared. Another violation of planetoid taboo. This reeked of Anessi's conniving. The blue alien and the Emperor had endangered the tribe, the factory, his family, the universe. He turned his fierce gaze up to the bloody sun, every fiber of his body ready to get even with the blue knave. The monster crawled toward the camp. An arrow whizzed by MakSym's ear. "Run!" MakSym shouted. He ushered his troops back into the field.

The children scurried farther up the trees. They gawked at the giant spider's pink eyes. It had only two main body parts, consisting of head and thorax, but it was enormous. It it approached the field stretching its long legs with seven segments ending in a claw. The children pressed themselves against the tree trunks. Any Gynoid reassured the Feridids, cowering in despair, ready to surrender.

An arrow whizzed past Valentine. "Git doon!" she yelled.

Lying on the ground, MakSym looked at Valentine and tried to remember an Earth expression . . . his eyes lit up, when it popped into his head, "Can I borrow your car?"

Valentine's hand was shaking as she handed him the rover key card. Her eyes held his. Then he left.

"Cover me!" He ordered. His archers took aim. He whispered something into his head archer's ear. The Feridid gulped down his fear and nodded.

MakSym was off. He ran from tree to tree, approaching the rover. *If only Anessi were here to fight his own battle!* The enemy's stones pelted the ground around MakSym. The giant spider was almost upon him. His archer drew an arrow and hit the giant creature's gelatinous eye. Several more Feridid arrows took out two of the offenders, enabling MakSym to jump into the car. He started it up and turned the vehicle around. Standing up on the seat, he yelled, "Now!"

The archer drew an arrow and hit the side of the rover. The arrow bounced off. Any grabbed a bow and arrow, strung it in one swift move, and hit the back of the vehicle, piercing the petrol tank. Fuel leaked from the rover. MakSym drove around the field with the leaking tank spewing petrol on the ground around the giant spider. He dove from the car and rolled away on the ground. The rover barreled into the center of the circle of petrol, toward the gesticulating spider.

The giant arachnid took the rover for pray and attacked, biting it with venomous fangs. The primates let out a war cry as the spider launched a cord of sticky silk toward the vehicle. *Splat!* It stuck to a metal side panel. The monster lassoed the machine with sticky bolas. Its giant appendages pulled the rover in. It unclenched its fangs and injected venom into the driver's seat.

"My rover!" Valentine covered her eyes as the monster began to metabolize her rover, flooding it with digestive enzymes and grinding it up with its jaws.

"Everybody down!" MakSym lit the back of the arrow aimed at the liquidizing car. He shot it into the air. The arrow struck the fuel-soaked rover. *Kaboom!* The rover burst into flames. Fire leapt from the explosion and ignited the ring of fuel the rover had leaked around the field. The explosion billowed out of the field, throwing hairy spider legs in every direction. A fang fell by MakSym's foot. "Blech!" He shuddered breathing in the stench.

"Take it," Valentine said. "Ye earned this spoil o' war. Keep it as a talisman." She gave him that mollowy look of thanks he'd seen so many times, never in real life.

He wiped the fang clean on a bush and attached it to his belt.

The orange flames mounted as high as a man. They raced around the circle of fire and trapped the invaders inside a wide circle. They threw down their weapons and bowed their heads to the ground in supplication. The survivors waited for the rain to put the fire out. This would be their last attempt at challenging MakSym's tribe.

"Survival of the fittest," MakSym said.

Valentine hung her head in sorrow over the loss of life. The Feridids bowed at her signal and began to hum in prayer.

A blue shadow flitted beyond the trees. An enormous blob on centuran back lumbered after it. "There!" MakSym cried, pointing to the small, blue figure riding out of the underbrush. Every fiber of MakSym's body stood ready. Anessi was fleeing on a centruan leaping over logs and rocks as they made their escape. MakSym had to choose: his long-life foe, the Emperor, or the infinitely resourceful Anessi. He ran through the brambles after Anessi. Time slowed as MakSym's adrenaline kicked in. He sprang into the clearing where a centuran was nibbling the grass in slow motion. In a few super swift strides, he chased down the animal and mounted it, yelling, "Yah!"

Anessi galloped in slow motion ahead, bouncing on the centuran's butt. MakSym charged over logs and burning grass to catch up to the scoundrel. "Yah!" he urged the centuran on, coming up beside Anessi.

"Get away from me, savage!" the little blue man blurted.

As fast as lightning, MakSym unhooked the cord at his belt and swirled his lasso in the air. The loop fell over Anessi's head. With a yank of the cord, MakSym tethered Anessi's arms to his body and pulled him off the tall centuran. A loud snap resounded as Anessi hit the ground. With a broken leg, he could only sit in the middle of the burning field and moan. "Your silly creatures are sitting on a priceless oil reserve!" Anessi wailed.

"I'll let the other embassies know how you feel about it while you sit in jail."

"Argh!" Anessi cried, tearing his hair out.

Valentine's eyes shone with pride from across the burning field. *We've scored a mighty victory today!*

MakSym turned his face to the sky. The Emperor of Earth and Ocean was lurking somewhere out there. MakSym shook his fist. The Feridids combed the woods, but found nothing.

"You can't stop the Emperor," Anessi sneered. There will always be another planet to excavate.

Three Feridids ran to MakSym's aid. They hoisted Anessi onto MakSym's centuran and brought him and the other prisoners back to the village, where they locked them in their oubliette. At sunset, they joined hands in prayer for the spirits they'd sacrificed in self-defense.

WHAT IF SHE SAID 'YES'?

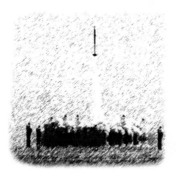

The only reason for time is so that everything doesn't happen at once.

—Albert Einstein

MAKSYM'S TRIBE SET UP THEIR TENTS in the field between MakSym's parents' houses. The Porters heard the Feridids chattering and came out to help. "Dads!" MakSym called.

His dads came and sandwiched him, sitting on a log. "When was the last time you had a bath?"

MakSym's spine tensed. "Dads, I know we haven't always seen eye-to-eye."

"Indeed, I've been busy," the Porters agreed, all four eyes on their son. "A shower every now and then can't hurt," the older one threw in.

"I can take care of myself, now, Dads. I've had to."

"I know I haven't always been there for you," old Porter said.

"It's OK. Really. It was hard, but I had to find my own way, my own work, not just busywork. Dads, do you realize that what Starliament and the Emperor want us to do is not the work that needs to be done?"

"That could be," young Porter said.

Old Porter said, "You know, you're always welcome here. Stay overnight, use the shower."

"Thanks. The thing is, now there's too much at stake. Why haven't the fertile planets switched to clean energy? The technology is there. It has been for ages. On Earth, since the invention of the windmill in the seventh century B.C."

" 'Cheap' and dirty fossil fuel is really the most expensive, after it pollutes water and food supplies," young Porter observed.

MakSym pressed his palms to his knees. "We need your help, Dads. Starilament shouldn't be giving money to oil corporations. The government is actually *paying* them trillions of salts every year to take over the universe."

"Who has time to save the world?" old Porter scowled. "Most people can't even see past their own addictions." Young Porter chimed in, and they said in unison, "There's nothing *we* can do about it."

"That's what corporations want you to think—that you're helpless. Be strategic: they did it; we can, too."

"I have faith that Starliament will do the right thing," old Porter said.

"Yeah, after they've done all the wrong things."

MakSym saw a smile creep across the younger Porter's face. Encouraged, MakSym got up and paced back and forth in front of the two Porters. "Dads, you haven't worked your whole lives for nothing. You're celebrities. You're on top of the hierarchy. Use your positions! You know how Starliament works. You have friends there. Yda's there. She could help convince them. Get them to stop giving money to oil companies."

"You make it sound so easy," old Porter said.

Young Porter mumbled under his breath. "What do we have to lose so late in the game? Why not come out of retirement, and give it a try?"

Old Porter scratched his stubbly chin.

The younger took up the cause. "It's a shame to pass on polluted land to our kids. The Emperor will just defile planet after planet. He doesn't care if there's already cleaner technology available. He'll keep on drilling for fossil fuel and pushing it on less advanced life forms, just to win the silly government subsidies."

Old Porter looked his son in the eye. The smile was contagious. "I suppose we have nothing to lose."

"Slaggy!" MakSym clapped him on the back and scooped both dads into an awkward embrace. They went back to the house. In his father's study, MakSym stood over them as the Porters called Yda and set to work on the diplomatic negotiation to halt the oil subsidies.

MakSym hugged his dads. "Maybe I will have that shower." When MakSym finally left his father's house and was halfway down the path, he turned and waved goodbye. Time was running out. Then he had to check on the next phase of the plan. They had to stop the Emperor from killing other planets. He found Any at the factory. She had begun production! "How are the Feridids taking the new line of androids?" he asked.

"A lot better than I am!" Any said. "When they saw the first shiny Colorado, the Feridids couldn't help but ogle over him."

MakSym sighed with relief.

The Colorado android spread MakSym's teachings among the young Feridids with surprising ease. That evening, MakSym watched the children gather around the first Colorado, all sitting with their legs crossed Indian style. Nothing could match the tireless patience and logic of a droid, gently showing the Feridids the path toward harmony with Nature.

Valentine came up to the circle. "He works!" She hugged MakSym.

"He's slaggy," MakSym said. But he sighed and hung his head.

"What's the matter then?"

"What if we can't find a way to fuel the ship? It'll take an enormous amount of energy to get them to the exoplanets."

Valentine looked away, unwilling to admit it was a long shot. "Have faith in your Feridids. Just keep working on it," she said. "Phira will be the Beta site for automated environmental protection." He held onto her belief in him and worked with the Feridids every day.

Valentine spent the next three moon phases adapting each android for life on the habitable planets. Tightening, rewiring, programming, testing, re-testing.

The etchings streaked the ground at the ancient starport. An advanced civilization had carved these gigantic etchings a meter deep into stone for a reason. Did they still work? On the afternoon of the blue moon Valentine and MakSym walked in the etching grooves holding their son's hands. The breeze blew through the boy's hair, as red-gold as a field of *alee* at sunset. The boy was not just from Phira, but of Phira. *Avia* planed over the runway. In the distance, orange treetops rolled all the way to the sacred Feridid tomb on the next peak. "Where have those two Porters wandered off to?" Valentine said.

"There's Granpa! Up there, beside himself," the boy said, pointing to the two Porters hovering over a bag of *hokkas* with Tweetie, Cuppy and Wuhvie in a ball of fur at their feet.

"Porter?" Valentine's voice shook with worry. According to Yda's report, the Emperor's forces were already landing on the exoplanets. There was no time to lose. She prayed that the launch would work, that the droids would make it to the exoplanets and be able to build clean wind and solar alternatives to dirty fossil fuels. She scanned the airfield shading her eyes from the glow of the red dwarf sun.

The *hupchas* leapt down from the bleachers and circled the boy, who chased them around and let them pretend to bite him. The grandfathers left off shucking *hokkas*, and launched into their *avia* calls. *Avia* were known to imitate sounds. They answered Porter's alarm clock in the morning tweeting in a high-pitched, *Ti-ti-ti-ti!* Porter had Van Gogh's ear for music and whistled Beethoven out-of-tune. Cuppy sat bolt upright and cocked his furry head. He hoped no *avia* were around to hear the nonsense these two old men were spouting. Porters could really muck up a melody. But three *avia* swooped down and answered with their own out-of-tune Beethoven, apparently also excited about the launch.

MakSym climbed the steps. The Porters stopped their whistling and announced, "Starliament has agreed to temporarily divert their subsidies from fossil fuel to alternative energy sources, as a sort of a test run. You've only got one Grod year to prove yourselves." They patted their son on the back, hesitating to ask the obvious question: How is that army of droids going to get off the ground?

Valentine hugged the two Porters. "You did it! You influenced Starliament!"

The Porters hemmed and hawed, afraid of their own success. "Be careful. The Emperor's not happy that Starliament has cut off his fossil fuel subsidies."

"The droids are ready for that," Valentine said. "It's time. All systems are go." She turned to her son. "Stay here and guard yer grandpas," nodding to the two old men, "while we take the droids to the Launchpad."

"Can I come with you?" the boy asked, hanging on the railing.

"Your Grandpas need you here." Valentine said. She knew the risks, and prayed that nothing would go wrong. "We can't keep Auntie and Grandma waiting. Bye now. Give me a kiss for good luck."

The boy kissed his mother's cheek. She hugged him. MakSym knelt down and looked his son in the eye. "We need you to oversee the launch. Tell your Grandpas what you see. Their eyesight isn't so good." MakSym winked at the two grandfathers.

"Ah yes," old Porter said. "We've been waiting for you to come and oversee the launch. Very important duty, right Porter?"

"Absolutely," the other Porter said, sure that no launch was taking place today. "Best take it seriously."

The boy stood a little taller, his hair shining red in the dwarf sunlight.

The older grandpa's eyes cleared as he beheld his grandson. Tweetie lay at the boy's feet, nested in a tangle of legs and tails. Behind them in the blond *alee* field, three laughing Feridid's drove a tractor around, halfheartedly trying to harvest the grain. The field's downward slope made this a challenge, and the tractor nearly toppled over. A female chattered at them and urged them off down the hill toward the ship where the other Feridids were circulating through the grooves of the etching.

A silver river that wasn't there before glinted in the sunlight. The troop of droids joined a procession of spotted Anys switching their feline tails, each flanked by two fuzzy, brown, six-legged, fan-swishing *huppies*. With their droid families, they formed pods of four. The procession entered the mothership. "Oh!" the boy said, waving to a silver android in his father's likeness. The boy and his grandfathers watched the silent march toward the payload section, the androids' metallic skin awash in the red sunlight. They watched Kenza and Grandma Eleanor went into the ship to direct the silver stream of droids.

"They're leading each pod to its own saucer inside the ship!" Boy said. The smaller saucers inside the rocket's payload section were programmed to land on habitable exoplanets.

"That ship'll never get off the ground," Porter mumbled.

"Yes it will!" the boy cried.

"Well, it would help if they had something to fuel it," Porter said.

"Papa says it will. Why is Papa 'The One', Grandpas?" The question filled the purple twilight.

"MakSym, was always special. His mother and I knew it the moment he was born. You could see it, looking at his pleasing proportions, not just his body, but also his mind. His head was perfectly shaped."

"And Starliament chose him!"

"Not exactly. He chose his own work. Whether Starliament will fall in, no one can say."

"How did he know what to choose?"

"It was the thing that was nagging at him the most."

The boy tossed a *hokka* to Tweetie, who caught it and chewed it up, watching the boy. "Is it good?" the boy asked, half expecting an answer.

The furry chewed gratefully on the *hokka* sinews with his back teeth. *Yes, wonderful, Little One, how lucky we are to be together.* Tweetie helped the boy concentrate and understand so he could explain what he saw to his grandpas.

"Do you remember anything from the blue planet?" the boy asked.

"I would have to empty the old hard drive to remember Earth," old Porter said.

The boy laughed. He knew his Grandpa didn't have a hard drive.

"Your head fills up as you age. I have to forget lots of things to make room for new stuff. Otherwise, my memory overflows with facts and dates while I try to verify the true and refute the false. They say it's not so good to boil everything down to its essence, but I run OK on general impressions. At least I have room for potential."

The boy considered this for a moment. "I have a riddle. What makes a brain a brain and not a lung?"

"You got me," Grandpa said.

"Memory." The boy threw out his chest.

"Memory. Good one. A brain is quicker than a lung, indeed."

"But not as quick as a droid," the boy said.

His older grandpa yawned, and the younger one yawned, too. Old Grandpa began rambling as he shucked another *hokka*.

The boy turned to the younger grandpa.

The younger grandpa's lips didn't move. He was remembering Earth, how the once-blue oily sea loomed up in the windshield of the spaceship, the planet so polluted that it resembled hell. He decided to say, "The ship skimmed over the blue sea."

"So traveling into the past *is* possible!" The boy was excited and wanted to hear more.

"Oh yes."

"It is!" the boy cried. "But then how come there aren't a lot of visitors all around us."

The two grandpas looked at each other. "Haven't you ever wondered why you have two grandpas?"

The boy looked from one to the other. *Doesn't everybody have two grandpas?*

"Visits from the future are rare, that's all," young Porter said.

"But how did you get into the future in the first place to rescue yourself in the past, Grandpa?"

"In the first place, yes. That's always the problem." Old Porter closed his eyes.

The boy looked to his younger grandpa, but he was also dozing. The boy's small hands shook his grandpas' shoulders. Old Porter yawned. "Let me ask you a question," Old Porter said. "Why does there have to be a first place? What if 'in the first place' there was no time to stretch everything out?"

The boy shrugged. "Infinity, I guess."

"Could be, could be. We're important to each other, but we're not so important that we get the one and only universe."

"We don't?"

"No."

The boy looked around. "It's the only one I see."

"Well, you gotta look for signposts that show where life has been planted."

"Where?"

"Well, now, to find them, you'd need a lot of energy and a fast ship," the younger grandpa said.

"Like that one down there." They eyed the glinting crowd gathered around the spaceship.

Porter shook his head. "That one's a dud. It doesn't have any real fuel."

"Papa says petroleum won't get you very far. But the breath of the tombs, heroes' tombs—now there's a fuel that light years are made of!"

"Spirit fuel?" Porter wasn't so sure.

"Yeah. Essence. From souls."

The grandpas' eyes closed again. *Hogwash.* The boy stood at the edge of the bleachers and watched the wild Feridid dance on the launchpad below, their almost-animal life blood in tune with Nature, feet stomping on etched stone, on the soul of Phira. MakSym and Valentine joined the Feridids in a circle around the spaceship. MakSym bowed, and they all gave thanks, paying homage to the red sun. The circle of creatures began to hum, their dance rising and ebbing in the twilight. "Grandpas, look!"

The tomb on the side of the hill glowed white with luminescent vapor. The egg-shaped *sema* opened, and out of the tomb came a wisp of smoke. Souls of heroes beyond value. A stream of spirits zoomed out. They gathered and soared up over the rocket. The spirits formed a cloud that grew heavy with the energy. It swarmed with the souls of generations of man, and a few recent Feridids. Fossil spirits. Soul fuel. The cloud's leaden belly grew heavier. It dumped a thundershower on the dancers. The Feridids and humans whirled faster around their circle under the rocket ship. The spirits broke free of the cloud and swept around the fields, drawing energy from the land. Nature sprouted a magnificent rainbow in the sunshine after the rain as the spirits zoomed back and spiraled around the rocket ship.

"Look at her!" the boy shouted, pointing to a long cloud shaped like an Egyptian queen.

"Where?" The grandpas started from their sleep.

"There!"

Expecting to see nothing special, the Porters followed the boy's little finger to a cloud shaped like Cleopatra. At first the Porters could see only what they had been conditioned to see. "She has a white dress and long arms." As the boy described the scene as he saw it, the mist cleared from the Porters' eyes. They noticed the clouds swirling into a white dress. Forms began to take shape, swirling around the rocket, and the Porters saw what ought not to be there. Their jaws dropped.

"And there's a lumberjack." The boy pointed to a cloud of soul energy limping like an old man. "He's hugging Mommy! Right there, with that cat lady dancing in the bubble!"

His grandfathers leapt from their seats to get a better look at the lumberjack and Any Gynoid vapors encircling MakSym and Valentine. "You mean those clouds over there? Oh yeah. Will you look at that." Who would believe that the energy from dead souls could be harvested for space travel?

Tweetie's six paws pattered up and down, his fan of tails spread in excitement. He butted his furry head against the boy's thigh. The boy scratched Tweetie's ears. Transfixed, the boy and his grandfathers watched the spirit clouds whirling around Valentine. She lifted up her arms as if to hug the lumberjack cloud. Any's soul bubbled and wafted over them and then rejoined the rest of the soul energy, swirling faster with the Feridid's joyous dance. "Why are you crying, Grandpas?"

The Porters blew their big noses. "Maybe."

The spaceship rocked, charging up. It rumbled and shook as the hairy throng danced around it in the crevices of the etching, igniting soul fuel.

"What if she said yes?"

"Who, son?" The two Porters asked simultaneously.

"Nature."

"She is saying yes, boy."

"She is saying yes," young Porter agreed.

Down below, the etchings went wild with color reflecting the orange sky. A blue aura burst from the rocket. Soul energy lifted the ship off the ground. It hovered for a split second and then, *whoosh!* The rocket soared up through the clouds and out of the atmosphere.

"We did it!" The boy threw himself into the Porters' arms. They scooped him up, laughing in utter disbelief, and tossed him back and forth trying to launch him into the sky. Tweetie, Cuppy and Wuhvie pranced around barking. The Porters joined the chase, and soon they were all running around in a circle. Boy and the Porters and *hupchas* waded out into the grass, flopped down and watched the launch pad where the rocket had been.

Rolling, playing, lying on their backs, looking up at the sky. It was almost bedtime. The boy's foot was already asleep under Tweetie's muzzle. He just had one more question for his grandfathers. He better not wait any longer. "Are computers smarter than humans?"

The two grandpas put their hands on the boy's shoulders and sighed. "We'll tell you about that after you get your name," old Porter said.

The boy looked out over the blue and orange *hokka* fields with anticipation. He'd heard that sometimes they gave you your grandpa's name, if they knew it. He secretly wished they'd call him 'Porter'.

TOPICS FOR DISCUSSION

1. How would you say Boy changed over the course of the book? Do you get the impression that Valentine liked Boy in the beginning? What brings them together in the end?

2. Discuss the theme of the environment. Why is Nature capitalized throughout the novel?

3. Discuss the common reaction, "There's nothing *we* can do about it." Can you relate this to the initiations in the book, and if so, how?

4. To what extent have humans taken on the role of God in creating living computers and droids, and to what extent are they freed, limited or enslaved by their creation?

5. Scientists predict that many of the jobs we know today will disappear in the near future. What kinds of work can humans do that computers can't? Comment on the Emperor's statement implying that 'appliances drain all the money out of the economy.'

6. What is the difference between prison and slavery?

7. At the ending of 'Slavery', the renegade family is given jobs on Grod working for Starliament, an organization sympathetic to the Emperor of Earth and Ocean. Do organizations hire people in order to deactivate them in

real life, and does this theme come up anywhere else in the book?

8. Is it moral for the *hupcha* to put ideas into Boy's head, or do the ends justify means?

9. Why does Eleanor elicit a shock from the alien, Yda, in *"Comment Aimer une femme?"* What facets of Eleanor's character are revealed in her relationship with the alien? Does their interaction show a change in her perspective?

10. To what extent is Any Gynoid a living being? To what extent have we outsourced out brains to computers, or become robotized through the use of computers? How do computers light the way, or spell our doom? Could they be used to automate environmental protection today?

11. Mrs. Dodgewisdom prepares students for their roles in society with busywork, and the Anys shout orders just to keep the Porters out of trouble in 'Word'. Discuss the function of busywork in *Nature's Confession*.

12. To what extent is Nature self-destructive? Does she confess in the novel, and if so, to what?

13. What happens to Porter after he leaves Grod? Why do you think he feels compelled to orbit his family in later stories?

14. How does the form of the novel renounce the organizing authority of an omniscient narrator? Does a variety of voices help depict things like the subjectivity of

experience, a democracy of points of view, impressionistic shattering?

15. Does the work that needs to be done pay more than busywork in real life? Why does Starliament send Mom to Phira to do work that doesn't need to be done? Is corruption, like the corruption of Staliament, inevitable in big organizations, and what kinds of forces get people back on track doing work that needs to be done?

16. What does the author show in the depiction of different kinds of relationships from traditional romance, to self-discovery, to platonic acceptance, sibling love, and procreation, including clones, droids and fur-ball spores?

17. Can you think of any real examples of underdeveloped civilizations with natural resources being exploited by more developed outsiders who are polluting?

18. What is 'soul energy' a metaphor for? What kinds of known renewable energy might bring us closer to 'spirit fuel'?

19. Should governments subsidize oil, coal and other fossil fuels?

20. Eleanor clones herself and has Kenza with no help from a man; Any makes the sedative to knock out the conflicted Porters during the raid on the Corporate facility; yet the grandson wishes to be named 'Porter' in the last chapter. In this context, discuss utility versus uselessness; what makes us human/animals; and the meaning or irrelevance of human endeavor.

More books from Harvard Square Editions:

People and Peppers, Kelvin Christopher James
Dark Lady of Hollywood, Diane Haithman
Gates of Eden, Charles Degelman
Living Treasures, Yang Huang
Close, Erika Raskin
Sazzae, JL Morin
Transoceanic Lights, S. Li
Love's Affliction, Dr. Fidelis O. Mkparu
Anomie, Jeff Lockwood
A Little Something, Richard Haddaway
Fugue for the Right Hand, Michele Tolela Myers
Calling the Dead, R.K. Marfurt
Growing Up White, James P. Stobaugh
Parallel, Sharon Erby

About the Author

JL Morin grew up in inner city Detroit and wrote her Japan novel, *Sazzae* (Gold medalist in the 2010 eLit Book Award, and 2010 Living Now Book Awards winner) as her thesis at Harvard. She took to the road, traveling to Australia and around the world, a way of life that fueled an interest in the origins of cultures, worked as a TV newscaster and wrote three more novels. Adjunct faculty at Boston University, J. L. Morin, was nominated for the Pushcart Prize in 2011. She is the author of *Travelling Light*, and 'Occupy's 1st bestselling novel' *Trading Dreams*, a humorous story that unmasks hypocrisy in the banking industry and tosses corruption onto the horns of the Wall Street bull. She writes for the Huffington Post, Library Journal, and has written for The Harvard Advocate, Harvard Yisei, the Detroit News, Agence France-Presse, Cyprus Weekly, European Daily, Livonia Observer Eccentric Newspapers, the Harvard Crimson and others.